Praise for *The B*

"A thrilling and beautifully .... with a strong sense of time, ..., and more than enough twists to keep one guessing. Readers will be as hard-pressed as I was to put this one down once they begin."

Anna Lee Huber, *USA Today* bestselling author

"An English murder mystery set in the 1950s, plus a friends (and sometimes enemies)-to-more romance? Naomi Stephens is an author to watch!"

Julie Klassen, bestselling author

"What an absolute delight of a novel! Deftly combining the quirky humor of Father Brown with gravitas and shocking twists, *The Burning of Rosemont Abbey* kept me laughing and pondering alongside the insightful and amusing heroine. Plus, romance! Naomi Stephens has a new fan in me!"

Sarah Sundin, Christy Award–winning author
of *Embers in the London Sky*

"Escape to a quaint English village where a young woman's twin brother has mysteriously vanished. Reminiscent of Agatha Christie, *The Burning of Rosemont Abbey* is a fast-paced blend of mystery, romance, and faith that will keep you guessing until the very end. I loved the richly layered details of life in a 1950s country mansion as Louisa delves into her complicated family history to solve a long-simmering mystery."

Elizabeth Camden, RITA Award–winning author

"Imagine a delicious intrigue rich in colorful, quirky characters, devilishly clever banter, and simmering with a romantic chemistry that will have you swooning! This perfectly paced British whodunit will by turns keep you grinning, gasping, and guessing until the very last page. Thoroughly captivating!"

Kate Breslin, bestselling author of *In Love's Time*

"I'm a fan of atmospheric, well-written whodunits that are peopled with unforgettable characters. Naomi Stephens's *The Burning of Rosemont Abbey* checks all the boxes for me. Readers who grew up with Nancy Drew and Agatha Christie will become fast friends with Louisa Everly. Be warned, this book will keep you up past your bedtime."

Susie Finkbeiner, author of *The All-American*
and *Stories That Bind Us*

"Twists abound in this engrossing, suspenseful, and atmospheric mystery. Readers will be drawn into a labyrinth of intrigue that deepens with every chapter. Layered with memorable themes and multifaceted characters, *The Burning of Rosemont Abbey* is a deftly plotted and thoroughly satisfying tale. Fans of Agatha Christie will be captivated."

Amanda Barratt, Christy Award–winning author of *Within These Walls of Sorrow* and *The Warsaw Sisters*

"Here's one for the top of your reading pile! Vivid writing, compelling characters, and a classic mystery that would make Agatha Christie break out in a hearty round of applause. I enjoyed every minute of *The Burning of Rosemont Abbey*, and you will too."

Michelle Griep, Christy Award–winning author of *Of Gold and Shadows*

"Smashing good fun! This historical mystery hits all the notes—a touch of romance, a heroine full of sass and verve, a cast of characters to utterly charm me, and a mystery that kept me guessing until the very end! I want to reread it right now!"

Roseanna M. White, bestselling author of THE IMPOSTERS

"Naomi Stephens has crafted a delightful, atmospheric mystery full of all the twists and turns an armchair sleuth could want. Readers will adore following the lively heroine and endearing cast of side characters as they puzzle out the clues to discover whodunit. Highly recommended to fans of Golden Era detective fiction."

Amy Lynn Green, author of *The Foxhole Victory Tour*

"Stephens leaves the reader guessing with this delightful homage to Agatha Christie where the mystery gets more intricate with each page and every character is a suspect. Fast-paced and beautifully plotted, *The Burning of Rosemont Abbey* is a novel sprinkled with clues, seeped in timeless truths, and capped off with a twist of an ending you'll never see coming."

Jennifer L. Wright, Carol Award–nominated author of *The Girl from the Papers*

The
BURNING
of
ROSEMONT
ABBEY

The BURNING *of* ROSEMONT ABBEY

NAOMI STEPHENS

BETHANYHOUSE
a division of Baker Publishing Group
Minneapolis, Minnesota

Published by Bethany House Publishers
Minneapolis, Minnesota
BethanyHouse.com

Bethany House Publishers is a division of
Baker Publishing Group, Grand Rapids, Michigan

Printed in the United States of America

Library of Congress Cataloging-in-Publication Data
Names: Stephens, Naomi, author.
Title: The burning of Rosemont Abbey / Naomi Stephens.
Description: Minneapolis, Minnesota : Bethany House Publishers, a division of
    Baker Publishing Group, 2024.
Identifiers: LCCN 2024006116 | ISBN 9780764242472 (paperback) | ISBN
    9780764243189 (casebound) | ISBN 9781493446599 (ebook)
Subjects: LCGFT: Detective and mystery fiction. | Christian fiction. | Novels.
Classification: LCC PS3619.T476766 B87 2024 | DDC 813/.6—dc23/eng/20240215
LC record available at https://lccn.loc.gov/2024006116

Scripture quotations are from the King James Version of the Bible.

This is a work of fiction. Names, characters, incidents, and dialogues are products
of the author's imagination and are not to be construed as real. Any resemblance
to actual events or persons, living or dead, is entirely coincidental.

The verse quoted in the epilogue, page 318, is from the poem "Holy Sonnets: Death,
be not proud" by John Donne (1572–1631).

Cover design by Dan Thornberg
Cover image of woman by Lee Avison, Arcangel

Baker Publishing Group publications use paper produced from sustainable forestry
practices and postconsumer waste whenever possible.

24 25 26 27 28 29 30   7 6 5 4 3 2 1

This book is lovingly dedicated to my parents,
who have always encouraged me and my love of reading.

And to Jenny, for recommending so many marvelous
mysteries while I was writing the book,
and because you understand the forsythia bush reference.

Built on the Rock the Church shall stand
even when steeples are falling.

Lutheran Service Book, Hymn 645

1

England, 1956

Louisa felt him die.

Through the years, she'd heard many strange stories like this, of twins who could sense when their sibling was suffering or dying without being physically present. She'd never understood why people went out of their way to tell her stories like that; she'd always thought they were ghastly.

In many of these accounts, the experience was said to be visceral, violent, a physical blow that brought the living sibling to their knees or wrenched a cry of startled anguish from their lips.

For Louisa, it was deathly quiet.

It was the switching off of an engine. A telephone conversation cut mid-word. It was an emptiness, an absence that started in her heart and spread outward like a bottle of spilled ink.

She hadn't even been thinking about her brother when it happened but was brewing herself a nightcap cup of tea in the kitchen. One moment she was standing there in her newest gown of coral chiffon, pleased as punch because

David Ashworth had taken her aside at his family's party that evening, told her she put all other beauties to shame—

And then there was nothing else.

She hardly heard the teacup smash beneath her as she threw out her hands to break her fall, her body crumpling at a skewed angle on the hardwood floor.

Paul's name flew from her lips in an unconscious whisper as the emptiness traveled from her heart up to her head; it seemed to be turning off lights the higher it went, for she could no longer see. She couldn't think either. She was still there, in the room, and yet she wasn't. Every piece of her had simply stopped.

Seconds later, the emptiness began to release her. She could breathe again. Could clench and unclench her fingers. Had just enough sense to wonder if a twenty-six-year-old woman was too young to be having a stroke. She still couldn't see, but she could hear the *pit-pit-pat* of a dripping faucet, the scratching of wind-harassed branches against the kitchen window. And, drowning out all else, the shrill pitch of a woman's scream.

"Help! Help!" cried the voice. "Miss Everly has *swooned!*"

The screech at the end made Louisa's ears ring. She blinked a few times, forcing the room back into focus. Dimly, she lifted her left hand. A triangular shard of pink floral china was wedged in the center of her palm.

It didn't hurt exactly, but the sight of oozing blood did nothing for her dizziness. Neither did the housemaid, Biddy, who was now pacing and tossing about a multitude of questions in rapid succession: "Miss Everly? Miss Everly, can you hear me? Are you ill? Have you hit your head? Did you dance too much at the party this evening? Oh, heavens, you're bleeding as well! And how will we get that blood out of your new gown? Why don't you speak, Miss Everly? Do you think you need to see a doctor? *Can* you speak? I'll send for the doctor at once!"

This time the silence was welcome as Biddy scurried out of the room. Louisa took the opportunity to stand unassisted. Her senses were snapping the rest of the way back to attention, but she wasn't finding the adrenaline much of an improvement. Trembly and numb by turns, she clutched at the wall as she stumbled her way to the first chair she could find.

A moment later, she heard voices and footsteps quickening down the hall. But it was Aunt Agatha, not Biddy, who appeared in the doorway. "My dear Louisa! Are you all right?"

Louisa released a breath. Her aunt had the finest alto in the history of the Rosemont Abbey choir; even when she was only speaking, there was something soothing about her deep, resonating voice. And though what she said rarely amounted to much, Louisa sometimes thought she'd have made a smashing radio announcer for the BBC.

Aunt Agatha was still wearing her gown from the party that evening, a French ensemble that had arrived at the last possible minute. The dark blue taffeta rustled as she stepped to the sink and poured a glass of water for her niece. "How many times have I told you to ring for tea?" she said. "Mrs. Hobbs will be furious when she hears you've been in her kitchen again."

Pale and silent, Louisa held the glass in her uninjured hand as her aunt ushered her down the hall and into the sitting room. *This*, her aunt pointed out, was a far more suitable atmosphere for fainting, guiding Louisa to recline on an exceptionally garish floral settee.

"There now," Aunt Agatha said, carefully inspecting Louisa's hand before repositioning it so she wouldn't get any more spatters of blood on her dress. "Dr. Clarke is sending Dr. Fielding to see to your hand. He told Biddy to leave that piece in there, if we can, so it doesn't bleed too much before he can take a proper look." She sat in the chair beside Louisa and tilted her head. "What happened, my dear?"

Now that Louisa had some control over her faculties, she took a sip of water and tried to rationalize what had happened. Perhaps she'd only had a dizzy spell or some sort of breakdown. It made no sense to think it had anything whatsoever to do with Paul. She and her brother weren't close, hadn't been for years. Of course, they couldn't have looked more alike if they'd been forgeries of the same painting. They had the same mousy brown hair. The same pointed chins. As babies, their parents said they could hardly be told apart, except that Paul was always wailing and Louisa always hungry. And yet Louisa had never—not once—felt the strange, ethereal "twin bond" that so many people had asked her about.

And besides that, they'd gotten into the most devastating row that morning. Paul had been cruel, and Louisa had spoken spitefully in turn, and so if something terrible *had* happened to Paul, why on earth should she be the one to sense it?

But sense it she had, in a place as deep and profound as her own soul, and so she knew it was true: her brother was dead.

Shivering, she glanced at Aunt Agatha, who was as slender and sophisticated as a champagne flute in her evening wear. If Louisa told her aunt what she'd felt, what she now believed to be true, she had no doubt her aunt would ring up Uncle Archie, who had stayed behind with George Ashworth to finish a frightfully heated round of cribbage. And Uncle Archie, who was as rational and unbelieving a man as ever she'd met, was likely to send for a doctor of *another* sort.

And so Louisa only muttered something about feeling a bit dizzy, and her aunt told her to wait there and rest while she went out into the hall. Louisa had just glanced at the clock above the mantel—it was half past eleven—when Biddy reappeared with fresh water, wrappings, and instructions for seeing to the invalid. Together, they dipped Louisa's hand into the bowl. The maid paled as she helped rinse Louisa's palm with the cool water, dabbing away the blood. It didn't seem to be bleeding so terribly now, as they both took turns observing, but it was still another hour before Dr. Clarke's intern, a young mustached man named Dr. Fielding, stepped into the sitting room.

"Terribly sorry for the delay," he said. "The bridge is out near Epfield Woods, and I got turned around in the dark. I'm still learning my way around, you see."

He was followed by Aunt Agatha, who had taken the time to change into a more subdued gingham dress. "We understand completely, Dr. Fielding."

"Dr. Clarke sends his regrets, of course." He dropped his hat and bag on the nearest end table. "He's been out all evening seeing to Mr. Hexam's gout. They're old army chums. No disrespect intended, but I'm afraid the two of them put together could out-chatter a set of howler monkeys."

Aunt Agatha laughed as if she'd just heard the most charming demonstration of wit. Louisa did not. Looking rather pleased with himself nonetheless, Dr. Fielding knelt on the rug in front of her and gingerly took her hand. "How did this happen?"

"I felt light-headed," answered Louisa. "I didn't realize the cup had broken when I fell."

He leaned closer, peering into each of her eyes in turn. "You didn't hit your head, did you?"

"No."

"Perhaps it was too much excitement," her aunt suggested. "David Ashworth asked her to dance *three times* this evening, you know."

"Hm." Dr. Fielding pulled at his mustache, then popped open his bag and rummaged inside. "The cut doesn't look too deep." He pulled out a few squares of gauze and a set of tweezers and went to work, apologizing every now and then for causing any discomfort.

He needn't have bothered; Louisa was still fairly numb all over.

Within a few moments, the fragment was free, clasped tightly between the tweezers as the doctor held it up for inspection. "A fine piece of china," he observed.

"And no longer a complete set," lamented Aunt Agatha.

The floral shrapnel was tossed into a wastebasket, and Louisa was given a neat line of stitches and instructed to drink plenty of water and to rest.

"Any more of this dizziness," said Dr. Fielding, "and we'll want to see you again without the slightest hesitation."

Her aunt thanked him a dozen different ways, then off he went. Louisa would have waited in the parlor while her aunt saw him out, but then, almost as soon as the front door was opened, she heard another shriek: *"The Abbey!"*

Louisa was at the door in an instant, pushing her way outside to stand between her aunt and Dr. Fielding. The evening air was cool and still and would have been silent were it not for Biddy's sudden wailing somewhere behind her. Louisa fought back tears as she followed their gazes to the peak on the other side of the valley.

Her father's church, Rosemont Abbey, was on the top of the hill.

In many ways, the abbey was all Louisa had left of her father since he'd died in the war twelve years prior. In fair weather, if she stood on the top step of her uncle's house and squinted *very* hard, she could just barely see it, like a smooth, gray pebble someone had dropped on the horizon. Now it flickered red and glowed against the black sky like a hot, smoldering ember.

Though Louisa could hardly make sense of what she was seeing, she somehow managed to whisper: "It's on fire."

"May God help anyone caught inside," rasped Dr. Fielding.

Louisa's hand throbbed. An hour had passed since she felt something terrible had happened to Paul. Was this what she'd sensed? Could he have burned to death in the abbey? She felt herself sway, gripping the doctor's sleeve for support . . .

But it was poor Biddy who fainted.

2

Louisa had last seen her brother in the morning, some nine hours before the Ashworths' annual spring soiree. Her aunt was in the parlor arguing with the seamstress, and her uncle had dragged his valet out into the garden because the buttonholes supplied for the last three dinners he'd attended hadn't passed inspection. Uncle Archie had always been persnickety about his buttonholes.

Louisa had just finished having her new gown fitted for the last time and gone in search of her aunt, who insisted on giving her approval to the latest set of alterations, particularly the length of the hemline, which had been altogether too low at the last fitting. With everyone else in the house duly accounted for, Louisa was curious when she heard rustling in her uncle's study.

It was the only room in the house that was considered out-of-bounds, even to family. Unless, of course, one received a formal summons. As she made her way down the hall to investigate, she found the door nearly closed, all but an inch. She peered cautiously through the crack before bursting into the room.

"What do you think you're doing?" she hissed at her brother, shutting the door softly behind her.

Paul wore a faded blue button-down, wrinkled at the sleeves, and a tweed flat cap pulled low over his brow. He sat in Uncle Archie's chair in an irreverent forward slouch, his lean frame dwarfed by the size of the gleaming mahogany desk. He was rifling through one of the lower drawers when Louisa came in. Her words did nothing to startle him out of his progress. "Hullo, Lou," he said without looking up.

The name stung, just as it was meant to. Only her father had ever called her that. He'd wanted to name her Eloise, after a beloved aunt on his mother's side, but her mother had known an Eloise in her younger years who had given the name a much less inspiring association. She suggested they call her Louisa instead, for it had a similar ring. After a few days of strenuous negotiations, her father had drawn up the following compromise—that she may be christened *Louisa* so long as he was free to call her Lou.

Paul, whose namesake was of the apostolic origin, had grown up into a rather crass, disagreeable young man, and Louisa didn't hesitate to tell him as much.

He laughed at her insult as he shut the drawer, hard enough to rattle the antique lamp on the desktop. "And you're a snob, Louisa Everly."

Louisa's brother had the deft hands of someone who often cheated at cards, but she knew him well and caught the slight shifting movement as he slipped something out of the drawer and into his pocket.

Before she could question him, he lifted his eyes and spotted her new chiffon gown. It was all the proof he needed to uphold his former insult. Sneering, he pulled a pack of cigarettes from his pocket. "Going out?"

She didn't think he truly cared to know, and so she didn't

bother answering. "If you need money, you don't have to steal it, you know. If you only asked nicely, Uncle Archie would help."

"I'm not inclined to ask nicely." He jammed a cigarette into the corner of his lips and struck a match on the arm of Uncle Archie's chair. "Nor do I want his money, for it always comes with strings."

"The expectation that you behave like a respectable human being, you mean?"

He blew out a long line of smoke as he stepped clear of the desk. There were flecks of white paint on his trousers and a few splatters of it on his work boots. "I did my time in this cursed house, and I'm done with it. Some people may not mind being puppetized and paraded about, but I happen to mind tremendously."

Louisa had been doing her best to keep the conversation at a whisper, but now she heard a noise in the hall and cracked the door, wondering if Uncle Archie was already returning from the garden. But no, it was only the butler on his way up the stairs with his master's dress shoes, which had been freshly shined for the party that evening.

They were running out of time. Any minute now, Uncle Archie would return and find them both in his study. As such, Louisa wanted to be done with the conversation as soon as possible, but she also didn't want to lose the argument at hand. "They can't exactly help it that they have money," she said. "It's been kind of them to look after us all these years, especially now that they don't have to. They may not always be right or perfect, but if they have certain expectations of me, then so be it. They've been good to me—to *both* of us—and there's nothing wrong with being the slightest bit thankful for it."

Paul's laugh released another cloud of smoke as he moved to leave the room. He reached for the door handle, and Louisa was now close enough to him that she could smell the stale alcohol on his breath. Despite her irritation, she began to worry.

"Where are you going?"

"Nowhere that is likely to result in my marrying a rich fool." He met her eyes. Here, at least, was one of the only noticeable differences in their features, for his were gray while hers were blue. "Tell me. Do you really think David Ashworth will look at you in that gown tonight and propose on the spot? Aunt Agatha certainly thinks so. But of course, all those rich men, they wouldn't look twice at you if she and Uncle Archie weren't so *benevolent*, trussing you up and promising a financial windfall to the richest bloke who will have you. I suppose it is lucky that they so enjoy showing you off—their niece, the lowly vicar's daughter, and orphaned no less! The wealthy love their charities, don't they?"

Louisa's face flushed, whether from anger or from mortification she couldn't decide, for she was feeling both in equal measure. "You're horribly mean."

"If I wanted to be mean, I wouldn't try to warn you, would I?"

"Warn me about what?"

"You're always saying I'm up to no good, and I suppose you're right. I've never pretended to hide my vices, and so you know exactly what they are. But there are truly terrible people all around you, Louisa. You can't see them because they have stacks of money or lofty positions to hide behind, but they're there, and I mean to prove it."

Louisa couldn't help but roll her eyes. It was hard to give credence to anything her brother said on this topic, for she'd heard many such rantings, especially in recent years. "I think you're drunk."

"Think whatever you'd like." He flicked his cigarette stub into the fireplace. "I'd hate for you to be distressed when you have to be looking your best at the party tonight. Aunt Agatha would never forgive me for hurting your chances with David Ashworth."

Now Louisa was seething. When their parents had died, she and Paul had promised to look after each other. But then they'd moved into Everly Hall and begun growing apart like a tree split at the root. It wasn't only that Paul had run off and started a whole new life without her as soon as he was old enough to do so. He was an adult and could make his own decisions. But he'd left that first night without so much as leaving word—without asking her to come with him—and now he kept reappearing, time and again, to quarrel with her.

Louisa knew better than to voice any of this out loud, for Paul loved to fling her words back on her, and so she struck him with a question: "Would you have been happier if I'd run off like you, homeless and penniless those first few months, to sleep in the street and see what might have become of me?"

He didn't answer. Beneath the unbuttoned top of his collar, Louisa spotted a thin silver chain. She didn't have to see the icon beneath his shirtfront to know it bore St. Jude's likeness—the patron saint of lost and desperate causes. It had been given to him by a Catholic priest who had attended their father's funeral. She and Paul had been only fourteen years old at the time, and she'd never seen her brother without it.

"I may be a snob," she said at last, "but you're a hypocrite."

"Louisa—"

"No. You think you're superior because you don't rely on

uncle's money, because you spend your time at the pubs instead of at parties, but I tell you there's not the slightest difference. I loved mother and father too, you know. I don't miss them any less than you do because I stay here. I don't spit on their graves by wearing a fine dress or by dancing with a few rich fools, as you call them, but you very well might by living the way you do."

The words were now coming too fast to stop, and Paul made no effort to silence them. He leaned against the doorframe with his head bent down so that Louisa could no longer see his face. At one point, she thought she saw him flinch, yet this only spurred her on, making her want to hurt him more.

"You're an angry, thankless fool, Paul Everly, and a drunkard and a thief. Mother and Father would both be ashamed of you. For my part, I wouldn't care if you drank yourself into oblivion or even to death. I hope I never have to see you again."

Those were the last words she said to her brother.

3

The first sound Louisa heard the next morning was the rhythmic crunching of wet gravel.

She hadn't been asleep, not really, but she felt as though she'd been pulled from a nightmare nonetheless. The argument she'd had with Paul had turned into a cold and bitter echo in the aftermath of the fire, and sorrow was a merciless companion. She still hadn't told anyone what she had felt, for she feared she would sound as if she'd taken leave of her senses. She'd lain awake in bed all night, waiting for the front bell to ring, certain she'd soon receive word that Paul had been killed in the fire at Rosemont Abbey.

And so she wasn't the least bit surprised when she heard a motorcar pull into the drive an hour before Mrs. Hobbs would have finished laying out breakfast. Her suspicions were further confirmed when she went over to the window and, peeling the curtain back from the glass, saw a black Wolseley parked outside, the front placard starkly inscribed with one word: POLICE.

The driver had already exited the car. Louisa caught only a glimpse of his gray fedora before he was shielded by the portico beneath her. Her heartbeat throbbed in her fingertips as she snatched a dress from the cupboard, smoothed out her slept-on curls, and sprinted down the stairs. She skidded to a breathless halt at the end of the hall, attempting to compose herself, but was spotted by a footman, who tucked his chin and pretended not to have noticed her mad dash.

When pressed for information, he told her that the inspector had been shown into her uncle's study, and that her aunt and uncle had both gone in to speak with him. The door was halfway open when Louisa reached it. As she slid into the room, she glanced at the desk and felt as if she were slipping into a dream. Just yesterday, she'd found her brother sitting in that very spot. In his disheveled shirt and flat cap, he'd looked like a fallen king in a throne much too big for him.

Her uncle was a more natural fixture, the sort of man who drank brandy at all hours and hung a great deal of importance on the curve of a well-crafted mustache. He filled the space with ease, speaking down on the visitor with thinly veiled contempt: "Well, of course he did it. No doubt in my mind whatsoever that he did."

The inspector stood opposite the desk without flinching, his back to the door. There was something about his stance, the set of his shoulders. Louisa felt a pinprick of recognition a second before he turned. And there he was. Brown eyes, gray suit, right hand tucked idly in his pocket.

Malcolm Sinclair.

"Ah, Louisa." Her aunt smiled mildly, motioning her into the room. "I'm sure you remember Mr. Sinclair. He's an inspector now, can you believe it?"

"Detective Inspector," he corrected, a flash of humor lighting his dark eyes.

Louisa stared at him, too much on her guard to wonder what exactly he'd found so amusing about the situation. She hadn't known that Malcolm had become a police officer or that he'd returned to Wilbeth Green, but his sudden reappearance felt both dreadful and strange, for he and Paul had once been inseparable friends.

That was nearly twelve years ago.

Back when Louisa's family was still whole. When they lived in the brick vicarage behind the abbey. In those days, the boys were always spoiling for mischief of some kind or another. Stealing bicycles and leaving them in funny places to be found later. Smoking outside the police station in Sutherby. Once they'd caught a fish in the creek behind the abbey and left it flapping about in poor, nervous Mrs. Pennyweather's bathtub. In the face of such antics, Louisa's parents had developed an eclectic repertoire of reproofs and reprimands, yet it was clear they had a fondness for Malcolm. He ate dinner at the vicarage at least three nights a week and was often sent home with leftovers to share with his family.

When Paul and Louisa moved into Everly Hall, Uncle Archie's first order of business was to put a stop to any unsuitable friendships. In the early days, she and Paul had received many lectures about not carrying on too closely with the wrong sort, and a boy like Malcolm Sinclair had two strikes against him. Not only was he the son of a greengrocer, but there was Scottish blood on his mother's side, which, according to Louisa's aunt, accounted for much.

Paul had cut ties with Malcolm, as ordered, but this wasn't exactly proof he was falling in step either. He despised his uncle's money and influence and was far too mortified to let his old friends see any evidence of it in his new life. The dandyish clothes he was forced to wear, the private tutors, even the posh estate that bore his family's name (and to which his own friends would never be invited)—it was all an intolerable insult. Which was not to say Paul had surrendered without some demonstration of dissent. He'd had the final word, more or less, by emptying the contents of his uncle's brandy cabinet into his aunt's hydrangea bushes, which had never fully recovered from the assault.

"Miss Everly." The formality of Malcolm's address was a sharp reminder that nothing was as it once had been. "I wish that I could be visiting you under pleasanter circumstances."

"Have you come about the fire?" she blurted. Having found her voice, she had no patience for the flood of disquieting memories his sudden presence had stirred.

"Yes."

There was darkness in his voice. Louisa was now certain they'd found Paul's remains, that Malcolm had come in some official capacity to tell her the news. "Please," she said, knotting her fingers tightly together to keep them from trembling. "If something has happened to Paul, tell me quickly while I can still bear it."

A torturous silence followed as his eyes narrowed. "Why should you think the fire has anything to do with Paul?"

"Well, doesn't it?"

His lips parted as if to answer, but then he stopped short, shook his head, and seemed to try a different tack: "Did he tell you he was going to be at the abbey last night?"

The question confused her. She might have been able to think more clearly if he wasn't looking at her so closely, as if waiting for her to give something away. He hadn't taken a single step, and yet she still felt as though he was crowding her. "Not exactly," she said. "I just had a . . . a feeling. Do you mean you haven't found him?"

"We haven't. But it's very important that we do."

"Why? Do you think he's been hurt?"

"No. But we have strong reason to believe he may have set fire to the abbey."

Louisa faltered, her mind fumbling as she tried to keep up. "An accident, you mean?"

She saw something then that she'd never seen in Malcolm. Was it reluctance, she wondered, or something else? It was there for only a second, too fleeting to tell, a quick downward glance when he could have easily answered her question but didn't.

The suspense, she found, was to be just as fleeting. Uncle Archie wasn't the least bit reluctant to share terrible news where his nephew was concerned, and so he supplied the answer without even bothering to stand up from his desk: "He means he burned it to the ground, Louisa. On *purpose*."

4

Louisa stood motionless as all three sets of eyes settled on her at the same time. When she didn't answer, Uncle Archie slid open a drawer and produced a pipe, which he lit in an agitated huff. Aunt Agatha was more maternal. She gave the seat beside her a meaningful pat, as if she thought Louisa might faint again.

Louisa wasn't in the slightest bit of danger. In fact, now that the shock was receding, she found the suggestion so absurd that she even laughed.

Her uncle looked up sharply, pipe wedged between his lips. "Have I said something amusing?"

A moment before, Louisa had struggled to find her voice, but there wasn't a weak spot to be found in it now as she answered: "Paul would never burn the abbey."

In what was more or less his second language, her uncle harrumphed, smoke billowing from the side of his mouth. The pipe jabbed upward and downward, punctuating each word as he spoke: "A sister's sentimental opinion won't hold as much water as evidence in court. And according to the inspector here, there's plenty of that."

"The inspector can show me all the evidence he'd like. I still won't believe it."

"You haven't yet heard the details of the case," Malcolm cut in. "How can you be sure he wasn't involved?"

Louisa glanced at Uncle Archie, who was still puffing angrily on his pipe, and then at Aunt Agatha, who looked as she always did when she was disappointed in her niece's conduct—like she'd found water spots on the crystal again. If Louisa told Malcolm that her brother had died before the fire, she'd have to explain how she knew it was so, and she didn't think her aunt and uncle had it in them to hear it.

"Paul had many faults," she said at last. "But he loved our father, and he was as devout as a man in his circumstances is able to be. He would never set fire to the church."

"When was the last time you spoke with your brother?"

"Yesterday morning. Around nine o'clock, I'd say."

Malcolm slipped a thin, worn notebook from the inside of his jacket pocket. He flipped a few pages. "And where was this?"

"I found him here. In the study."

Her uncle stood in an affronted rush, barricaded thankfully by the desk, his face growing redder by the second. Aunt Agatha stepped between them, drawing Louisa's gaze. "But you never said anything about it, my dear. Was that why you were so out of sorts last night?"

Malcolm, who had been writing in his notebook, paused with the stub of a pencil poised over the page as he glanced up at her. "You were out of sorts?"

"Yes. Well, no. It wasn't because we quarreled."

"You quarreled?"

"We often do."

Uncle Archie harrumphed again, pulling at his mustache as he dropped back into his seat. "Yes. Well. I, for one, would like to know what the two of you quarreled about yesterday."

Louisa didn't answer. She was generally patient with her uncle's moods, but this wasn't his interrogation. And though she fully expected Malcolm to put the same question to her, as any sensible inspector would, she really wasn't sure how to answer.

Perhaps Aunt Agatha had surmised as much, for she crossed the room before anyone else could speak a word and set a gentle hand on Louisa's shoulder. "My niece has been through a terrible shock," she said to Malcolm. "I wonder if the rest of your questions might keep for another day."

Malcolm paid no heed to Aunt Agatha as he went on studying Louisa, his pencil tip still suspended an inch above the page as if he wasn't quite sure how to describe her for future reference. And was that blank, unflinching stare how he looked at *every* suspect who came under his scrutiny? Louisa tried to withstand, but she lowered her eyes first.

In his own good time, Malcolm snapped his notebook shut. "If any of you should remember anything relevant—"

Aunt Agatha smiled, gliding forward as if to sweep him from the room. "Of course," she said. "Good day to you, Inspector."

He nodded and left without a word of thanks or farewell, which Aunt Agatha observed was remarkably bad manners. Her opinion of Malcolm clearly hadn't improved since the last time she'd seen him. It was right around the time that Paul was pouring Uncle Archie's brandy into the hydrangea bushes that Louisa overheard her aunt telling her uncle that she was concerned about the kind of influence a boy like Malcolm might have on Louisa. For a woman of Agatha's standing, it was an understandable anxiety. By the time he was fifteen, all the girls in Wilbeth Green had gone a bit mad for Malcolm at one time or another because he had charm, slightly wild hair, and he'd laughed generously in his youth; perhaps all of that was owing to his Scottish blood, too.

Still, Aunt Agatha needn't have worried about any romantic feelings developing between Malcolm and Louisa; they'd been so young, and there hadn't really been the proper climate for it at the time. Though Malcolm had been a regular at the vicarage, he and Paul rarely went out of their way to include Louisa in their antics, nor did they admit her into their confidence, as Paul always said she'd tattle. More often than not, she was on the receiving end of their mischief. Never anything mean or malicious, but often irritating, like the time her new church dress had ended up on the scarecrow in Foster's field.

But then Malcolm could be kind, too. Whenever he visited the vicarage, he was in the habit of bringing an apple for Louisa; he'd toss it to her from across the kitchen as he and Paul slipped out the door to go fishing. Once, when they were eleven or so, Paul had called her down to the fishing dock, thinking it would be a great laugh to toss her into the lake. But then, at the crucial moment, Malcolm shoved Paul in instead, howling with laughter as his friend emerged sputtering.

And then there was the day of their mother's funeral, six short, painful months after their father's—Malcolm had found Louisa sobbing in the woods behind the abbey and sat beside her on the cold, wet ground until she could speak again.

"Don't tell Paul," she'd pleaded.

So far as she knew, he never had.

And maybe this was why, when Louisa was asked to fetch

tea so her aunt and uncle might speak privately, she slipped out through the kitchen door and ran after Malcolm. She caught up with him as he was opening his car door. He heard her coming from a good way off and stared at her over the hood, brows raised.

Louisa wasn't sure what she'd run out to say. Malcolm had been only sixteen when his family had packed up and moved to Oxford, and no one could have been more surprised than she was to learn of it. Now that he was in front of her, standing so straight and so serious, with not a hair out of place, she couldn't decide if his presence was comforting or if it somehow made everything worse. The passing of twelve years had changed him, certainly, and yet she couldn't see Malcolm without expecting Paul to come tromping along after him.

She circled around to his side of the car. "Paul didn't burn the abbey," she said, a pleading note in her voice as she struggled to catch her breath. "You know he didn't."

Malcolm shut the car door. He glanced once at the window to her uncle's study, then took her by the arm, carefully, and led her behind a small cluster of trees. "What did you two argue about?"

At first, Louisa thought he might have been asking out of concern, but then she saw that the notebook had reappeared in his hand. "I should hate to have it on record," she said, hesitating. "We both said unfortunate things."

"Such as?"

Digging the toe of her shoe into the gravel, her cheeks warm, she murmured, "He called me a snob."

Malcolm paused, his pencil hovering before he wrote this down, with a bit more diligence than she would have liked. "And?" he pressed.

"Well, isn't that enough?"

The pencil tip paused again. "I mean, what did *you* say that was unfortunate?"

"Oh." She looked down again but was determined to tell the truth, at least. "Well, I called him a hypocrite and an angry, thankless fool, a drunkard, and a thief." When she'd finished this recitation, she lifted a glance toward Malcolm, and for just one moment she saw the familiar upward turn of his lips.

"I don't see you writing any of those down," she observed flatly.

"I'll remember. Was he very angry when he left?"

"Not angry enough to burn the abbey, if that's what you mean," she shot back, as suddenly out of temper with him as she'd ever been after finding herself the target of one of his and Paul's pranks.

Malcolm sighed and seemed to be looking past her, to Everly Hall, which stood like a stately chaperone behind them, its walls and high medieval arches clothed in Cotswold stone.

"I don't like this any more than you do," he said after a moment's consideration. "You know I don't. But I have to follow the evidence."

He sounded so confident, so sure, that Louisa's resolve nearly faltered. "Is there really very much?"

"Yes, plenty. Most of which will be in the papers by tomorrow morning. It would probably be best if you and your family avoided town for a few days."

Louisa's laugh was faint but bitter, drifting out of her like a puff of wind. "Am I allowed to request an early edition?"

At first, Malcolm said nothing. He took an age closing up his little notebook and slipping it back into his pocket.

"Turpentine," he supplied at last, "was used as an accelerant. The same brand Paul used for his painting projects. The cans we found at the site matched those from his work stores."

"Any number of suspects might have access to turpentine."

"Yes, but Paul had told the vicar he'd be at the abbey last night. Said he'd left some materials in a cupboard in the church that he needed for another job. Reverend Hughes returned to the vicarage a little after twelve-thirty—he'd been at the Ashworths' party, as I'm sure you know, and got delayed in returning home by a lengthy conversation with a parishioner. By the time he returned to the vicarage, he found the church already on fire. He might even have gone in to try to put it out, but he received a nasty knock to the head before he ever made it to the front door."

"Good heavens!" Louisa cried. "Is he all right?"

"He was pulled a safe distance from the abbey. He'll have a sore crown for a couple of days, but he was otherwise unharmed."

Louisa pressed a hand to her chest, trying to slow her breathing. "Did the vicar say it was Paul who did it?"

"He didn't see his attacker, no. Just the back of him as he ran off."

"So it might have been anyone."

"Perhaps. Except this was also found at the scene."

Watching her closely, Malcolm slid a small envelope from his pocket and tipped it up. A thin silver chain unraveled quickly in his palm, and Louisa's heartbeat quickened as he lifted the trinket for inspection. There hung Paul's necklace, the icon of St. Jude slowly spinning. It was an old piece, but she could still make out the worn engravings—the club in the saint's hand, which was a symbol of his martyrdom, and the flame above his head in remembrance of Pentecost.

"We found it outside the abbey." Malcolm's voice lowered. "It looks as though he ripped it off and left it there to be found. See where the chain is broken?"

She saw the severed chain and reached for it instinctively, but Malcolm stepped back, swinging the necklace up to close his fist around it. Louisa folded her arms. If anything, she was now even less convinced that her brother had burned the abbey. Not only did the timeline not match her own experiences from that night, but she knew her brother. He hadn't attended services in years, though he did plenty of odd jobs around the abbey, always free of charge, and he and the vicar had been on friendly terms for ages. On occasion, they were even seen sharing a pint at The Three Foxes.

"He didn't do it." The pleading note in her voice had been rooted out, replaced by cold defiance. "He cared for that charm too much to have left it behind. Besides, someone might have ripped it from his neck in a struggle and left it there deliberately."

"Framed him, you mean? With what possible motive?"

Louisa snorted. "You of all people know he was no saint, Malcolm—nor does he work alone when he decides to get himself into trouble."

At that, Malcolm stepped closer. And though Louisa did her best to hide it, she stiffened. She knew this wasn't an interrogation, and yet it was, and she had no recollection of him being quite so formidable. As he stared at her, she felt and fought a sudden impulse to reach up and run her fingers through his neatly combed hair, wanting to rumple it so he'd somehow still resemble the Malcolm she once knew.

"I can tell you're holding something back," he said. "I don't know what that might be, or why, but as far as I'm concerned,

Paul's already pulled you into this mess. But I think you're smart enough to know you aren't doing him any favors by concealing his whereabouts. Because if he's as innocent as you say in the matter, then where on earth has he gone?"

"Oh, stop talking to me as if I were a suspect!" she snapped. "If I knew where he was, you can be sure I would tell you. Far better he be in prison than . . ."

"Than *what*?"

Dead.

Louisa's heart revolted at the prospect of speaking that terrible word out loud. She covered her face with her hand, might have retreated to the house, but Malcolm gripped her arm, anchoring her to the spot.

"What is it?" he insisted, his fingers pressing as if to squeeze the truth from her. "Just tell me."

"He's dead."

Malcolm released Louisa's arm so quickly she nearly tripped down into the sludge of wet gravel. "What do you mean he's dead?"

"Paul. Paul's dead," she repeated. It was the first time she'd spoken the words out loud. They sounded twice as true as they'd only felt previously, and so she believed them all the more.

"How do you know?" Malcolm demanded.

"I felt it happen." She saw doubt flicker in his eyes and spoke in a rush, hoping to stem the tide of disbelief: "I know how that sounds. I *know*. But it's the truth. I felt him die."

"When?"

"Last night, after the party. I was standing in the kitchen, and I felt it. I've never felt surer of anything in my life. That was at half past eleven, but you say the vicar saw his attacker run off well after midnight. So, you see, Paul couldn't have done it."

"Who else have you told about this?"

"No one." Her voice faded as she looked away. "I didn't think anyone would believe me."

Malcolm stepped back. Then he shook his head. He was still holding Paul's necklace and stared down at the icon in the center of his palm for a long, hopeless minute. "I think your aunt may be right. You've been through the most terrible kind of shock, and I'm sure if you get some rest . . ."

Louisa had never felt quite so mortified, for no one had ever thought her to be truly mad before, but her scowl was severe enough to halt him mid-sentence. "You asked what I was holding back, and now I've said it. But I will thank you not to patronize me, Inspector Sinclair, but rather to do your job. Which is to discover what has happened to Paul, and who has burned the abbey. I implore you to find the culprit, *if you can*, but I don't mind telling you that I will make my way to the bottom of it one way or another."

"Stay out of my way, Louisa."

His voice deepened with the warning, but there was a faint smile tucked in there too, which made Louisa wonder if Malcolm knew, as she did, that there was little chance of that.

5

Three days passed before Louisa was permitted to leave Everly Hall. A smattering of reporters from various counties had set up camp outside their home, each hoping to secure the family's first official statement. Uncle Archie insisted the family keep a low profile while the first wave of scandal ran its course without them. Even visitors were not permitted. By then, the people of Wilbeth Green, who rarely agreed on anything, whether it was the forecast or the cost of a cabbage, were of a unified mind:

Paul Everly had burned down the abbey.

Newspapers for miles ran with early morning headlines about the former vicar's profligate son and the charred remains of the historic abbey. Somber to the point of relish, they divulged every damning detail for public inspection. The turpentine. The St. Jude necklace. The brutal bash to the poor vicar's head, and most condemning of all, the suspect's sudden disappearance. The case was as open and shut as a dead man's pocketbook; at least, that was what Uncle Archie said.

The fourth day was Sunday, and Aunt Agatha insisted that a few nasty newspapermen wouldn't keep *her* from attending

service. They'd received word that the Rosemont congregation was to gather at the usual time in a small clearing a safe
distance behind the abbey. Uncle Archie had not attended
for years—ever since his brother's death—and so it was to no
one's surprise that he stayed behind. Aunt Agatha reminded
him not to repeat his "dead man's pocketbook" analogy to
anyone, reporters or otherwise, and off she and Louisa went.

Louisa had worn her widest brimmed hat for the occasion,
and a pair of dark cat-eye sunglasses. She was trying to screen
herself from the cameras as best she could, but she heard one
reporter observe to another that she looked fabulous, like a
grim-faced movie star.

Long before they reached the abbey, Louisa could smell
the smoke and cinders. A little closer and specks of ash lay
scattered like frost on the grass beside them. They were not
quite halfway up the hill when Rosemont Abbey rose up out
of the early morning mist to offer her haunting reception.

The gray stone walls and central tower still stood, charred
black in places like the inside of a chimney. Stained-glass window frames were empty on all sides of the building, staring
out over the valley like a series of startled, gaping eyes. The
worst of it was that the roof had collapsed entirely, the force of
which had yanked some of the topmost stones from the walls
and undoubtedly crushed whatever was left of the sanctuary
within. Louisa closed her eyes and thought of the high-domed
ceiling above the altar, which had been painted a century ago
with golden images of Christ on His throne in triumph, along
with all the company of heaven. It seemed impossible that a
church that had survived the Norman invasion—and even
the more recent bombings by the dreaded Luftwaffe—should
fall in such a way.

Yet again the abbey had passed through trials of its own, as had many of its kind. It was stripped and shuttered under the 1536 Dissolution of Monasteries and might have remained uninhabited had the people of Rosemont and Wilbeth Green not purchased the building for a parish church in the 1850s. With the help of a few wealthy patrons, the abbey had undergone extensive restorations and, for its northern wall, received an ornate three-panel window depicting Christ's final moments in the Garden of Gethsemane. Scholars called it a Pre-Raphaelite masterpiece, and no wonder. Whenever it rained during service, it looked as though it were raining in the garden itself, as if the image had sprung to life when Louisa wasn't looking.

Now she stared at the blackened stones surrounding the empty casement. A skeleton, it seemed, without its soul. She reminded herself that it was only a window, easily replaced, but the grief only burrowed deeper as she pictured her parents standing together on the path beneath it. Paul was capable of many things, she thought, but he would never have destroyed this place. Not for all the world.

The rest of the congregation was already gathering in a clearing on the other side of the cemetery fence. A few chairs had been set out in rows, with a makeshift altar constructed out of someone's kitchen table and a flouncy lace tablecloth. As people made their way to the clearing, they moved among the headstones in shifting clusters, some of them crying, others whispering busily together.

Heads turned when Louisa and her aunt arrived, but Aunt Agatha forged a fearless path ahead, stopping only once to remind Louisa to remove her sunglasses. Louisa slipped them into her handbag as the bells began clanging in the next town over at St. Stephen's Church. Several people standing near Louisa lifted their heads as they heard the faraway echo. Rosemont's bells, which usually tolled in tandem to mark the turning of the hour, were markedly silent.

It was at that moment that Reverend Hughes stepped forward. He was a friendly-faced fellow, tall, stout, and in his forties. Shadowed by the abbey ruins, he looked paler than usual, his left eye bruised, but he still wasn't nearly as grave as Louisa might have expected. He waited for the last bell to finish tolling at St. Stephen's, and then he began:

"It is a hard and heavy loss we feel today. But we would do well to remember that the things of this world—yes, even the most beautiful things—are fleeting. Our hope is and remains in Christ alone. The walls of Rosemont Abbey, these many ancient stones, are not the true stones with which He builds His church. And so we do not despair this morning, nor should we. Many of God's people have sojourned much longer and farther than this without a home . . ."

His voice, which had carried easily to this point, now trembled to a halt. He looked down, and then he looked up at the abbey, and whatever he saw there seemed to renew him.

"As those baptized in His holy name, we rejoice that God dwells in us. That even though our bodies will someday fail us, will fall to ruin as surely as the walls of our beloved Rosemont, we have the promise and triumph of salvation. Let us thank God for this good and perfect reminder. For pulling our eyes heavenward when it is so terribly hard to look at the ruins around us."

There were murmurs in the back. Louisa peeked over her shoulder and spotted a few suited stragglers lingering on the path near the abbey's remains. Reporters, she realized after a moment's inspection. There were only a handful of them, and they kept themselves at a distance, but Louisa still had to turn away quickly as one lifted his camera in her direction.

Glad for the cover of her hat's wide brim, she stared forward, unwilling that they should have anything to photograph but the angry line of her straightened back. She couldn't tell if the vicar had seen the journalists or if he thought, as she did, that their presence there was a mark of gross disrespect. If anything, the vicar's voice softened as he went on:

"I must implore you, brothers and sisters, to make no hurried judgments about what has happened here, nor to let yourselves fall prey to idle gossip. Whoever set fire to the abbey—and we don't yet know who that is—is no more a sinner than any of us who are standing here today. As we gather, let us examine our own hearts, truly and honestly, and so pray like the tax collector, 'God be merciful to me, a sinner.'"

The rest of the service was a study in simplicity. There was no sanctuary, yet they gathered. There was no organ, yet they sang. A few people wept through the prayers and wept again when Reverend Hughes called them forward to receive the Lord's Supper. Through it all, Louisa sought comfort in the liturgy, but her last fight with Paul circled like a restless scavenger over the deep waters of her conscience. It was a painful thing to forgive the dead. Harder still to realize that her own brother might have died before he had forgiven her in turn. But her restlessness went deeper than even that.

In the past, Louisa had rarely struggled to confess her sins, nor had she ever doubted herself forgiven when the words of absolution were spoken. It wasn't that she was any more a sinner now than she'd ever been before; she'd only been too young perhaps to acknowledge the full weight of her own words or to recognize the subtler shades of sin within herself. She was finding it all rather inescapable now. The longer she examined herself, and most especially her relationship with Paul, the more evidence she found of a sinfully proud and unforgiving heart.

Distressed, she clenched her eyes shut and prayed as the vicar had encouraged. "God, be merciful to me, a sinner . . ." Though she whispered these words to herself again and again, the prayer felt frail and insubstantial, overshadowed by the relentless memory of her own heartless words: *"I wouldn't care if you drank yourself into oblivion, or even to death. I hope I never have to see you again."*

The reporters were gone by the time the service ended, but this was small consolation when Louisa had yet to exchange pleasantries with a whole congregation who undoubtedly believed her brother was an arsonist. Most people were still kind to her, remarkably so. Some went out of their way to ask her how she was holding up. Others inquired if there was anything they could do for the family as they waited for word. No one spoke of Paul by name, not directly, but as Louisa approached the cemetery gate, she overheard Mrs. Kittle, the head of the Mothers' Union, speaking to Mrs. Shaw: "And to think he was fixing your roof only last Thursday. I shudder to imagine him lurking up there, and what he might have done if he'd found a grievance with *you*, dear!"

"He did a fine job on my roof," sighed Mrs. Shaw. "A pity I'll have to go to the trouble of finding someone new."

"Well, he can't be *all* bad," interjected Mrs. Gale, who had only just entered the fray. "Dr. Clarke's wife told me that he painted the surgery a few days before the fire, and that he only billed them for half the price on account of her sending a lovely dinner round to thank him."

"A dinner!" Mrs. Shaw was scandalized.

"Stuffed haddock, I think it was. She said he was so kind and polite. And she felt sorry for him."

"Well, I'm sure she's rethought *that* position," said Mrs. Kittle sniffily. "He always was a bit wicked, that one. We've all known it, haven't we, ever since he stole the school roof money?"

The school roof money! Louisa nearly laughed. This story was dusted off and recirculated every time Paul did anything the slightest bit troublesome. He'd been only twelve at the time of the theft, and no one had been able to pin it on him directly. Still, Paul had been seen riding his bicycle near the school that evening, and he'd never said outright, not once, that he *hadn't* stolen the money. Which was all the evidence most people needed to assign blame. Louisa had never believed it herself, at least not fully. After all, how had a twelve-year-old, who'd made off with all that cash, managed to spend it surreptitiously in a place as tight at the margins as Wilbeth Green? It wasn't like he had hundreds of extra comic books stuffed in the back of his closet; Louisa had checked.

As she and her aunt drew closer, someone in the group coughed pointedly, after which Mrs. Kittle broke off in the middle of her sentence and leapt forward to snatch Aunt Agatha's hand. "Oh, you poor, miserable dears! How sorry I am for all of you! I always said that boy would burn something to the ground, didn't I? A shed or a barn perhaps, like a proper vagrant might do, but never a *church*! Is there anything we can do for you? Anything at all?"

Aunt Agatha's smile held an inspirational degree of civility. "My nephew has yet to be convicted of any crime, Eustace. Should it ever come to that, and I pray that it doesn't, you may offer us your sympathies, such as they are, at that time."

Louisa, who had never heard her aunt speak defensively of Paul, felt a cheer of gratitude rising in her throat as they strode away from the cemetery. The vicar was greeting a line of parishioners on the path ahead. As soon as he caught sight of Louisa and her aunt, he begged pardon from those still waiting to speak with him and ushered the two women a few steps away from the path, safely out of earshot.

"I can't say how sorry I am for everything your family has been through," he said in a low voice. "I tried to pay a visit the other day, but I was told you were only accepting calls and visits from immediate family."

"Quite right," said Aunt Agatha. "We've been inundated by concerned parties, you see. I hope you weren't offended at being sent away?"

"Not at all! I only wanted to offer support in case there was anything I could do to help."

"Why, you dear man. Thank you! But *we* should be the ones offering to help *you* in the wake of all this senseless damage. Rosemont always was a stunning beauty. Incomparably divine!"

"Nothing has fallen that can't be rebuilt."

"And your head?"

He gave it a cautious tap. "No cracks, or so I'm told. I've always been said to be a touch hardheaded, it shames me to admit, but I've never been grateful for it until now."

Louisa looked more keenly at the vicar. As far as she knew, and she had only the scant details Malcolm had deigned to share, he was the last known person to have spoken to her brother before the burning of the abbey.

"I understand Paul told you he would be at the abbey?" she said.

"He did, yes."

"And when did he tell you that? Was it that morning?"

"Well, no. He told me that evening. At the Ashworths' party."

A bolt of surprise shot through Louisa. "At the party!" she echoed. "Good heavens, what was he doing there?"

"I'm not sure, but I came upon him at the back of the house. He was quarreling with your uncle, and rather heatedly. I-I'm sorry, Miss Everly. I thought you knew."

Louisa didn't know, not a bit of it, and wondered why her uncle, who had been ranting about Paul for the last three days, hadn't thought to mention such an argument. Or that Paul, who had always detested the Ashworths, had turned up at their party, for that matter.

"And you didn't see Paul at the abbey that night?" she asked.

Aunt Agatha touched her shoulder. "I think we've taken up enough of the vicar's time," she interjected. "He has many good mornings yet to say."

"It's quite all right," the vicar said. "If it was Paul who set fire to the abbey, I didn't see him well enough to recognize him."

"Just the back of him?"

"Not his back really. I was on the ground, you see, and only just coming to. I saw his shoes as he was running off."

His shoes. Louisa perked up and thought back to that morning in Uncle Archie's study. Paul had been wearing his brown work boots at the time. She'd noticed them, and those spatters of white paint, as he stepped away from Uncle Archie's desk. "What sort of shoes were they, if I may ask?"

"Louisa!" her aunt scolded more directly. "Reverend Hughes has already given his statement. To the *police*."

"I don't mind answering, not in the slightest." The vicar closed his eyes for a couple of seconds, then shook his head. "There was nothing remarkable about them, Miss Everly. They were black, possibly wingtipped. The same as one might find in dozens of closets from here to Oxford."

"In decent condition?"

"I'd say so. I'd have worn them to service myself."

That settled it. For Paul to have burned the abbey, he would have had to return home at some point during the day to change his shoes. But Paul rarely, if ever, wore dress shoes. That had to mean—well, hang it all, Louisa didn't know what it meant, not precisely. The only thing she knew for certain was that Malcolm wanted her to stay clear of the investigation, as far from it as possible, and likely for good reason.

But first she was going to have a long, careful look in her brother's closet.

6

verly Hall had ten bedrooms, five receiving rooms, a
library, and a lounge. There was a swimming pool in
the back, a stable full of prizewinning horses, and gardens and walking paths aplenty. Most incoming staff took a few weeks to learn the ins and outs; one maid a few years back had gotten herself locked inside a rarely used stairwell for nearly four hours before she'd had the good sense to wave her white apron out the window as a distress signal.

All this square footage had meant less than beans to Paul. He'd called the place a veritable prison and, shortly after reaching the age of majority, taken up residence in a shoebox of a room above an old vacant garage, which he'd used as a workshop for repair and paint jobs around town.

Louisa had no trouble gaining entrance. Paul had told her that he kept a spare key under a rusty paint can beside the woodpile. She was to use it only in the case of an emergency if she was ever truly in trouble. It was as close as he'd come in recent years to looking after her. As she slid the key out from its hiding place, she wondered if Paul had ever imagined that *he* might be the one in trouble.

She found the stairs to his flat at the back of the building. The entrance faced the woods, completely out of sight of the main road. Though the evening breeze smelled sweetly of spring, the air outside the garage was an acrid mix of rubber, wood, and paint thinner. As Louisa climbed the rickety stairs, the fumes stung her nose, and one of the steps near the top, half-rotted through, made a swift but unsuccessful assassination attempt. Louisa pitched forward as it cracked beneath her, then flailed out an arm to straighten her balance. She was beginning to understand just how out of place Paul had always felt at Everly Hall. In her plaid swing skirt and green cashmere cardigan, she felt like a mis-shelved book, an intruder in a world that had only ever belonged to him.

After everything that had happened, she knew it would be hard, emotionally, to see her brother's room, and she thought she'd braced herself for it accordingly. But nothing could have fully prepared her for the garish red police sign fixed to the door: DO NOT ENTER.

Louisa hesitated as her errand made an unpleasant pivot from taking a look around to breaking and entering. She'd known all along that her brother's flat was considered a crime scene, but she didn't realize the police were treating it as such, not in the official sense. Though if the authorities were looking at the lodgings as belonging to a suspect rather than a victim, then maybe she could find something to subtly redirect their gaze...

Her hands were cold all of a sudden, the key slipping against her clammy palm as she slid it into the lock. The mechanism was stiff and out of joint, but she somehow managed to pry it free. The door hinges proved less stubborn, though they gave a rusty squawk.

Louisa wasn't sure what she expected to find in her brother's room. When she was angry with him, she'd often imagined him living like the wastrel he so wanted to be, with empty whiskey bottles scattered all around and a good deal of mold, dust, and disorder.

This was not the case.

The room reeked of cigarettes, but everything was otherwise tidy, clean, and well-kept. She flipped the light switch a couple of times to find the power had been cut, and so the room held tightly to its shadows. It was a narrow space and not an inch of it unused. At one end of the room, his bed was made up well enough to pass military inspection, a patchwork quilt tucked in neatly at the corners. At the other end, a thin worktop, a sink, and a square cabinet all crowded in together. Most of the dishes had been done, she noticed as she stepped across the room. There were two unwashed water glasses in the sink and a small stack of clean pots beside the hot plate. She snooped quickly through the cabinet but found nothing at all remarkable.

His desk was tucked behind the door, a polished plank of wood affixed to a few stacked whiskey crates. An assortment of paintings and framed photographs hung on the wall above it. Most were familiar to her, for they'd hung on the walls of his room at Everly Hall. But there was one in particular that caught her notice: a black-and-white photograph, slightly faded, which was taken during the war. Louisa's heart filled with sorrow as she gazed upon her father's handsome face. As a chaplain, he'd heard many last confessions, seen countless men killed on the battlefield, though he'd done his best to shield his family from the worst of it. His letters were always so calm, so cheerful. But then the terrible headlines had descended more and more rapidly, like bombs heralded by sirens, until Louisa couldn't help but fear the worst. She never expected her father would be taken from them by something as commonplace as a heart attack, and only a few months before Armistice Day.

It was all so dreadfully unfair.

In the aftermath of his loss, her family had received letters from many men abroad, each telling of how deeply they had loved and respected Captain Everly. One of the soldiers who'd been with him in his final moments had traveled all the way to Wilbeth Green to pay his respects. He'd brought a stack of letters for Louisa's mother, those which she had sent to her husband while he was overseas, and a few things for Paul as well—his father's shaving mirror, his prayer booklet, and a small parcel of photographs.

Louisa had never seen this particular photograph before. Her father was wearing his uniform and his black chaplain's scarf, his right hand raised to bless a dozen or so men who were kneeling in the dirt with their heads bowed low over their boots. She touched her fingers to the cheap frame, then dropped her hand as another photograph caught her attention. This one was of her and Paul when they were much younger. Eight or nine years old, they sat together, legs caked with wet sand, smiling wildly at the camera. The lake behind them— Swallows Lake—was a favorite family haunt from summer holidays before the war. Though he'd teased her for it, Paul had taught her to swim that day when she'd been too afraid to jump in after him.

Renewed grief tightened her throat, but she forced herself back to the task at hand. Her aunt and uncle, who thought she'd gone out to borrow a dress from Tilly Harbrook, were likely to wonder when she'd be returning.

Spotting a small assortment of objects on the bedside table, Louisa crouched to take an inventory. There was a wooden ashtray with a small forest of cigarette stubs, a half-empty bottle of scotch, and a cherry-red Dansette record player on the shelf below them. His record collection was stacked in a precarious slant on the floor beside it, most of them fairly current, with older titles wedged in baskets throughout the room. Louisa thumbed through the records, humming a few of the songs and remembering how they'd sounded when Paul still lived at Everly Hall, when the gaudiest strains of jazz had been reduced to a smothered echo behind his closed door.

The room was growing darker now, but Louisa had come prepared. She popped open her handbag and pulled out a torch. Clicking it on, she repositioned herself in the center of the room and looked around more urgently for any sign of her brother's shoes.

There wasn't anything like a wardrobe in the room, just an assortment of hats and button-up shirts hung on a row of pegs, and a few pairs of pants folded over the back of a chair. Louisa rifled through the pockets, feeling a good deal of loose change and pocket lint before extracting a matchbook. She flipped it over in her palm and saw a logo printed on the back with the outline of a cat's green eye and three words in white: THE BLIND CAT.

There was no address, nothing at all to indicate what kind of establishment it might be. Louisa whispered the words, hoping they would sound more familiar if she heard them spoken out loud. She thought it might have sounded like the name of a restaurant or pub, but she'd never heard of a place called by that name, and her brother was a regular patron at

The Three Foxes, which was located at the end of the high street in Wilbeth Green.

She tucked the matchbox into her pocket and might have retreated altogether had she not realized she hadn't yet checked beneath the bed. It was a rather obvious and embarrassing oversight for someone sleuthing about for clues, but Louisa pardoned herself as a novice as she reached under the bed, unearthing a few bins of clothes, some extra blankets—

And shoes!

Black shoes, to be precise, and not a speck on them, the kind Paul would have worn if he'd succumbed to her pestering about attending Sunday services from time to time. She slid them out from under the bed and scrounged deeper, until her fingertips met the wall. But the paint-splattered work boots were nowhere to be found. She scuttled her way back out from under the bed and stood, brushing dust from her skirt as she pondered the state of things.

If she was to believe the order of events as she'd been told, then her brother would have had to change his shoes twice that day—once before burning the abbey and again after knocking out the vicar. She supposed it was possible. But why? Every so-called clue at the abbey seemed to have been left deliberately by Paul himself as a vengeful message. And yet, after setting the inferno, he'd taken the time to return home, to wash every speck of evidence from his shoes, then put them back in their proper place? It made no sense. Unless, of course, Paul hadn't been wearing his black shoes that evening. In fact, Louisa was quite certain that her brother hadn't changed his shoes at all, that he'd been wearing his work boots until the moment he died.

As soon as she thought it, the room was illuminated by a

bright flash of yellow light. She nearly took it for a sign that she was thinking in the right direction, and so she felt dense as a potato when she heard the steady whir of a car with blinding headlights sliding into the drive below.

She clicked off the torch and crouched down quickly so she wouldn't stand shadowed in the window. That was as far as her good sense got her, for panic was settling in rather quickly. She'd parked her car up the road, hoping to keep her visit discreet, but that didn't mean it hadn't been spotted. A wider sweep of light slid across the room as the car rounded the building, and then the engine cut and there was only darkness.

Footsteps soon followed, slow on the steps, terribly slow. Quick as she could, Louisa set down the torch and shoved her brother's shoes back under the bed. They were evidence, of course, and if she truly believed that her brother was dead, then she had to believe he was murdered, and what might that mean for anyone caught snooping?

As if to answer, the door was pressed open by a cautious hand, the rusty hinges sounding the alarm. The room seemed darker now than it had even minutes before. Louisa groped along the worktop. She grabbed a pan at random. Clutching the handle, she lifted it over her head, ready to strike. She'd ceased to breathe but stood to face her fate even as she pressed her other hand over her mouth so she wouldn't have to hear herself scream.

A second later she was wincing, blinded by the high beam of a torch as the intruder, now blocking the doorway, aimed it in her face.

7

I s this what you call staying out of my way?"

Louisa's nerves, durable though they usually were, were unprepared for the relief that came with realizing she was not about to be murdered. At first, she thought she might cry where she stood or else succumb to hysterics, but the prospect was so appalling that she threw up a defiant hand, screening her eyes from the glaring light. "Must you shine that thing in my eyes?" she snapped.

Malcolm lowered the torch, the light pooling the floor between their feet. As Louisa waited for him to speak, she fretted over the dust on her skirt and, more pressingly, about the unmistakable police notice on the front door. Malcolm would be well within his rights if he arrested her for trespassing, but it was the thought of his inevitable lecture that made her think it almost might have been better if he was, as she had first feared, an assassin sent to bump her off for snooping.

"I thought I made it clear that you weren't to meddle."

Louisa had forgotten she was still holding the pan, so she

gave a nervous squeal when Malcolm tugged it out of her hands. Still, he sounded far more irritated than angry, which Louisa thought was promising.

Surely he couldn't arrest her on the grounds of irritation alone.

"I wasn't meddling," she protested. Then, with a spark of inspiration and a defiant lift of her chin: "I was looking for a record."

Malcolm didn't dignify that lie with any sort of cross-examination. Instead, he laughed, which didn't do much for Louisa's poise. Paul had always said she was a rotten liar. Said it as though this was the most pulverizing kind of insult. But even if that was the truth, it didn't mean Malcolm had to appear so utterly disbelieving. What had started as a lie of self-preservation turned to one of salvaging pride as she improvised further: "There's one that holds special meaning for the both of us"—this much at least was true—"and I didn't want it to go walking off. You know how things can go missing when homes are abandoned for too long."

"Trespassers," he agreed, "cause all sorts of trouble."

Louisa scowled outright. "It wasn't my intention to trespass or to 'meddle' in your investigation. Why would I? You've already said the case is more or less a foregone conclusion."

She squinted again as he flashed the light back in her face. "I never said it was a foregone conclusion," he said tightly. "Only that I can't ignore the evidence in front of me simply because I don't like the kind of conclusion it suggests."

"And what about your history with Paul? Is your personal knowledge of a suspect to have no bearing on your conclusions about him?"

He brushed past her without replying, leaving nothing but

darkness behind him. Refusing to be ignored, Louisa trailed after him. "I didn't realize you'd returned to Wilbeth Green," she said. "After you left so suddenly, without a proper good-bye, I might have thought something had happened to turn you against it."

One extra flicker of courage and she might have asked why he hadn't told her he was leaving. She'd wondered about it often enough. But as she stared at the shadow of him in the darkness, so much taller than she remembered, she decided that their younger selves had been very young indeed.

"Where are you staying?" she asked instead.

"I've been put up in a room," he answered, "above one of the local establishments."

"While you look to settle in somewhere more permanent?"

"I don't plan on being here long enough for that."

"Oh? Why's that?"

He opened the cabinet and glanced inside. "I was on the fast track to Scotland Yard, but some of the higher-ups—well, they felt I was too young for it. They had me sent here to prove myself."

"But you'd rather be in London?"

Once again he didn't answer. His torch beam swept ahead, moving from the cabinet to the bedside table. Louisa thought he was trying to decide what she might have touched or carelessly rummaged in her hunt for clues. Since he hadn't arrested her—at least not yet—she didn't see any harm in guiding him: "If you're looking for evidence," she said casually, "then I would encourage you to question the vicar about his attacker's shoes."

"His shoes?"

The confusion in his voice gave Louisa no small amount of

satisfaction. "Yes, his shoes. Whoever bashed the poor vicar on the head was wearing a fine pair of black shoes."

"And?"

"And I saw Paul in the morning, before the party, and he was wearing his work boots. They had paint all over them."

"So he changed them before he crashed the party, perhaps even to slip in unnoticed. No great mystery there."

"You could be right. But I'm assuming Paul would have been in a terrible hurry after setting fire to the abbey—wouldn't you think so?"

"Undoubtedly."

Encouraged by his agreement, Louisa reached under the bed and held up the black shoes. The pristine leather gleamed beneath Malcolm's torch as he drew closer. "So why, after leaving behind all those *beautiful* clues for you to find, should he take the time to return to his room, wipe these clean, and tuck them under the bed?"

Malcolm frowned at the shoes, then shook his head. "Maybe he has more than one pair of black shoes."

"You do realize we're talking about *Paul*. I've known him all my life and only ever seen him wear this sort for funerals."

"I still think you're reaching."

"Am I? It would have been pretty foolish of him to return here after setting the fire, and especially after leaving his necklace at the abbey. Are there any witnesses who can put him in this room after the fire, or any evidence to suggest that he returned here at all?"

"No, but—"

"My uncle spoke to Paul at the party, as did the vicar. There was quite a crowd that night, so he might have been spotted by any number of witnesses. You should ask if anyone took notice of Paul's shoes. If he did change them for the party, as you say, then it should be easy enough to prove, and that might explain it. But if he *was* wearing his work boots to that party, well, then you have to explain the strangeness of it all, don't you?"

Malcolm didn't acknowledge the sense in this, but he didn't argue either. With an air of triumph, Louisa pressed the shoes into his hands, motioning to the door. "It's getting late," she said. "If I don't return home soon, my aunt will be ringing up the police."

"I don't suppose it would make her feel any better to know you're with the police."

Not if her aunt knew the officer in question was Malcolm Sinclair. Louisa didn't dare admit this out loud, but Malcolm laughed as if she had. "I can drive you back," he said. "Unless you think even that would be too much for the woman's sensibilities?"

"Good heavens," said Louisa, "there's no need to risk it. I parked just up the road." She reached for the door and turned the knob, but her fingers dropped away when she realized Malcolm wasn't following. "Aren't you coming?" she asked.

"I'm waiting."

"For?"

"For you to remember what you've forgotten."

As far as Louisa could remember, she hadn't forgotten anything. She nonetheless gave the room a hurried glance, then shrugged at Malcolm.

A thin taper of moonlight shone through the window beside him. It cut through the shadows, revealing the faint curve of his smile. "The *record*, Louisa."

The record! Her mind jolted as she found herself cornered and caught by her own miserable lie.

"I can help you look if you'd like." His smile had moved, very subtly, from his lips to his voice. "I'd hate for you to have come all this way for nothing."

Coming clean would have been painful at that point, unbearably so, and so Louisa snatched the torch from Malcolm's hand and flipped through the nearest stack of records. By some small miracle, she spotted The Andrews Sisters within seconds; this was the very record she'd been thinking of when she'd improvised her story moments before. As she slid the album out from the rest of the collection, Malcolm came up behind her, reading over her shoulder:

"*This* is the record?" He paused. "Doesn't seem very sentimental to me."

He probably thought he'd caught her spinning another ridiculous story, but Louisa was glad she didn't have to lie now. "Our eighteenth birthday was a disaster," she explained with a distant smile. "Paul got into the most dreadful argument with Uncle Archie. He called him a rotting old vampire—which really was quite terrible—and said he couldn't wait to move out on his own. I was always trying to smooth things over, so I asked Paul if there was anything he wanted to do to celebrate our birthday, and he said, 'The only thing I want is a good, stiff drink!'"

And so Louisa had gone straight to her room, dug out one of her old records—*Rum and Coca-Cola*—and slid it beneath Paul's door. She knew it was a rotten pun and probably not the most desirable of gifts. Unlike Louisa, Paul had never been a fan of The Andrews Sisters. But then, much to her surprise, he'd thrown open the door while she was still standing there, laughing himself to stitches even as he accused her of landing the tackiest punch line this side of the Atlantic. And for that moment at least, all was well. He and Louisa had sat in the library until midnight, playing cards and drinking soda as they listened to every Andrews Sisters record Louisa had in her collection.

She did her best to explain all of this to Malcolm, then lapsed into silence when she was done. How silly she must have sounded to him, like any other suspect gabbling wildly to cover a lie.

He surprised her with a look of ponderous sadness. "For what it's worth," he offered, "I hope you're wrong. About Paul. That is, I hope he's all right so you can see him again."

"In prison, you mean?"

He sighed. "If it should come to that."

Clutching the record to her chest, Louisa followed him outside onto the landing, where she felt the scrape of a flat object catching beneath the toe of her shoe. As Malcolm turned to lock the door, she dipped down and scooped the item into her hand, her fingertips examining what felt like a tiny, smooth button. It might have been nothing. Might have fallen off one of the officers searching the area. Or it might have been a clue. She slipped it discreetly into her pocket just in case Malcolm decided to confiscate it, then kept on down the weather-beaten stairs. He was only a half step behind her.

When they reached the bottom, he insisted on walking her to her car. She thought he was being gallant, but he stepped in front of her door at the last moment, blocking her from reaching for the handle.

"What are you doing?" Louisa demanded. "Stand aside."

"I will. Just as soon as you hand over that key."

She glanced at his hand, which he now held out in silent expectation, then up into his eyes. "Forgive me," she said, unwilling to give anything away so easily, "but I'm not sure what you're referring to?"

His laughter rose to the occasion. "Whatever key you used to get into Paul's flat. I'm assuming he left one to you, but you'd better leave it to me now."

"Am I detecting an *or else*?"

"Or else you might be tempted to return. In which case I'd have to arrest you for trespassing. Or perhaps tampering with a crime scene." He leaned a little closer. "From where I'm standing, Miss Everly, I can see more than a few possibilities."

Now it was Louisa's turn to laugh. "You're welcome to arrest me for anything you'd like, *Inspector*."

She brushed past him, half expecting to be seized and searched for her lack of cooperation, but Malcolm only tugged open her door, as quiet and accommodating as a chauffeur, and shut her up securely inside.

And that might have been an end of it, a clean and comfortable stalemate, had Louisa not cranked down her window after starting the car: "I realize," she said, "that you haven't thanked me yet, but you're *quite* welcome for the hint about the shoes."

As soon as she said this, she stepped down hard on the gas pedal, and Malcolm slid back at the last possible moment, just as her wheels began to stir the gravel. Heedless of his potential pursuit, Louisa gunned the car up the road, watching him in her rearview mirror for as many seconds as the darkness allowed before relaxing in her seat.

She hadn't planned on making such a devilishly dramatic

exit. Truly, she hadn't thought that far ahead. But there was something about Malcolm, something that felt mildly inconvenient at the moment, and so she focused on the road instead, her thoughts merging with the low drone of the engine as it growled like a beast that was hell-bent on getting away.

8

I t's as I always say, isn't it? There's no greater comfort for low spirits than a fine new pair of heels."

Louisa's new kitten heels, which were a happy shade of lemon yellow, clicked a pretty tune as she crossed the stone terrace to where her aunt, who had indeed always lived by a certain "new heels mantra," smiled approvingly. Louisa had bought the shoes months ago; she was only waiting to find the right dress so she could give them a suitable debut. But when Aunt Agatha learned that David Ashworth and his mother were both coming for tea, she told Louisa it was time to put on her finest dress and give her new shoes a proper walkabout.

The table had already been set. In the Everly household, tea was as precise a science as biology or chemistry. It was all about balance, about proportion. Unless the weather failed to cooperate, and it rarely dared to do so, Aunt Agatha always served tea to her guests on the terrace, which was less to do with personal preference than with pride. Apart from the raising of Louisa and Paul, she'd never had children of her own but had spent years tending to her garden with a kind of parental diligence. Louisa had always supposed it was only natural that her aunt would want to show off her agricultural efforts to her guests. But now, as Louisa sat in the chair nearest the lavender, her aunt paused, considering her with a gardener's judging eye before announcing, merrily, that her niece was "as pretty as a primrose."

Louisa told herself that it was only a compliment, the same as many she'd received over the years, but she couldn't help recalling what Paul had said to her at their final meeting: *"I suppose it is lucky that they so enjoy showing you off."*

She stared down at her white lace gloves, wrestling against the memory until her aunt set her hand over hers on the table. "You've been through so much, my dear. I fear it may be too soon for you to be receiving visitors?"

"Oh no!" sputtered Louisa. "It's so kind of them to call on us, and I would hate to show even an ounce of rudeness to Mrs. Ashworth."

"Or to her son," her aunt added in a smiling undertone.

Moments later, the sound of an engine came hurtling up the drive, followed by the closing of several car doors and the unmistakable trill of Mrs. Ashworth's cheerful voice.

"I think I hear her now," said Aunt Agatha. "The little dear."

There was nothing notably "little" about Mrs. Ashworth. She was actually quite tall. But she was also the sort of woman who, no matter the topic at hand, always seemed to be commenting on the weather. Had she been poor, the upper crust would have called her insufferable for it, but alas for them, she came from old money, and so she was referred to as "the little dear." Uncle Archie was somewhat less tactful; when he heard that Mrs. Ashworth would be joining them for tea, he came straight to the point and called her a bore, to which Aunt Agatha firmly reminded him that David Ashworth would make anyone a fine son-in-law.

"Agatha, *darling!*" Mrs. Ashworth wore a pillbox hat festooned with pheasant feathers, which fluttered merrily as she bustled through the open French doors. "How very attractive your garden looks—" she stopped to bestow a ceremonious kiss upon each of Aunt Agatha's cheeks "—and how *perfectly* accommodating of the sun to be shining down for your little tea!"

Aunt Agatha nodded her agreement, but her smile was the slightest bit pained as she turned away, motioning for a servant to fetch the tea tray.

Wearing a tweed suit and a pair of thick-rimmed sunglasses, David appeared in the doorway at the same moment the servant was departing. There was a brief confusion of shuffling feet and overlapping apologies. David was still chuckling about it as he removed his sunglasses and stepped onto the terrace. Just the sight of him was enough to set Louisa more at ease, for he was becoming so charmingly familiar to her, his sandy hair slicked to the side of his temples and a smile so effortlessly bright it would have been right at home on a big band orchestra stage.

He'd brought a bouquet of roses and pink dahlias for her aunt, which were marveled over briefly before being handed off to another servant, who went scurrying in search of a vase. David's smile, brightening when he saw Louisa, faded as he drew near enough to look into her eyes more fully. "Poor kid," he said, taking her hand. "How are you holding up?"

"Well enough," she answered, squeezing his fingers.

"Any word from Paul?"

"Not yet."

His mother, who heard this little exchange, sighed momentously as she sat. "This must be such a trial for you, my dear, and yet you mustn't allow it to weigh you down too terribly. As my mother used to say, worrying is a waste of fine weather—and *such* fine weather it is!" She smiled up at the clouds as the dahlias, now arranged in a china vase, made their triumphant return to the terrace. The servant needed a moment, and a few subtle signals from Aunt Agatha, to position them acceptably on the table.

"Oh, but they *are* lovely!" Louisa's aunt remarked when this was finished.

"Well done, David!" agreed his mother.

The next arrival was a brightly colored floral teapot with a swirl of steam curling upward from the spout like a puff of smoke from a dragon's snout. As Louisa's aunt poured, David reached forward and accepted a strawberry scone when Louisa held out the platter. "You have a fine garden, Mrs. Everly," he said. "You must put a good deal of work into it."

"Thank you." With an expert hand, Aunt Agatha stirred two cubes of sugar into her cup, her spoon failing to clink the edge of the teacup even once. "I do work at it quite a lot. Of course, our dear Louisa helps me from time to time."

Louisa had helped once, to be precise, and it was three years prior. She'd yanked out a whole row of fledgling forsythias, which had looked no different from ordinary weeds to her. Her aunt had smiled patiently and said she understood, yet she had not requested Louisa's help since that day.

"It's a miracle the flowers are getting on as they are," remarked Mrs. Ashworth. "The mornings have been so unthinkably cold. Since the night Paul set the fire, I mean."

Fighting the impulse to wince, Louisa took up a triangular

sandwich and set it neatly on her plate. Aside from Malcolm, she hadn't shared her suspicions about Paul's disappearance with anyone. And yet the people of Wilbeth Green were as ready and willing as a jury to hand over the guilty verdict. Shifting the universal opinion wasn't going to be easy. Still, Louisa had to try.

"We don't know for sure that he set the fire," she said. This was safe enough to say surely, for her aunt had already said as much to Mrs. Kittle.

"Really?" David's eyebrows rose. "I didn't realize there was any sort of debate about it."

"I prefer not to leap to any conclusions when my brother isn't here to give a full account of himself." Louisa didn't mention that she'd leapt to plenty of other conclusions in the meantime. Her aunt would likely have a coronary if her niece brought up as coarse a subject as murder at the tea table.

"He left the necklace, didn't he?" challenged David. "And the turpentine? Forgive me, Louisa, but were *those* not an account of his movements? Or at least of his intentions?"

"They were a message," she agreed. But then she saw the way that David nodded, as if he'd just won a hand at cards, and so she felt just gutsy enough to add: "Whether that message came from Paul or from someone else remains to be seen."

"How terribly cryptic!" cried Mrs. Ashworth, her pheasant feathers all aflutter.

David pondered for several seconds, then slunk back in his chair and shook his head. "If Paul didn't burn the abbey, then who else would have done so?"

Unable to answer without sharing what she'd felt on the night of the fire, Louisa stirred and stirred her tea, grateful for the reprieve when Aunt Agatha leaned forward and offered

David another scone. "The best any of us can do," she said gently, "is pray that my nephew will return to us when he feels the time is right. Beyond that, I prefer not to discuss arson during tea. It really *isn't* the thing."

After that, the conversation made a swift and graceful pirouette to the subject of Lady Westlock's newest hat, which really *was* the thing. After all, it had a splendid arrangement of flowers, as Aunt Agatha observed for some time.

"Though not very likely to stand up to any sort of rain," mused Mrs. Ashworth.

9

After tea, it was suggested that David and Louisa should stroll through the gardens while the older women finished their gossiping. There was a charming stone footbridge behind the stable, which offered a gorgeous view in early spring. Casually, Aunt Agatha inquired if David had ever seen it. To no one's surprise, he hadn't, and so the course for the suggested stroll was set as neatly and efficiently as the afternoon tea table.

David smiled and hooked Louisa's arm through his as they walked, but he was much quieter than usual, and so she wondered if she ought to apologize for her aunt's obvious scheming. No doubt, the woman thought a little gentle prompting was all it took to make a proposal materialize out of thin air. But while Louisa liked David immensely, their relationship had never progressed beyond the standard flirtation or the slight brush of his cheek against hers while they were dancing. She didn't want him to think she was naive in her expectations of him, or that her affections were more attached than his. In fact, the idea of a proposal at that moment was so absurd, so unthinkable, that she could hardly draw breath when David stopped in the middle of the bridge and, very slowly, reached into his pocket—

He pulled out a silver cigarette case. "D'you mind?"

In twenty-six years, Louisa had never experienced anything so disastrously anticlimactic. Quashing the urge to laugh, she motioned for him to go ahead and smoke. His silver lighter flashed in the sunlight as he popped it open, and for a moment he leaned against the bridge, staring out at the fields as he smoked in silence. Louisa rested her arms against the railing beside him and followed his gaze. It really was a striking view. Clusters of Queen Anne's lace burst up through the tall grass, and daisies, and most vibrant of all, a sweeping array of bluebottles—"bachelor buttons," Louisa had heard them called.

David cleared his throat and tapped his cigarette, peppering the creek below them with ashes. "I'm sorry if I sounded contrary about the fire."

"Oh." This wasn't at all the conversation Louisa had hoped for, but she nonetheless found a smile, however faint, to reassure him. "It's all right."

"No, it's not. I should have been more mindful about what you're going through. Of course you want to wait to be sure. To have all the answers. He's your brother, after all. I just don't want you to suffer through any false hopes, you understand."

"Yes, I understand." She paused. "Did you happen to see Paul that night? At your family's party, I mean?"

As Louisa waited for him to answer, she looked out over the field. There was no breeze that day, so the flowers stood perfectly still, as though they too were holding their breath. David took a final drag of the cigarette, then dropped it, unfinished, to the creek below. "I wish I had. Maybe I could have stopped him if I'd been able to see how out of sorts he was."

"He wouldn't have listened to you. Paul never listened to anyone with money."

"I suppose you're right." He smiled at her, and they turned from each other at nearly the same moment, leaving the bridge and the wildflowers behind them as they meandered back toward the house.

With each step, Louisa watched the horizon until the topmost stones of Everly Hall stretched back into view above the trees. "Does your mother know?" she inquired as they passed the stable.

"Know what?"

"That you smoke. I've heard her call it a filthy habit."

"She pretends not to know." He angled her a look, lightly bumping her shoulder with his own. "You won't tell her, though, will you?"

"And part with a perfectly fine bit of blackmail? Not a chance."

He laughed under his breath as they reached the gravel drive, then briefly consulted his wristwatch. "What do you think? Have they had enough time to finish their gossiping?"

"I doubt it very much. Our walk will have given them twice as much to gossip about."

"In which case I shouldn't want to rush them." He took her hand, lacing her fingers between his, and tugged her behind the third topiary to the left of the path. When he leaned in, she thought he was about to kiss her cheek, as he usually did, but perhaps their stroll to the bridge had inspired something after all, for he anchored her against him at the last moment, his arm pulled in tightly around her back.

"Will you go for a drive with me tomorrow?" he murmured, his breath tickling her forehead.

"Where?"

"Oh, I don't know. Anywhere. I can bring the Bentley after dinner."

Leaning into his chest, Louisa smiled up at him. It wasn't the proposal Aunt Agatha was hoping for, but it was, for now, entirely enough. "I'd like that very much."

David was still holding her. There was a look on his face that Louisa hadn't seen before, but she'd been hoping very much of late that she might. Her heartbeat stuttered as he tipped her face and tucked her in even closer, his lips hovering thoughtfully over hers.

"Ahem."

Louisa turned sharply and flushed to a humiliating shade of scarlet when she realized that the butler, Joseph Fernsby, was standing behind them. He was a lanky middle-aged gentleman with a long face and remarkably poor sense of timing. If he ever laughed, and Louisa highly doubted it, he only ever did so in secret.

"Pardon me," he said, "but there's an inspector here who wishes to speak with you, sir. He's waiting in the billiards room."

David's hands dropped from Louisa's waist. The billiards room was on the first floor, facing the drive, and had a splendid view of the narrow space behind the third topiary. Louisa glanced over just in time to see a shadow turn itself away from the window.

Was Malcolm waiting there?

Her face went redder as she wondered if he might have seen, from that very spot, the intimate moment Fernsby had so clumsily interrupted.

"He wishes to speak to *me*?" David laughed and straightened his tie. "How irregular."

"He did say it was a matter of some urgency."

Louisa had never heard Fernsby's voice rise above a low drone—it was ill-suited for inspiring any true sense of urgency in anyone—but David nevertheless excused himself from Louisa's side and went with Fernsby back to the house.

Louisa watched them go but didn't move an inch herself. She knew she ought to return to the terrace. Her aunt was likely to come looking for her if she knew David had been summoned away. But Louisa also knew that Malcolm would only request an interview with David if he thought it would shed light on her brother's disappearance.

Curiosity on that score trumped any sense of caution and compelled her to move forward. Of course, listening in at the door would have been too risky. It was right next to her uncle's study, and he was likely hiding in there until Mrs. Ashworth was gone. But the billiards room window was open a crack. The right side of the casement and the wall beside it were covered with creeping vines and an assortment of flamingo-pink rhododendrons. The shrubs provided the perfect cover, dense and tremendously tall. Glancing up the drive once to ensure she was alone, Louisa clambered in from one side and skirted the narrow gap between the shrub and the wall.

As she went, she sent a brief plea heavenward that she wouldn't be spotted by her aunt, for there was nothing at all dignified about climbing through rhododendrons. It was scratchy and awkward, and her progress was halted once or twice by the overgrown branches that clawed at her curls. By the time she reached the billiards room window, she was in a state of mild dishevelment, brushing dirt and a few fragments of dead leaves from the hem of her skirt.

And as she did so, she heard Malcolm's voice, which carried clearly through the open window beside her: "There's no sense in lying to me, Mr. Ashworth. I can assure you we already have a credible witness to the fact."

Louisa stilled. She peered cautiously around the corner and barely suppressed a squeak of surprise when she found Malcolm standing much closer to the window than she expected. Mindful of his recent threats to arrest her, she shuffled back out of sight, but not before she spied David on the other side of the room; he stood near the furthest corner of the billiards table, turning a white cue ball over and over in his hands and looking as though he'd like nothing more than to hurl it straight at Malcolm.

"I fail to see the relevance of it," Louisa heard him say as she repositioned herself next to the window. "Am I under suspicion for something?"

"We're trying to determine where Paul might have gone," answered Malcolm. "Anything you might remember from that night could shed light on his state of mind."

"You have a whole pile of burned rubble to show you the state of his mind."

"His whereabouts then."

"He didn't tell me where he was going."

Louisa's whole body went deathly cold as those words registered. David had told her, in no uncertain terms, that he hadn't seen Paul on the night of the party. What was he trying to hide from her? Dragging herself back up, she risked another glance around the edge of the window frame. Malcolm had crossed to the other side of the room. He'd taken two cue sticks down from the rack on the wall and, smiling sharply, held one out to David. "Why don't you tell me what he *did* tell you, Mr. Ashworth, and *I'll* decide if it's important."

Louisa leaned closer, desperate to catch every word of David's answer, but she heard another mix of voices in the distance—her aunt and Mrs. Ashworth. Were they looking for her? Irritated by the interruption, she glanced in the direction of the garden, then back into the room just in time to watch Malcolm line up his aim over the side of the billiards table. There was a silence. Then the cue ball went cracking into the rest of the formation, scattering balls in all directions and impressively sinking two of them into the pockets at the end of the table. As Malcolm straightened, David glared at him. And though he still hadn't answered Malcolm's question, Aunt Agatha's voice was now drawing nearer. Fearing she was about to be the subject of a search party, Louisa reluctantly slid out from behind the shrubbery, smoothing her hair and her skirt and trying to appear as normal as possible.

"There's a call for you, Miss Everly."

With a faint cry of alarm, she spun on her heel and once again found herself face-to-face with Fernsby. He looked bored. Chronically unamused. So much so that Louisa might have thought delivering messages to people hiding in the rhododendrons was a usual part of his daily duties. And though her uncle always said that the measure of a good butler was in not knowing he was there to begin with, this really was taking things a bit too far.

"Good heavens, Fernsby!" she hissed, plucking a stray flower petal from her hair. "You nearly frightened the life out of me!"

"There's a call for you," he repeated, his gray eyes hooded. "In the house."

She sighed heavily. Since the fire, the telephone was *always* ringing, with many well-intentioned neighbors wanting to know how she was getting on in the aftermath of "the incident," as it was already called in the local vernacular. She'd learned to be on her guard about every call. One reporter had been so desperate for a statement from the family, and so cunning, that she'd pretended to be one of Louisa's old school friends. She might have gotten away with it too if Louisa hadn't put her to the test and realized the woman couldn't recall the name of Thomas Canfield. He was the first boy to have kissed Louisa, or rather tried to, at the church's spring fete. That was fifteen years ago, and yet there wasn't a soul living in Wilbeth Green who wouldn't remember the vicar's daughter pushing the Canfield boy into the cake table right as Mrs. Kittle was being awarded for Best Victoria Sponge.

Though Louisa was wary of being duped again, she followed Fernsby inside and picked up the handset. "Hello?"

"Miss Everly! Miss Everly, are you there? Ah, yes, there you are! Bravo. Reverend Hughes here. If it's convenient, I wonder if you might stop by the vicarage tomorrow."

"Certainly!" she said, surprised. "Is anything the matter?"

The line crackled with static, making his voice sound far away: "I have something!"—*crackle!*—"something from Paul!" Louisa crammed a hand against her open ear and closed her eyes, struggling and straining to hear him through the din: "—shouldn't like to speak about it just now," he was saying, and she thought he sounded nervous, as if he was afraid of being overheard, but then he added hurriedly: "These telephones are so awkward, you know!"

"Yes!" She shifted the receiver to her other ear. "Yes, I understand completely. I can be there tomorrow. Around ten?"

"Mrs. Watson!"—*crackle!*—"the shrubbery!"—*crackle!*—"most remarkable sense of hearing!"—*crackle!*—"noon?"

"Yes!" she shouted. "I'll be there!"

"Cheers!" the vicar bellowed back.

He hung up at once, but Louisa stood in the hall with the handset slack in her hand. The vicar had something to show her. Something from Paul. Was it a clue perhaps? She could only hope. There was nothing she wanted more than to discover the truth about what had happened to her brother, and that was becoming more complicated by the minute.

David was lying to her. She wasn't sure why or about what, but Malcolm seemed to know, and now she found that Paul had taken the time to slip something to the vicar prior to his disappearance.

"There are dangerous people all around you," her brother had warned on the day of the fire. *"And I mean to prove it."* At the time, she'd been so sure this was only the paranoid raving of a drunken man. But now? Now she wasn't sure of anything.

Or anyone.

10

Mrs. Watson was still busy trimming the vicarage shrubbery when Louisa arrived the next afternoon. A squat row of bulbous boxwoods had already come under her shears and were looking much more themselves, but the lilac bush near the gate was proving more of a challenge. Shears in hand, the eighty-four-year-old woman balanced her frail frame on a stool, trimming vigorously near the top of the bush while the vicar paced on the patch of lawn beneath her. "Mrs. Watson," he entreated. "Please. *Please!* You must let me do that for you!"

"No need to fuss!" Mrs. Watson answered. "I'm *perfectly* at home up here! I'm a whole head shorter than Napoleon—been balancing on chairs my entire life!"

The vicar shook his head and muttered defeatedly: "Would that I could talk some sense into her."

Anyone else would have been too far away on the stool to have heard him, but Mrs. Watson laughed and wagged her shears at him. "If it hasn't happened yet, it likely never will! Now here comes Miss Everly. So you must stop your fretting, Vicar, and off you go for your tea."

Their afternoon repast had already been set out in the kitchen, featuring a tin of biscuits and a Battenburg cake to rival all Battenburgs. "Mrs. Watson is a woman of many talents," the vicar observed as he set to slicing it. Beneath the thin, silky layer of white icing, the cake was a dainty patchwork of pink-and-yellow squares.

Louisa hardly heard the vicar's pleasantries as she poured their tea. This was the first time she'd set foot inside the vicarage since her parents had died, and quite without thinking she'd sat in her usual chair at the table. Since the war, things were used up until they were broken beyond all hope, and so the house was, in many ways, unchanged. The furniture was the same. So too the curtains, which were patterned with a floating array of faded apples and pears. Even the teapot, which Louisa held in her hand, was still serviceable enough. It was an old Brown Betty, chipped beneath the handle from where her mother had once accidentally bumped it against the bottom of the sink while washing.

Whichever way Louisa looked, she was stricken by this strange and spectral sense of sameness, and yet there had also been a vanishing. Her mother's floral apron no longer hung on the peg beside the sink. Her father was always forgetting his reading glasses on the worktop near the bread box, but they were nowhere to be seen, nor were his books, or his hat, or Paul's fishing pole, which they were always tripping over on their way up the stairs because he never remembered to put it away properly.

Louisa heard herself ask if the vicar wanted milk, but what she really wanted to ask was *how*? How could so many things remain the same in a place where everything that had once mattered to her was gone?

She put on a smile as she handed him his cup, but he wasn't fooled, not for an instant. "This can't be easy for you," he said, the corners of his kind eyes crinkling. "Sitting here. Like this."

"It would be easier if I had some answers," she admitted.

He pushed back from the table and went to the cabinet. "I'm not sure if this will help," he said, reaching into the top drawer, "but I hope it does in some way. Paul left this in my care; I'm not at all sure what it means."

He handed her a plain white envelope. The words *Hold on to this for me* had been written in Paul's unmistakable scrawl. Inside, she found an old black-and-white photograph. It was creased at one corner as though it had been worried over many times by nervous hands. In the picture was a young woman. She wore a collared pullover sweater and an oval locket, her dark hair tucked, all but a few finger curls, beneath a linen bucket hat. Louisa thought the woman might have been sitting on a beach, for there was a blur of gray waves visible just past her shoulder. With her closed-lipped smile and lovely dark eyes, the woman left a somber feeling floating in Louisa's stomach. She flipped the photograph over and read the message written on the back: *Don't be stingy. I want what I'm owed, or I'll peddle your secret to every paper from here to London.*

"When did Paul give this to you?" she rasped.

"Mrs. Watson found it under the cabinet in the entryway when she was sweeping. He seems to have slid it under the door, but it must have been brushed aside when I entered. I'm afraid I have no idea how long it might have been there."

"Does it mean anything to you?" asked Louisa. "The photograph?"

"Not a thing. That's why I called for you. I hoped you might shed some light on it."

Louisa flipped the photograph over again. She could see three possibilities as to its meaning. Her brother might have been blackmailing someone. She hated to admit it, but this didn't exactly seem out of character. Perhaps Paul's victim no longer wished to be blackmailed and had gotten rid of Paul before he'd had a chance to deliver his next threat. But the handwriting on the photograph didn't match the writing on the envelope. Each letter was carefully written, nothing like her brother's crowded chicken scratch, which Louisa had recognized at once. This made her wonder if Paul was the one being blackmailed, yet she failed to see what this picture would have to do with it, as it was decades too old to be proof of any current dalliance. Which brought her to the third possibility: perhaps Paul wasn't the victim or the blackmailer. Perhaps he'd merely stumbled upon the blackmail scheme and was trying to bring it to light. In any event, he wouldn't have slipped the photograph under the vicar's door unless he feared the photograph might fall into the wrong hands.

Unless he felt that something terrible might happen to him.

Louisa had entirely forgotten the vicar was still in the room. She nearly jumped out of her seat when he stepped closer, his angular features honed by a look of quiet anticipation. Paul had trusted him, which made her want to trust him as well. But there wasn't much to trust him with. At least not yet. So far most of the clues she'd found were small enough to fit in her cardigan pocket. The button. The matchbook. She'd taken to carrying them both on her person, reaching for them at odd moments and pondering what, if anything, they meant.

Her fingers shook as she drew them out and set them down on the table beside the picture. With a low hum, the vicar slid into the chair opposite her, squinting curiously at the items as if she'd emptied a puzzle box onto the table. "What are we looking at?"

"I'm not sure," said Louisa, "but I know that Paul didn't burn the abbey."

She waited for him to answer dubiously. To demand to know how she could have entertained such a preposterous suspicion. Any number of people she knew might have laughed outright or, more delicately, called her nerves into question. Instead, the vicar's frown lines deepened as he read the message on the back of the photograph.

"I've doubted as much myself," he admitted at length.

Louisa could have buried her face in her hands. She could have wept. And she very nearly did, for here, at last, was an ally. Or, at the very least, someone who didn't think she was entertaining silly and sisterly notions about Paul's character.

"Are you all right?" The vicar spoke in a quiet voice, as if he was wary of spooking her, and Louisa realized it had been several minutes since she'd drawn a full breath.

Feeling dizzy, she blew out slowly through her loosened lips. "Yes," she whispered, "I'm all right."

Though the vicar nodded, he didn't exactly look convinced. "I know that your relationship with your brother was strained," he said. "Paul wanted it to be otherwise, and I'm sure it hasn't been any easier for you. If you should ever wish to talk—"

Louisa stood abruptly and shook her head. She never dreamed that Paul would have spoken of her to the vicar. It might have been easier for her to imagine that he never really thought of her at all.

Easier, perhaps, but not likely.

There was a courtesy mirror on the far side of the kitchen,

near the back entrance, and Louisa's gaze was pulled and fixed there. It was impossible to look in the mirror without thinking about Paul; their features were so hauntingly similar. Perhaps everything would have been less painful if they hadn't been twins, if they hadn't looked so much alike and yet been so different in every other possible way.

Or perhaps, like most things in their relationship, it wouldn't have made a difference.

For now, all Louisa could do was move forward. She could focus on the fire and who had set it, and when the last of the cinders were swept away, when the truth of it all came out, then she could face the rest of it.

She broke the spell cast by her own reflection by lowering her eyes, then stepped back to the table, eager to press onward now that she had some traction. "I have a question that may sound very strange, but it's important. You said you saw my brother at the Ashworths' party?"

"We spoke in passing."

"So you saw how he was dressed."

"Yes, of course. The same as he usually is."

"Not dressed for a party, then?"

"Well, not the sort of party I would usually attend," he admitted with a chuckle.

"I wonder if you happened to take notice of his shoes?"

The vicar looked out the window in a slow, thoughtful way before his eyes widened with sudden realization. "Boots!" he said. "But of course! My assailant at the church—"

"Black shoes," Louisa finished for him. "Yes, exactly." She paused a moment, allowing this information to click into place, then tapped the matchbook. "Have you heard of this establishment?"

"The Blind Cat? I'm afraid I haven't. Could it be a pub perhaps?"

"If it is, it's one I've never heard of."

"It's a boxing club." Louisa and the vicar both jumped as Mrs. Watson strode briskly into the room. "Do forgive me, dear," she said, brushing her old arthritic hands on her apron frills. "Couldn't help overhearing."

"Mrs. Watson!" scolded the vicar, but Louisa merely smiled. She couldn't really fault Mrs. Watson for snooping when she herself had climbed into a rhododendron bush to eavesdrop on Malcolm's interview. As Mrs. Watson cut herself a piece of the Battenburg cake, Louisa picked up the matchbook. "A boxing club," she repeated thoughtfully, turning the matchbook with her fingertips from corner to corner. That certainly sounded like Paul's kind of haunt.

"Yes, and a rather dodgy one at that," said Mrs. Watson. "Lots of drinking and gambling and everything else you warn against in your homilies, dear vicar, and for good reason!"

"Do you know where it is?" Louisa asked hopefully.

"Oh, certainly. It's in Chitwell. Next to a mortuary at the end of Harlowe Street, though I do hope the boxers haven't a frequent need of *those* services."

"Er, Mrs. Watson?" The vicar cleared his throat delicately. "May I ask how you, um, came to know about this particular establishment?"

"I have twelve grandsons," she answered, as if this explained everything.

"And?"

"And they tell me *all* the nonsense."

Louisa laughed. She couldn't recall the last time she'd laughed without feeling that wayward tug of sorrow. But she thought it was fitting that she should do so, after all those years, while sitting in her family's kitchen. "It sounds like your grandsons have made a sport out of shocking you," she observed.

"I'm eighty-four years old," Mrs. Watson said, spooning a hefty bite of cake into her mouth. "Nothing shocks me anymore except the state of the vicarage shrubberies."

11

It was no longer a matter of whether Louisa got caught. It was now a matter of *when*.

She was supposed to be out driving with David. Of course, given the conversation she'd overheard between him and Malcolm, she'd wanted nothing more than to plead a headache and postpone, but nothing short of a broken limb would have convinced Aunt Agatha to allow it. Louisa would never have been permitted to drive all the way to Chitwell on her own either, but that's precisely where she was, with a map sprawled on the seat beside her as she navigated the rain-slickened streets.

Chitwell was two hours east of Wilbeth Green. On the map, which Louisa had snuck from her uncle's study, it stood out like a tiny blemish on the farthest fringe of Oxford. She thought she'd have plenty of time. Time enough to track down The Blind Cat and ask a few harmless questions. Time enough to return for dinner and keep her driving date with David.

She would have made it back in time, but she forgot that the bridge was still out near Epfield Woods. And then she got herself lost, twice. An unexpected dash of rain only made matters worse, for the cold, gray drizzle made every street in Chitwell look much the same as any other. The same muddy lanes. The same faded storefronts packed in close on the street like herrings in a tin. She'd passed four fish-and-chips shops and twice as many pubs, and they all would have looked abandoned were it not for the dimly lit windows that only hinted at life still flickering within.

In her mint-green gown and her aunt's teal-blue Cadillac, Louisa stood out more than she would have liked, but it couldn't be helped, for she had to be dressed and fully ready for dinner the moment she returned home. And though she felt bad fooling her aunt, it was easily done. She told her she was going shopping for the afternoon with Tilly Harbrook—who always found it rather thrilling to provide any sort of alibi—then secured her freshly coifed curls beneath a green satin scarf and went on her way.

Her new kitten heels came along, too.

She *was* growing rather fond of them.

As she eased the Cadillac onto Harlowe Street, she glanced nervously at the clock. The minute hand was edging dangerously close to six. She'd already missed dinner and was disastrously late for her drive with David, which meant her aunt would have been ringing up Tilly and then, quite possibly, the police.

Guilt swelled within her, then ebbed when she peered through the rain and spotted The Blind Cat exactly where Mrs. Watson said it would be. It was a scrappy-looking brick front squashed between two much larger establishments. One was the mortuary, as Louisa had already been informed, and the other a butcher shop. Both seemed to be doing their best to shoulder the boxing club out of the way, but still it stood there with its grimy windows and a leaky gutter, spitting a stream of rusty water upon the step below.

Not wishing to draw too much notice, Louisa parked down the street from the butcher shop and cut the engine. She hadn't realized how nervous she was until she unclenched her hands from the steering wheel and found that her wrist-length leather gloves were steeped in sweat. "Get ahold of yourself," she muttered, yanking them off. "You're only here to ask a few questions."

To ask a few questions of a potential blackmailer. A potential *murderer*.

And yet she owed it to Paul to discover the truth. To clear his name if she could. Since they'd been children, no one except their parents had ever believed his side of any story. No one had ever seen or acknowledged what was good in him because it was far easier to point out his faults. Even Louisa had done as much to him in her own way.

But not anymore.

Plucking up her handbag, she shoved open the car door. Her first step forward led her into a pool of mud. It sucked her left heel downward like quicksand and threw her balance to the side. She caught herself on the hood of the car but nearly slipped off the front. For a moment she stood there, blinking through the pelting rain, a scream of aggravation gathering inside her. She didn't believe in omens, but if she did, she wasn't sure this one boded well.

With an indelicate grumble, she yanked her foot free and trotted the rest of the way up the road. She sidestepped the leaky gutter, climbed the front step, and stared at the entrance with a dwindling sense of fortitude. The door looked as though it hadn't been replaced since the turn of the century. The varnish had been stripped away by rough weather, as colorless as driftwood, and though Louisa thought she saw what looked like a bullet hole near the doorknob, she resolutely ignored it and let herself inside.

She nearly gagged as she stepped into the room. The air was thick with smoke and stank of sweat and vomit. The odor settled over her like a putrid shroud as she closed the door behind her. When she was later questioned by her aunt and uncle, there would be no hiding the sort of establishment she'd been to, for it would take two washings to get the stench out of her dress.

Most of the room was taken up by the boxing ring, which was elevated on a short platform. Two men stood in the center, hemmed in by a series of frayed ropes. One man was tall, the other short and stocky and cradling a bloodied nose. The two of them circled each other slowly, this way and back again, their stances tense and predatory. Louisa dropped her gaze a moment before the taller man lunged. She tried to block out the crunching sound of pulverized bone, wondering with useless worry if Paul had ever found himself in the ring.

"You lost, sweetheart?"

Louisa looked up. There was a bar to the right lined with stools and a few tables tucked in at odd angles around the perimeter of the ring. The room wasn't too crowded, only six men or so. As she crossed the space, they stared back at her and laughed, sharing a generous round of crude epithets at her expense.

The one who'd addressed her sat at the end of the bar, a half-finished pint in front of him. He was a young, lean man with green eyes. Eyes the color of money, Louisa thought as she drew near enough to make them out. And how easily she could picture him sitting in that very spot, counting stacks of it over and over again.

"Where exactly are you trying to get to in Chitwell all fancied up like that?" His smile did nothing to soften his sharpness. "I'd offer directions, but I must admit—I'd almost hate to let you go."

A warning shot. As his men laughed approvingly, Louisa's limbs began to tremble, but she planted herself and questioned him in her steeliest voice: "Do you run this establishment?"

"You seem to think I do."

"Perhaps you can help me, then. I'm trying to find out what's happened to my brother."

"And you think whatever happened to him might have happened here?"

Louisa glanced sideways at the two men in the ring. They were leaning forward now, bulky forearms balanced against the ropes, watching her with interest. The short one had stuffed a rag against his nose, and it was growing redder by the second.

The man at the bar followed her gaze. "I suppose we may not measure up to your silk and champagne standards," he said. "But I can assure you that I run a legal business here."

"You can assure me all you'd like," Louisa replied, recklessly turning her back on the men in the ring. "I'm not the sort to pretend to be stupid. Or blind. I know trouble when I see it."

To her surprise, the man laughed. "Who's your brother?" he asked.

"Paul Everly."

She studied him carefully but saw no spark of recognition in his eyes. She supposed he could be conning her, but she'd come prepared for another possibility—that Paul had used an alias to protect himself. Opening her handbag, she slipped out an old photograph and held it up for examination.

The man angled forward in his seat and plucked the photograph from her fingers. "Johnny Brimfield? *He's* your brother?"

The men were murmuring again. One of them cursed and spat on the floor. Louisa shifted back, attempting to be discreet as she glanced at the door, gauging the distance and the possibility of escape. Yet her heels felt pitiful and flimsy beneath her; fashion might have ordered the day at Everly Hall, but it would be useless here if the present conversation spiraled into an outright chase. "You sound as though you know him well," she said, stalling.

"I know him to be a cheat."

"How much money does he owe you?"

"More than he can honestly repay." The danger in his voice was no longer disguised by false pleasantries. He dropped Paul's picture as he stood, crushing it beneath his boot when he strode forward.

Up close, the man was much taller than Louisa might have guessed, but she managed to keep the rush of terror from entering her voice. "And what exactly were you willing to do to get it back?" she demanded. "Were you blackmailing him?"

The man's lips curled. "I might have done," he said, his gaze lowering to her mouth, "had I known he had such a pretty sister."

He took hold of her arm. His grip was light, but Louisa couldn't bring herself to move or to push him away. She fought the sob crowding in her chest as she wondered if the hand that held her now had killed her own brother. "Did you . . . did you *kill* him?" This time her voice emerged distressingly weak, almost a whisper, but there was no way to ask that question without something breaking inside of her.

All at once, the man's smile vanished. Louisa couldn't tell if he was angry or if she'd merely surprised him, but she flinched when his hand tightened on her arm. "You telling me he's dead?"

"I believe him to be so. Yes."

He swore as he released her, then rounded the bar and snatched a bottle of Scotch whiskey down from the shelf above him. He poured two generous glasses and then, to her amazement, pressed one into her hand. "Well," he said with a vehement laugh, "there goes my money!"

He drank the contents of his glass as if he'd spoken a toast, but Louisa clutched hers without drinking, trying to decide if she was being tricked. The man's bitterness seemed genuine, especially when he plunked his empty glass upon the bar, but it might have been a ruse.

"You didn't do it?"

He made an offhand signal, dismissing his men like rats to the gutters. "If your brother's dead," he said once they were alone, "it wasn't my doing. I might have wanted to a time or two, but dead men can't pay their debts, and that's the truth."

Louisa believed him. She had no grounds for it, none whatsoever, but she did. "When did you see him last?"

His eyes shifted to the boxing ring, where two new men were hard at work thrashing each other while the rest gathered on the perimeter, shouting crude but vigorous support. "Oh, about a month I'd say. He came to me for a loan, and not his first one from me either. We came to an understanding, you might call it, but then just as soon as he got his hands on the money, he disappeared." He turned his attention back to her, his eyes tracing a line from her satin scarf to her kitten heels. "You look as though you might find the means to pay on his behalf if I put the screws to you, what with all that finery. Rich parents, I suppose? Your brother was wise to keep that secret."

"Our parents are dead."

He snorted. "As if I needed another reason to feel sorry for you."

"Sorry enough that I can go?"

He tilted his head, considering. "If you tell me your name first. I feel as though I ought to know it."

Louisa considered lying, but she supposed this was a point-less precaution when she'd already given her brother's full name. It would be only too easy for the man to track down her family, and she had no doubt whatsoever that he would. "It's Louisa."

The shrewdness returned to his eyes in double measure. "Well, off you go, Louisa, and quickly. Before I change my mind about you."

She didn't wait to be told twice.

12

By the time Louisa left Oxford, the rain had stopped and the roads were shadowed beneath the gathering darkness of a starless night. There was another car on the road behind her, its headlights small as fireflies in the distance, but the roads were otherwise clear. It would be almost nine o'clock by the time she returned home, and there'd be the devil to pay when she did. Louisa didn't waste the drive making up any excuses for her disappearance. Uncle Archie was better than her aunt at spotting a lie, and she knew it would only make matters worse. The best and only course was to tell the truth and grovel beneath the fruitless hope that she wouldn't be banned from driving the Cadillac until her thirtieth birthday.

She passed a large ramshackle barn and turned right. The cows were too tired and lazy to pay her any notice, but three farm dogs bounded from fence post to fence post, barking at her in rapid succession. Moments later, she heard a reprise of barking and glanced in her rearview mirror. The car behind her had turned as well. The headlights were still way off, but she thought they were closer than before.

A pulse of panic fluttered in her chest.

What if the man from the bar had changed his mind about her after all and sent one of his underlings to bring her back? She'd read novels where characters had seen too much for their own good. They were usually pitched into the nearest, most convenient body of water, and though she couldn't think of anything she'd seen worth being murdered for, the Thames was still a touch too close for comfort. Her heartbeat fairly tripled at the thought of her lips slipping beneath the silent current, but she drew a measured breath and adjusted her grip on the steering wheel. Whether she was being followed or not, paranoia wouldn't do her a crumb of good. It was late, certainly, but she had no reason to suspect every car that happened to share the road with her that night.

When she came to the next few junctures, she recalled the route she'd traced on the map earlier and turned left, then right, toward Wilbeth Green. Eyes fixed on the mirror, she held her breath as the car behind her rounded slowly through the turns—left, then right. The headlights were now so close she couldn't glance into her mirror without squinting. She drove faster, even as she told herself that she'd only been swept away by a wild and silly suspicion. She'd probably have a good laugh about this in the morning.

The engine in the car behind her disagreed. It revved as her pursuer gunned forward to match her pace.

Louisa was no longer measured. Terror hurtled through her as she kicked off her heels and slammed on the gas. Her assailant gave a single warning, two sharp blasts from his horn, but she didn't ease up, not for a second.

Shadows swooped and blurred like specters past her windows, her headlights plowing a narrow path through the

95

darkness ahead. She couldn't breathe. She'd never driven so fast in all her life, but her aunt's Cadillac purred magnificently, as if it had been waiting all this time for just one good and glorious chase.

As Louisa raced toward the next intersection, she prayed that the cross street would be empty. When at last she came upon it, she feigned right, then turned sharply to the left at the last possible moment, dust whirling off her wheels in all directions as she went pelting up the road.

Her assailant tried to follow, but the road was too wet from the rain, the gravel too slick. As Louisa gained speed, she heard the sideways skidding of wheels behind her, and in an instant the glow of headlights vanished from her rearview mirror like a candle snuffed by a puff of wind.

She was shaking now, so violently that she could hardly hold on to the wheel. She squinted from the road to the mirror and back again, trying to distinguish one scrap of darkness from the next. A full minute passed without the car reappearing behind her. Then five. After ten minutes, she slowed to a more reasonable speed. If she could have caught her breath, she might have taken some pride in the victory of escape. After all, she'd never given anyone the slip before, and it *was* rather gratifying. But then, just as she was passing the fingerpost sign for Wilbeth Green, a pair of blinding headlights swerved out of the darkness to the left of her as a strange, shrill bell deafened her ears.

With what little breath she had left in her body, Louisa screamed, but the shock had otherwise scrambled her senses. Hardly thinking, she slammed on the brakes and skidded to a stop, the front of the car nearly nose-diving into the ditch beside her. The sudden stop pitched her sideways, her right shoulder slamming into her window as a hulk of black and chrome skidded up alongside her door.

She found some relief when the clanging siren cut away, but her ears were still ringing when she heard far more ominous sounds: first the slamming of a car door, then the steady crunch of footsteps traipsing through a slurry of mud and wet gravel.

Whoever it was now stood just outside her door.

Panic spiking, she fumbled blindly for the lock, but the door was yanked open and pulled beyond the reach of her scrabbling hands. A swirl of cool evening air entered the cab, mixed with the haziest hint of aftershave as her assailant shadowed her exit.

"Out of the car." The voice was low. Gruff. Unmistakably Malcolm.

Though Louisa's senses were rallying, her mind was still struggling to catch up with the rest of her. She had no idea what he was doing there, was still trying to make sense of him when he gripped her arm and hauled her up out of her seat.

She came up shouting, unable to distinguish relief from anger: "You nearly ran me off the road!"

Her voice was strong, thank goodness, but her legs were shaking more than she realized. She stumbled sideways through the mud on her stockinged feet, might have tumbled straight into the ditch if Malcolm hadn't firmed his hold on her arm and deposited her against the hood of the car. "Catch your breath before you rail at me."

Louisa shrieked in outrage as the bottom of her dress was soaked with cold rainwater. For his part, Malcolm didn't sound the slightest bit unnerved or out of breath, which likewise irritated her. She supposed there wouldn't have been anything remarkable about the pursuit. Not to him. He chased criminals for a living, after all.

For Louisa, it was perhaps the single most harrowing episode of her entire life.

"Why did you chase after me like that?" she demanded.

"I spotted the Cadillac a while back and thought it was you. I kept a distance, just wanted to make sure you were heading toward home. But then you started driving so peculiarly. At first I thought you'd lost your mind, but then I feared that maybe you weren't driving at all—that maybe someone had nicked your car." He leaned in through the driver's seat and yanked her key out of the ignition. "Why'd you run?"

"I thought you were someone else."

He drew up short, eyes tightening. "Anyone in particular?"

"Yes—I mean, no. Not exactly. What are you doing all the way out here anyway?"

He locked her door and slammed it shut, then pocketed the key. "Looking for you, as a matter of fact. I'm sorry to report that your accomplice didn't stand up to any sort of questioning. As soon as Miss Harbrook was told you hadn't returned home, she caved to hysterics and admitted that she hadn't seen you all day. Your aunt and uncle saw no other choice but to call the police."

Louisa narrowed her eyes. She felt monstrous for putting Tilly in such an awful position. Doubly so for worrying her aunt and uncle. And yet she couldn't help noticing that Malcolm hadn't given a thorough enough explanation of his appearance on the road that night.

Not by half.

"I didn't tell Tilly where I was going," she said. "Come to think of it, I didn't tell anyone. How did you know I'd be here?"

He flicked something onto the hood of the car, which she snatched up into her hand. It was the matchbook from Paul's room. She'd tucked it away—safely, she thought—beneath a chaos of scarves in the top drawer of her bureau.

"You searched my room?"

"Your aunt permitted it."

Louisa flushed with embarrassment as she pictured Malcolm's hands rummaging through her things. And what else might he have uncovered or noticed in the course of his search? She'd hidden each of her so-called clues separately, out of what she'd thought at the time was an overabundance of caution. The button, which she'd tossed in with a drawer of hairpins, would have seemed unremarkable enough, but she did fear he might have found, and perhaps confiscated, the photograph with the blackmail note she'd tucked inside one of her green Wellington boots. "Did you find anything else of interest?"

"Yes. You have too many novels and a truly perplexing number of lipsticks. Whatever do you need so many for?"

"So many novels, you mean? Or lipsticks? As I'm sure you're aware, they serve decidedly different purposes."

He speared her with a look. "I'm surprised you can sound so casual when your aunt and uncle have been beside themselves with worry. And for good reason, as it turns out. I'm familiar with The Blind Cat. From my time in Oxford. Thomas Sykes, the proprietor, is a notoriously dangerous man. We have a file on him that's heavy enough to sink a body in the Thames, and don't think he wouldn't. Tell me you didn't go through with it, that you weren't half so foolish as to go in there by yourself."

Given how the evening had unfolded, Louisa conceded the

fairness of this rebuke. "Perhaps it was foolish of me to go there by myself," she acknowledged, "but not entirely fruitless. This Mr. Sykes, as you call him, was more forthcoming than you'd think. Terrifying, of course, but also rather . . . not."

Startled, Malcolm's chin jerked, his thumb falling from where he'd hooked it in his jacket pocket. "You mean you actually spoke with the man?"

"I was following a lead."

"You don't have leads, Louisa. *I* have leads. Leads I'm not following at the moment because I've been forced to come all this way to bring you home."

"I am sorry for worrying everyone. Truly I am. But the man I spoke to, whom I now believe to be Mr. Sykes, said that Paul had debts. Sizable ones. Which means he might have any number of enemies. Now, I'm not sure what *you* classify as a lead, but it might be worth scribbling down if you have your little book with you."

Malcolm swore under his breath, but he nonetheless dug his notebook out of his coat pocket and jotted something down, muttering to himself as he did: "Of all the rash, reckless, *incomprehensibly* stupid . . ."

While he expanded on his list, Louisa considered telling him about the blackmail note Paul had slipped to the vicar. Indeed, she rather thought she should. And yet she couldn't stand the idea of Malcolm taking the evidence and shutting her out from the rest of the investigation.

And what if the police decided that Paul was the blackmailer?

Instead, she pointed to the bottom of Malcom's page: "Before you get the wrong impression, I'd also like to go on the record by saying that Mr. Sykes had nothing to do with my brother's disappearance."

Malcolm's pencil halted mid-word, as did his muttering. "How can you be sure?"

"Because he told me he didn't."

"And you believe him. Simple as that?"

"Simple as that."

He winced, as though physically pained by her naivete. "Louisa," he said, "do you truly believe that your brother is dead? That he was murdered?"

Her voice cracked as she answered: "I know what I felt."

He sighed and stepped forward, his dark eyes softening at last. "Then you can't trust anyone. Not even the people who are closest to you. If you truly believe that your brother is dead, then you have to assume that anyone with ties to him has a motive for his murder. And for yours should you keep poking around."

Louisa, whose pride hadn't yet fully recovered from being called *rash*, *reckless*, and *incomprehensibly stupid*, crossed her arms tightly to her chest. "Really?" she challenged. "What's *your* motive, then?"

His glance turned into a glare as he flipped his notebook shut. "C'mon," he muttered. "I'm taking you home."

"Thanks," she said, slipping down from the hood of the car, "but I'm more than capable of driving myself." She made it three paces toward her own door before she remembered that Malcolm had confiscated the key. Face flaming, she swiveled back around and tried to cover her oversight: "That is, if you'll be kind enough to hand over my key."

She stopped in front of him and thrust out her hand, but he only laughed, brushing easily past her. "I had a date tonight, you know. With Dorothy Simms. Instead, I've been tracking your movements for the better part of three hours. It's all made me feel somewhat . . . less than kind."

"Malcolm!"

While most of Louisa's gentlemen callers would have stumbled over themselves to open the car door for her, Malcolm was already sliding in behind the wheel. "I told your uncle I'd bring you home, and I intend to do just that. If you don't appreciate my methods, then you're more than welcome to wait here for the next *kind* soul who passes by."

"You can't be serious." She seized his door to keep him from closing it. "Malcolm, please. I'm sorry, all right? My uncle will fly into a rage if you leave me here, but he'll be even more livid if we leave the Cadillac behind."

"That's what I'm counting on."

Louisa shifted back on her feet and fumed. Malcolm thought she'd keep her nose out of things if her uncle was angry enough to make her life more difficult. It was a rather low move and not likely to work in the long term, but at the moment she could see no suitable alternative to going along with him. Wordlessly, she got into the car, though with the decided air of a captured dignitary. She sat straight and prim, as close to her window as she could, with her hands folded neatly in her lap.

Malcolm grinned as he leaned forward and started the car. "Oh, don't look so defeated," he said. "I've chased loads of criminals, but this was the first time anyone's ever given me the slip."

Though Louisa was loath to accept the olive branch, she scooted up marginally in her seat. "Do you mean it?"

"Of course I mean it. But don't let it go to your head. Most of them were idiots."

13

hitwell! Well, I'll tell you this once and never again, young lady, that no niece of *mine* goes driving around in some seedy, backwater slum like Chitwell. I hear the place is crawling with Irish these days. And with a dingy pub on every corner, ha! No wonder!"

"Archie, *please*." Smoothing a hand over her pale pink dressing gown, Aunt Agatha lowered herself down onto the sofa beside Louisa. "What your uncle is trying to say, dear, is that we were so dreadfully worried about you. You might have at least told us where you were going."

"And what about the car?" demanded her uncle, prowling like a wounded bear from one end of the room to the other. "A Cadillac will stick out like a sore thumb in a place like that. Just left there on the side of the road! What if it's vandalized? What if it's stolen? Did you ever stop to think about that?"

Once again, Aunt Agatha appealed to Louisa with a gentler translation: "What he *means* to say is that disappearing like that, without telling anyone where you were going, was dangerous. You might have been hurt, my dear, or lost, and we wouldn't have known where to look for you."

"Yes, yes," clipped her uncle impatiently, "and just where the devil is Inspector Sinclair?"

Here, at last, he paused long enough for Louisa to string together an actual reply: "I believe he had other pressing business to see to."

This was a lie, and no doubt about it. Malcolm had made it perfectly clear that he had no better place to be, but that he was leaving her there, in her bare feet no less, to face her fate alone. Her heels, which she'd kicked off during their chase, were still on the floor of the Cadillac. She'd only noticed they were missing when the shock had worn off. She still cringed to remember how pathetically she'd pleaded with Malcolm to go back for them. The Cadillac was only ten minutes out of their way at that point, and she couldn't very well return home in her ripped nylons. When outright begging failed to sway him, she informed him, grandly, that a gentleman would certainly go back for a lady's shoes, but this only succeeded in making him laugh. *"If that's so,"* he'd said, *"then maybe David Ashworth will fetch them for you."*

After that, Louisa was much too angry to ask him about the interview she'd overheard between him and David, or to admit that David had lied to her about having seen her brother at his family's party. She wondered now what Malcolm might have told her about David if she'd only set aside her pride long enough to press him about it. Perhaps he wouldn't have told her anything. Perhaps he would have laughed at her again. Perhaps he was off, even now, trying to salvage his date with Dorothy Simms—the thought of it made her inexplicably angry about her shoes all over again.

She looked back at her uncle, who was making a brief fuss about lighting his pipe. He always said the smell of tobacco helped him think more clearly, which remained to be seen, but it usually managed to reduce his temper to a discontented mutter. "I'd like to know what manner of police inspector drives up and deposits a respectable girl on the front step like a brown-paper parcel without so much as a knock on the door."

"Perhaps it's only instinct," Aunt Agatha put in. "After all, he used to be a delivery boy."

Uncle Archie's eyebrows drew together in a contemplative scowl. "Yes," he mused, puffing his pipe. "Yes, exactly! And he was always on that *bicycle*. Delivering potatoes, I think, and heaven knows what else for his father. You could hear the bell on that dingy old thing from three streets over—"

"Oh, never mind about the bicycle!" sighed Aunt Agatha, swatting a hand at him. "But what were you doing in Chitwell, Louisa? And at such an hour?"

Louisa gripped the edge of the couch. She knew the truth was not going to land particularly well, at least not with her uncle. Yet the time had come, with or without her shoes, to plant both feet and come out with it. "I was at a boxing club."

Her aunt released a little strangled cry, but the horror of this revelation rendered everyone in the room otherwise mute. This included the poor maid who had arrived at the worst possible moment to deliver a tray of tea. She set it down on the table with a disruptive clatter, then turned and scooted off without waiting to be dismissed.

Uncle Archie was struggling most of all. His pipe dangled, then dropped from his slackened lips. He caught it in his hand and then very slowly began to recover his faculties. "Boxing club?" he croaked weakly. Then with indignation: "Boxing!"

Louisa rushed to clarify further. "I was led to believe that Paul had been a patron at the club at some point. I was . . . well, I've been trying to discover what's happened to him."

"What do you mean 'what's happened to him'?" Her uncle's words were coming together more quickly now. "Everyone knows he's run off. It's all over the papers, isn't it?"

"I don't believe the papers," said Louisa. "So far the reporters have been more interested in selling a good story than in finding the truth."

"And the police? I suppose they're wrong as well?"

"To my knowledge, the investigation is still ongoing."

Her uncle's stare turned vicious, his lips twisting like he was trying to chew through a stringy piece of gristle. "Then what, pray tell, *do* you believe?"

Louisa teetered on a precipice within herself. If she spoke the truth, her uncle would no doubt think her foolish and irrational. And yet if she kept quiet, her brother would go down in Wilbeth Green history as an arsonist—more than that, as a blasphemer—and his killer would carry on as though nothing had happened. It was too late for Louisa to take back the hateful words she'd spoken to her brother before the fire. But she could speak better words now. Braver words. Insofar as she was able, she could protect him.

"I believe that Paul is dead," she said at last, though very quietly. "More than that, I believe he was murdered, and I intend to find out who did it and why."

"You can't just walk around suspecting people of murder," protested her aunt, clutching the collar of her dressing gown with a tense, white hand. "Think of how you'll shock the poor neighbors by acting like a constable. Why, it's all so . . ."

Her uncle had traded his pipe for a bottle of brandy, which

he now poured into the nearest glass with a generous hand. "It's vulgar is what it is," he spat. "I've always suspected you had good sense in short supply, but now I'm sure of it. Too much polish and not enough substance, that's what's wrong with you. *Murder,* she says! Ha! As if anyone will believe such absolute nonsense. Well, if you can't see what's two inches from your face, then I'll tell it to you clearly. Your brother burned down the abbey. Walloped the vicar on his head. Naturally he made a run for it, and it's no surprise, not to anyone who ever knew him. Your brother was an intemperate child—I always told your parents as much—and he grew into a rough, unpleasant, insulting young man without the slightest shred of gratitude or integrity. For my part, I wasn't a bit surprised when I heard about the fire. It all comes down to class, you see. Some people are born to make trouble for themselves and for everyone around them."

At first, Louisa was silenced by a quick burst of rage. She stared at her uncle, her hands fisted at her sides and her pulse beating wild with fury. "Perhaps that's true," she fired back. "And perhaps other people are born with their noses already pointed in the air, with a singular fondness for making tired, appalling speeches."

"Louisa!" hissed her aunt, but her uncle only smiled and drained the rest of his brandy.

Louisa knew what he'd say if she gave him the chance. That she sounded just like her brother. That she could dress up as fine as she liked, but she and Paul were cut from the same middle-class cloth, and here at last was the proof—as if he hadn't given them both every advantage and opportunity!

Well, she wasn't about to stand there waiting to be told. Ignoring her aunt's frantic pleas that the two of them apologize to each other at once, Louisa turned, her back straight as a chimney, and strode coolly out of the study.

She made it no further than the base of the stairs. Almost as soon as she was in the hall, she'd sensed something. She couldn't say what it was, or how, but she was struck by the strangest feeling of being joined by a silent somebody.

Of being *watched*?

Gripping the banister, she swung back around, but whoever it was had vanished in the time it took for her to blink, without a single breath or telltale footstep to suggest they'd ever been there at all.

That night, Louisa couldn't sleep, so she took a long, warm bath and sat on the rug by the fire in her room. Generally speaking, the fireplaces in Everly Hall were purely decorative. Her aunt had a severe and long-standing aversion to soot, and consequently to most chimney sweeps as well.

And yet the hearth in Louisa's chamber was often aglow. The warmth of sputtering flames reminded her of evenings in the vicarage. She remembered how her mother would brush out her hair when it was still damp from the bath and set her beside the fireside to dry. She remembered those long winter nights when she and Paul would hunker in close to toast bread while snow gathered on the ground outside slowly and silently, like one sheet of paper laid carefully over the next. She remembered her father dancing with her mother in the flickering light as Bing Crosby crooned from the radio in the corner.

Louisa lowered her chin, the heat from the fireplace warming her brow. Minutes before, she'd pinned her damp hair in dozens of tight swirls all around her head just as her mother used to do. Her aunt was always offering to take her into the hairdresser for a permanent, which Tilly Harbrook had recommended as well, but Louisa still preferred the slow and quiet practice of pin curls to the colossal heating contraptions.

Now she scooted in closer to the fire, preparing to paint her nails. She did some of her finest thinking when she was painting her nails. There was something about the ritual of it, the familiarity. It required steady hands and concentration. There was a rhythm, and when she was finished, there was something new, something to admire and appreciate.

As for polish, she had a wide assortment of shades in her drawer, though she generally favored reds. Simply Scarlet was a long-standing favorite for times of deep personal crisis, which was precisely why she chose it that evening. She leaned forward, applying a lavish coat to the nails on her left hand while she replayed her argument with Uncle Archie over and over in her mind, growing all the more unsettled as she remembered each of his wrathful replies.

It had never been a secret that her uncle disliked her brother. At times she knew he even resented him. But his speech that evening had rattled loose and exposed a far more dangerous sentiment—hatred.

She shifted on the rug, blowing on her nails to dry them as Malcolm's warning surfaced like a bobber in the back of her mind. He'd told her that she had to assume anyone with a connection to Paul had a motive for his murder, and what if that's exactly what she'd uncovered that evening? Was it possible that her uncle, in arguing with Paul, had gone too far? Just one shove in the wrong direction, one unthinking blow, and he might have been awakening from a fit of temper to stare down over his own nephew's body . . .

No, she thought, her whole body racked by a shiver.

No.

It wasn't possible. Uncle Archie was a boor. Everyone knew that. But he was no murderer. And besides that, he was their *uncle.*

Louisa thought of the year he'd secretly come around the vicarage with Christmas presents for her and Paul, as well as an orange and a whole bar of chocolate for each of them so they didn't even have to share. Paul and Louisa were too young to have known it at the time, but their parents were struggling to afford even the basic necessities that year.

When Paul asked where all the presents had come from, their mother had smiled and said in a secret-keeping kind of way: "Oh, it must have been Father Christmas." But Louisa had been watching from her window that Christmas Eve night and seen Uncle Archie, without realizing it was him, speaking with her father in the backyard. Her mother had laughed the next morning when Louisa, at age five, had asked why Father Christmas had been so cranky, and where was his red coat, and did anyone else know that he smoked cigars?

It was terrible to imagine that the same man had murdered his nephew and set fire to the abbey to cover it up. Far worse to imagine that her brother had looked up into Uncle Archie's eyes and realized what was happening to him. But if there was the slightest chance her uncle was involved—and, according to Malcolm, she had to entertain the possibility—then she had to follow the trail as far as it would take her, for at the moment she had no other suspects.

Of course, his anger alone would have been far too flimsy

for motive, and she hadn't the slightest shred of proof. At least nothing concrete enough to convince Malcolm or even to sway the court of public opinion should it come to that. She thought of the turpentine found at the abbey. The St. Jude necklace. If only she had evidence of a similar kind, something she could actually hold in her hand—

She sat up with a gasp, nearly bumping over the bottle of polish as a new memory impressed itself upon her.

Paul had pulled something out of her uncle's desk on the day of the fire and slipped it into his pocket. At the time she'd been sure he was stealing money, but now she wondered.

Could it have been the photograph?

If it was, then that brought everything into slightly better focus. Perhaps it meant that her brother was blackmailing her uncle, or that her uncle was being blackmailed by an unknown third party and her brother had discovered it. Since the handwriting on the back didn't match her brother's, she was strongly inclined to believe the latter.

She thought back again to the night of the Ashworths' party. Louisa had returned home with Aunt Agatha, but Uncle Archie had driven separately that evening and stayed behind to finish his cribbage game. She hadn't seen him before she'd felt Paul's passing. And though she still couldn't believe it, it was possible that he might have taken a detour on the way home.

He would have had enough time to commit murder and set fire to the abbey.

She was wrenched from this tangle of horrible thoughts by a scuttling noise in the hall, very much like the sound of a mouse nosing its way through the rafters. Glancing sideways, she held her breath and watched as a small, folded scrap of paper skated silently through the gap at the bottom of her door and bumped to a stop against the corner of the rug.

Louisa heard footsteps in the hall, fast but faint.

She leapt across the room and threw open her door. As she already expected, the hall was empty by the time she reached it. She slipped back into her room, checking the lock on her door before she snatched up the paper.

Her nails weren't quite dry, and her hands were trembling as she tore into the note, leaving a smear of Slightly Scarlet like a blotch of blood beside the three inky black words that had been written there:

I believe you.

14

Investigating was more of a challenge now that Louisa was no longer allowed to drive, but her uncle was immovable. He'd already warned Kenneth, the family chauffer, that under no circumstances was he to escort Louisa anywhere, nor was she allowed near any of the cars in the garage. He'd locked up the keys with a triumphant turn of his lips and warned Louisa six ways to Sunday that if she didn't stop making a fool of herself with all this murder business, he'd cut her off without a penny.

Naturally this made her rather certain he had something to hide.

Mostly, though, it made her want to take the bus.

Her aunt discouraged her from taking such drastic measures: "Your uncle just needs some time to process everything that's happened," she said. "As do you, my dear. You gave us quite a scare. Boxing clubs, imagine!"

Though Louisa still had her suspicions, she kept her head down, dutifully, and carried on as if nothing out of the ordinary had occurred. If her uncle was innocent, she didn't want him to know she'd been walking about for days suspecting him of murder. Even for a man as bad-tempered as Uncle Archie, this was likely to be hurtful. And if he *was* guilty, well, then she couldn't very well risk his finding out that she knew, for what if he tried to murder her as well?

Holed up in her room, listening to her records, Louisa gave every outward impression of waiting for her uncle's temper to thaw while at every opportunity she desperately scoured Everly Hall for clues. She started in his study. She read through his ledgers, his post, and even pieced together a few paper shreds from his wastebasket—a receipt for a season's worth of new hats, commissioned by her aunt and altogether obscenely expensive. Grumbling, Louisa brushed the scraps back into the wastebasket.

It wasn't that she expected to find a signed confession or anything so incredible as that. She only knew that she had to find something. Something she could bring to the police station to avoid being written off as a silly or overdramatic girl. (Or worse, a detective of the *armchair* variety.) The note on the photograph was sinister enough, but it wasn't conclusive, as it might have been directed at anyone.

She sank into her uncle's desk chair to think and was seized by an unexpected stitch of pain within her chest, which she couldn't fully account for until she realized she was sitting exactly where she'd found Paul on the morning of their final argument.

It was like sitting in a dream, like standing on the wrong side of a mirror. Holding her breath, Louisa looked at her place by the door, filled with the dreadful, empty hope that her twin brother might burst into the room to confront her, that perhaps they'd merely traded parts in a play in which neither of them knew they'd been cast. This was, she knew, even more improbable than finding a written confession, and so she forced herself not only to stand but to keep moving forward.

Going through her uncle's bedroom was riskier than being caught in his study, but Louisa searched there next, rifling efficiently to the bottom of every drawer. Her aunt's room was adjoined to her uncle's by a shared dressing room, and Louisa had been in there on numerous occasions. It was a bright blue sanctuary, airy and regal, each surface adorned with flowers, jewelry, and a fine collection of paintings and novelties that her aunt had selected with all the scrupulousness of a museum curator.

But this was the first time Louisa had ever set foot in her uncle's private chamber. With its gilded frames and burgundy hangings, the room spoke of wealth but revealed nothing of note about the man who inhabited it. After nearly ten minutes of searching, Louisa hadn't found a single personal object that might have distinguished her uncle from any man of similar standing. There wasn't even a photograph of her aunt on the desk or on the bedside table.

Louisa was in the process of lowering the lid of his mahogany cigar box when at last she spotted something curious: a nearly imperceptible seam near the base of the box. From a reasonable distance, it looked no different from the rest of the wood grain. Up close, however, she could make out the outline of a long, thin rectangle. Transfixed by her find, Louisa pressed her fingers against the seam, her breath catching as a thin panel of wood swung open on a tiny invisible hinge. Inside the compartment, she found a box no taller than the stub of a pencil and no wider than the length of her hand. It slid out easily, like a drawer, but was guarded against further inspection by a miniature keyhole.

Louisa was ecstatic, but she also wasn't sure how to proceed. In the event the lock still worked, she feared she had little hope of ever getting her hands on the key, for her uncle was likely to carry it on his person. Then again, she'd often heard that a hairpin could serve handily enough in a pinch, and in this respect she'd come prepared. A wayward curl toppled against her cheek as she drew a pin at random. Prying the prongs apart with her teeth, she huddled close to the box and went to work.

No matter how many times Malcolm questioned her, Louisa would never confess to him just how long it took for her to pick that lock, though even she was surprised when she finally succeeded. Her first thought when she opened the top was that her brilliant lock-picking labors might have been spent in vain, for there seemed to be nothing more than an assortment of banknotes stuffed inside. But as she tilted the box toward the lamplight, she heard something scraping against the bottom. She froze to listen, then paged through the rest of the notes in a hurry, stopping only when she felt the familiar coolness of a necklace chain against her fingertip.

Gently, Louisa lifted a round, gold locket out of the box. Her heart swayed in a startled rhythm as it swung from her hand. She had seen this locket before, but where?

The piece of jewelry was hardly worth a fortune and was in need of polishing. Still, it was lovely, the front patterned with a whimsical array of filigree forget-me-nots. When Louisa pressed the clasp at the side, she discovered the tiniest lock of dark brown hair bunched up inside. Her aunt, whose hair was just beginning to show strands of silver, had always been a blonde. Louisa's cheeks flamed as she snapped the locket shut. Before she could return it to the box, however, an astonishing realization leapt upon her: she knew *exactly* where she'd seen the locket.

She made it no further than that, for a door in the hall had just opened and shut. She heard footsteps in her aunt's chamber, drawing closer as whoever it was crossed the room and let themself into the adjoining dressing room. Holding her breath, Louisa swiveled her gaze to the dressing room doorknob. It jiggled only once, as though someone was testing the lock, then slowly began to turn . . .

Quickly, Louisa stuffed the banknotes back in the drawer and jammed the whole contraption, rather confusedly, back into the cigar box. By some small miracle, she remembered to snap off the lights and close the door as she scurried out of the room, her pulse throbbing in her throat as she flew back to her chamber, the locket clenched in her fist.

Louisa bolted the door, then marched straight to her bureau and pulled the blackmail photograph out of her boot. She squinted from the photograph to the locket and back again, but she only needed the first glance to confirm what she already suspected. For there it was, the very same locket, dangling from the woman's neck in the photograph.

Louisa sat slowly in the armchair behind her. Her uncle knew the woman in the blackmail photograph. He knew her well enough to have come into possession of her locket, a lock of her *hair*, and had gone to some length to conceal them both. Reluctant as Louisa had been to suspect her uncle of murder, she was almost more desperate to seize upon a reasonable explanation for the locket, if only for her aunt's sake.

The photo had to be several decades old, judging by the style of the woman's bucket hat and finger curls. Perhaps she and Uncle Archie had been sweethearts in their youth. If that was the case, the locket would have come into his possession well before he met Aunt Agatha. Or perhaps the woman had given it to him as a token of farewell, and he hadn't been able to bring himself to part with it. But no, Louisa was not convinced. A youthful romance wasn't the sort of secret worth blackmailing someone over, and it certainly wasn't worth killing for.

Even so, an illicit affair? Was her uncle still acquainted with the woman in question?

Louisa closed her eyes and thought of the note that had been slipped under her door. Someone in Everly Hall thought she was on the right track, but she had no idea if they meant the fire itself or Paul being murdered. And why work anonymously? Though Louisa was emboldened by this secret supporter, she had no way of knowing if she was veering off-track with the photograph.

As much as she hated to admit it, she needed to talk to Malcolm. Now that she'd connected the blackmail note to her uncle, she could no longer move forward without involving the police. And this was rather frightening because the simplest explanation that *she* could think of was that Paul, dangerously deep in debt, had seized the opportunity to blackmail his uncle and passed the evidence to the vicar just before he'd been killed for it. Granted, the handwriting on the back of the photograph didn't match Paul's, but he might have written in a neater hand so their uncle wouldn't recognize it. Heavens, but she hoped she was wrong about all of it.

The only hitch was how to go about handing over the photograph and the locket. She couldn't very well walk all the way to the police station in Sutherby, but neither could she imagine her aunt and uncle allowing her to borrow a car after she'd deserted the Cadillac in Chitwell.

Before she could decide what was to be done, she heard the pitchy chime of the front doorbell. Sliding the locket into her pocket for safekeeping, she cracked her door an inch. In the early afternoon hush, she heard Fernsby's footsteps echoing through the foyer below, his usual toneless greeting, and the muffle of a man's voice answering from the other side of the doorway.

Louisa held her breath as she clung to the doorframe and listened. If it turned out to be Malcolm, the timing would have seemed downright providential. Or it might be David Ashworth, who was still a person of interest in the case as far as Louisa was concerned. She still wasn't sure why he'd lied to her about seeing Paul on the night of the party, or if he was aware of her recent excursion to Chitwell. In any event, he'd rung for Louisa three times since that night. And each time her aunt had intervened to inform him that Louisa was indisposed with a headache—the only malady Aunt Agatha believed a lady of fashion should ever admit to. *"Just until you're sounding more like yourself,"* she'd said to Louisa, which Louisa took to mean that her aunt and uncle couldn't risk her nattering about homicide to perfectly respectable suitors.

To Louisa's relief, the voice at the door didn't sound much like David. It lacked his enthusiasm and charm, his youthful panache, something she would have recognized from a quarter mile off. Slipping out of her room, she tiptoed across the landing, leaning over the banister rail until she saw Aunt Agatha emerge like a butterfly from the sitting room below.

"Vicar!" Aunt Agatha's voice sounded merrier than usual. "What a happy surprise!"

As Fernsby disappeared from view, the vicar squashed his hat in his hands and stepped the rest of the way into the foyer. "I hope you'll forgive the intrusion," he said. "Your man seemed rather put out—perhaps I ought to have called?"

"Nonsense!" laughed Aunt Agatha. "It's never an intrusion, I assure you, and you mustn't pay any mind to Fernsby. His personality's as flat as a pancake, poor fellow, but such is the countenance of a capable butler, or so I've been told."

"I'm sure you are very fortunate to have him."

"Fortunate indeed. I've just now sent him round to the kitchen to ask about my tea. Perhaps you would like to join me on the terrace?"

"Nothing could be more pleasant," said the vicar, "but, alas, I have a meeting with the priest at St. Stephen's in less than an hour. I'm on my way there now, as a point of fact. But I'm preparing to make a certain announcement on Sunday, and I wanted your family to hear it from me directly first."

Her aunt paused. "And what might that be?"

They'd turned a bit, which was making it harder for Louisa to overhear the conversation. So she abandoned the banister and crept silently toward the top of the stairs, crouching low to stay out of sight.

"There's going to be a special church fete at the end of the month," the vicar was saying. "St. Stephen's has graciously agreed to allow us to use their property. All funds will go toward the restoration of our abbey. Given what you've already been through, I didn't want you to feel caught off guard about it on Sunday."

"That is very kind of you."

"Of course, everyone will understand if your family doesn't wish to participate or even to attend, if it should come to that. I know this is a very uncertain and painful time for all of you."

"I assure you, we wish to attend!" said Aunt Agatha. "What's more, you must tell us how we can be of use. I would be happy to provide floral arrangements—as I've done for past fetes. Would that be helpful?"

"Most helpful," the vicar replied, "and more than generous. I'll direct you to speak with Mrs. Ashworth about it. She's volunteered to be the head of our planning committee."

"Well, of course," said Aunt Agatha, "the little dear."

And though she smiled at the vicar very kindly and seemed to be ushering him toward the front door, he remained where he stood, turning his hat over in his hands and glancing down the hall toward the back of the house.

"Was there something else you wanted, Vicar?" asked Aunt Agatha, following his gaze.

"Yes, actually. I'd hoped to speak with your niece while I was here. I wanted to see how she's been getting on."

Aunt Agatha's voice lowered to a sympathetic murmur. "I'm sorry to say she's not been taking it particularly well. I don't think she'll ever fully come to terms with what her brother has done. In fact, she's drummed up some rather wild theories in order to cope with the news."

"Really?"

"Oh, yes, but I think she'll come out of it well enough. She's been keeping to herself these past few days, and I think the time to rest and reflect has been good for her. She's in her room now, listening to her records. I shouldn't like to disturb her, you understand. But I'm sure she'll be very grateful to know you've asked after her."

Louisa stood abruptly. Her aunt meant well enough, she knew, but what Louisa needed—*truly* needed—was an opportunity to speak with the vicar. Thus far, he was the only person who had openly admitted to sharing her suspicions about Paul. He knew her brother and had seen the blackmail photograph—

And he was halfway through the front door!

Louisa moved so fast she fairly catapulted herself down the stairs. "Just a moment!" she blurted. "Please don't go just yet!"

Her aunt gripped the doorframe and looked ready to faint at the sight of her niece, but Louisa still had to give credit where it was due: for a woman who believed anything worse than a headache was indecorous, she was handling Louisa's obvious display of eavesdropping fairly well.

The vicar's hand fell from the doorknob. "Miss Everly, are you quite well?"

"Yes!" panted Louisa, still endeavoring to catch her breath. "But I would very much like to speak with you, Reverend. In private, if I may?"

There was a pause as Louisa glanced in silent appeal at her aunt. And though Aunt Agatha was still shaking her head, she waved them toward her private sitting room. "Oh, very well," she sighed. "Your uncle is sure to be back at any moment, but I'll see to it that you won't be interrupted."

Louisa thanked her aunt, and just as soon as the sitting room door was closed, she sat down with the vicar and told him a great many things in a hurried whisper. She told him about her journey to Chitwell and her quarrel with Malcolm. She told him about David's lie and about the row she'd had with Uncle Archie and about the anonymous note that had been slipped under her door.

When she told him about the locket and the mysterious woman in the photograph, the vicar hummed in his usual way and settled back in his chair. "These are serious charges you lay at your uncle's door," he said, "and so I must caution you: as of yet, you have very little, if anything, to prove that your uncle killed your brother."

"But plenty of motive, don't you think?"

"I'll grant you that the photograph and the locket *are* concerning, but they might not mean at all what you think they mean. Have you spoken to him directly about any of this?"

"Do you really think that's safe? I can hardly believe the man's capable of murder, but I have to be careful. After all, Paul had the photograph in his possession. And now he's dead."

"But let's just say, for the sake of argument, that Paul *isn't* the blackmailer. And going by what I know of him, I don't think he is. But even if he somehow managed to *uncover* such a scheme, the real blackmailer would have just as much as your uncle to gain from your brother's death, if not more. Either way, this whole matter has gotten out of your depth. You need to take this photograph and the locket straight to the police."

"I would speak to Inspector Sinclair," Louisa said, "truly I would, but my uncle has forbidden me to drive anywhere. I haven't even been permitted to answer the telephone these last few days. I think he's afraid I'll start spouting off about murder to anyone who will listen."

"Which could be evidence of guilt," said the vicar, rubbing the side of his temple. "Or it could be genuine concern."

"Concern?"

"Well, yes. If he thinks you aren't coping well with all that's happened." He paused and lowered his hand from his brow, looking at her more intently. "How *are* you managing what's happened?"

Louisa shifted in her chair. "It's been frustrating. I wish

I could get my hands on more definitive evidence. And I wouldn't mind another suspect or two. I suppose it's always good to have some variety when you're working things out, and all the better if it means exonerating my uncle."

"I'm not speaking about the case, Louisa."

She shifted again and lowered her eyes. She might have told the vicar about the fight she'd had with Paul. She might have told him that she was having trouble sleeping or that she'd been avoiding mirrors so she wouldn't keep haunting herself with her brother's likeness. And yet it was far easier to stuff those thoughts aside like boxes in a cluttered room.

"Oh. Yes, I'm fine," she said clumsily. "But the fact remains that I'm barred from driving, and I can't think of a single thing that will make my uncle change his mind about it. As it is, Sutherby might as well be on the other side of the world. But perhaps . . . perhaps *you* could give Inspector Sinclair the photograph and the locket on my behalf?"

The vicar mulled this over, tapping his long fingers on the arm of his chair. Then a smile spread slowly across his face. "I know what's to be done." He said it with such solemnity that Louisa might have thought, were it not for his collar and cross, that he was a detective himself sitting there.

And even though he left abruptly without explaining a bit of his plan, Louisa was unspeakably glad to have him on her side.

15

Early the next morning, before Louisa and her aunt had finished their breakfast, Mrs. Watson came puttering up the drive to Everly Hall in a forest green Morris Minor sedan. As far as Louisa knew, Mrs. Watson had never driven a car, and she worried about whether the woman was tall enough to reach the pedals. Mrs. Watson looked half her usual size behind the enormous front windshield; only her eyes made it fully above the steering wheel, and they were covered by a pair of dark, owlishly round sunglasses.

"How peculiar," said Aunt Agatha, peering out the window from the breakfast room.

Mrs. Watson was still sitting in the car. For the next several minutes, she seemed to be figuring out how to open her door. When at last she emerged, she was so busy straightening her headscarf that she nearly forgot to shut the door behind her and most certainly forgot to turn off the engine. And yet Mrs. Watson walked at a surprisingly nippy pace. She reached the front door and rang the bell so hurriedly that Louisa and her aunt had to jump across the room and into their seats at the breakfast table to keep from being caught loitering too near the window. (When faced with an unexpected visitor, Aunt Agatha believed it was *always* better to look idle rather than interested.)

They weren't fully settled when Mrs. Watson swept into the room like a busy little breeze, with Fernsby puffing in hopelessly after, endeavoring, and failing, to announce her in time.

"Good morning, dearies!" said Mrs. Watson, tugging off her knit gloves as she shooed him away. "You'll have to forgive me for popping in like this without calling first, but I've just been over to St. Stephen's, and it's a *complete* catastrophe, I'm afraid. They told the vicar we could borrow their table linens since ours were lost in the dreadful fire, and of course he doesn't want to make a fuss, the dear man. But I've seen them with my own two eyes, and they're simply unsuitable. Checkered is fine enough for a picnic, of course, but for tea one simply must have white. And if one can, one *must* have lace. I'm sure you both agree."

Aunt Agatha had been doing her best to follow along, smiling politely at each turn in Mrs. Watson's speech, but the sudden silence at the end was harder to navigate. "Mrs. Watson," she said, "please sit down and tell us what you mean."

"Tablecloths!" clarified Mrs. Watson, remaining on her feet. "We need a whole new set of them, and we need them straightaway!"

"Yes, dear, you've said that. But what do you need them for? And what does this matter have to do with us?"

"We need them for the church fete, of course! The vicar told me that Louisa has graciously volunteered to help us with the tea tent, so I came over to enlist her just as soon as I realized the true state of things. And I'm sure you'll both agree with me that using checkered linens for a church tea, why, it's downright sacrilegious! Of course, the vicar said he doesn't think it is, not *exactly*, but there's tradition to be maintained, you realize, and there's what's right. Therefore, I need you to come with me, Louisa, to order new ones at once."

Louisa had no idea how to go about answering. In truth, she didn't know how she felt about checkered tablecloths versus lace ones for tea, and she was sure to be useless when it came to selecting anything proper from the catalogs. The only thing she knew for certain was that she had most definitely *not* volunteered to assist Mrs. Watson with the tea tent. This made her rather inclined to think the vicar, true to his word to help Louisa, had called in the only cavalry at his immediate disposal—an eighty-four-year-old parishioner with gigantic sunglasses and dubious driving skills.

And yet Mrs. Watson was very convincing.

Convincing enough that Louisa paused to replay her conversation with the vicar several times over in her head, trying to determine if she might have accidentally volunteered for the fete without realizing she had. There was only one way to know for sure.

"I'd be very happy to help," she said, sliding her breakfast plate aside. "That is, if my aunt can spare me?"

To Louisa's surprise, her aunt readily agreed and even remarked that a bit of industry out of the house might do Louisa some good in getting her mind off things. Minutes later, Louisa was stuffed into the front seat beside Mrs. Watson, with the locket and photograph tucked into her pocket just in case.

She held her breath as they pulled out from the drive, fully expecting the older woman to say something smart or conspiratorial. Instead, Mrs. Watson turned the wheel much too sharply, trundled over a rock, and protested: "Merciful heaven, this *car*!"

Louisa gripped the edge of her seat and resisted the self-saving impulse to seize the steering wheel. "I didn't realize you drove, Mrs. Watson," she said delicately.

"I wasn't fully sure of it myself until this morning."

"Really? Where did you get the car?"

"One of my grandsons lent it to me. I rang him up yesterday afternoon and told him about the tablecloth fiasco, and he's really the most understanding of my grandsons. You'd like him, I think, though he went and became a Catholic when none of us were looking, so you mustn't think of him as a prospect per se—unless you're interested in converting."

Louisa paused. "So we're off to order tablecloths, then?"

Mrs. Watson nodded, her foot growing fonder of the gas pedal. "I put great stock in linen," she said as she zipped around a curve. "The men might disagree, but a fine piece of linen is just as important as a handshake when it comes to first impressions."

Louisa had been hoping to make it to Sutherby so desperately that she sank back in her seat and tried not to look sulky now that linen really was to be the gravest, most pressing matter of the day.

"Is something the matter, dear?" asked Mrs. Watson, nearly running down a rabbit that had scampered across the road.

"No," said Louisa, "nothing at all, but . . . Oh! Mrs. Watson, you'll need to turn around. You've just passed the road to Bridge's."

Bridge's was a small but popular general store on the high street of Wilbeth Green. When it came to finery, Bridge's didn't have much by way of inventory, but they had a long shelf of catalogs and could order nearly anything from the nearest cities.

"I never go to Bridge's if I can help it," said Mrs. Watson, accelerating even more. "When it comes to linens, I only ever go to Flagman's in Sutherby!"

The police station in Sutherby was a two-story, corner structure made of brick, distinguished yet unadorned. When it was first built, there had been a mild sensation when it came out in the papers that they were putting in not one, not two, but *three* holding cells! And they were nearly always empty save for the occasional drunkard or vagrant.

The station served the four closest communities: Rosemont, Wilbeth Green, Camden Hills, and Sutherby. And though Sutherby was the largest of the four, the people of Rosemont had never forgiven them for getting a police station at a time when they themselves had been petitioning to have one built. (For there had been a rather alarming number of bicycle robberies that year.)

Louisa's reception in the front office was cheery enough. There were two constables working near the desk, and they were so unaccustomed to regular visitors, apparently, that they nearly tripped over each other to show her the way when she inquired about speaking with Malcolm.

His office was buried in the back of the building. It was a dreary room with gray walls and hunter green wainscoting, brightened only by a fireplace near the door and a single window in the corner. The desk was an old oak monstrosity positioned near the fireplace, the top littered with books and files. Though Malcolm was nowhere to be seen, Louisa supposed he couldn't have gone far. His jacket and hat were hung on a spindly rack to the side of the door, and there was a cup of tea, still steaming, tucked beneath the desk lamp as though huddling there for warmth.

Her heels clicking on the checkered linoleum, Louisa stepped the rest of the way into the room. Rather than sit down to wait, she gravitated toward the low table behind Malcolm's desk, which was covered with a number of curious items, each bagged separately and labeled as evidence. Louisa leaned over the desk to survey the lot. There were three dented canisters of turpentine and a pair of black shoes, the same pair she'd found under Paul's bed and handed off to Malcolm.

And there, again, was her brother's St. Jude necklace.

It took every ounce of self-control not to snatch it up and carry it home where it belonged, but her grief at seeing it curled up in an evidence bag shifted to curiosity when she noticed the crumpled-up pack of Chesterfield cigarettes, Paul's usual brand, bagged beside it. The packaging had been badly burnt, the bottom scorched nearly to bits. She suspected it had been found near or within the abbey's remains and wondered why the newspapers had not listed it along with the other evidence.

She lowered her eyes and spotted her brother's file on Malcolm's desk. After Malcolm's recent threats to arrest her, she knew better than to read it, but she still picked it up and weighed it in her hand. While she knew little about police files, she decided that Paul's wasn't as thin as she would have liked, nor was it as thick as she might have expected. She wondered if all the clues she needed to solve her brother's murder were hidden somewhere inside—

"Glad to see someone's gone back to Chitwell for your shoes."

Louisa, who had worn her yellow kitten heels on purpose, dropped the file as Malcolm strode into the office. His eyes were sharp, as always, but the knot of his tie was loose. If he noticed what she'd been up to, he didn't comment on it, but instead circled the desk and slid into his chair, paging through papers as though settling into his work.

He hadn't invited her to join him, but Louisa nonetheless dropped onto the chair opposite the desk, her voluminous skirt crushed between its narrow arms. "Malcolm," she began, "I have something to tell you. Something that I think will make you very angry with me."

"Doesn't sound like much of a change from our usual pace, does it?" He sighed and tossed down the file he was holding. "Oh, all right. Let's get it over with."

Louisa set the photograph on the desk in front of him. And then the locket. Malcolm's eyes narrowed as he picked up the photograph. He studied the image of the woman, then read the message on the back. "Paul slipped it under the vicar's door," Louisa explained. "It seems he left it to him for safekeeping."

"And when was it given to you?"

"The day before I drove to Chitwell."

Malcolm's eyes frosted over with fury. "You mean to tell me you've known about this for a week and you haven't thought to report it until now?"

"I know that was wrong of me."

"Wrong?" He slapped the photograph onto the desktop, got up, strode over and shut the door. "Withholding evidence is a *crime*, Louisa," he said, his voice lower than before, albeit no less furious.

Louisa raised her hands in surrender, yet she realized right away that this was a mistake. Malcolm looked ready to fish out a pair of handcuffs. "I know," she said quickly. "I know, and I'm sorry for it. I was afraid that if I showed it to you, you'd assume Paul was the blackmailer. I just needed a bit of time to figure some things out."

"And what about this?" He stalked back to the desk and snatched the locket.

"I found it yesterday in my uncle's room."

"Your uncle!" he echoed in a strangled voice.

"Yes. The night we came back from Chitwell, I told him I thought Paul had been murdered, and he lost his temper like I've never seen before. A little while later, this was slipped under my door." She handed him the note. "It would seem someone in Everly Hall shares my suspicions, though I can't for the life of me figure out who that might be."

Malcolm turned a shade paler than before. "I can't believe you didn't bring this to me straightaway."

"Well, I haven't even been allowed out of the house until today. Which is partially your fault for leaving the Cadillac behind. But I used the time to do some poking around. Turns out there's a locked compartment in my uncle's cigar box. I found the locket in there."

"How'd you get the compartment open?"

"I picked the lock."

He was inspecting the note again when his eyes lifted, observing her over the top of the paper. "Picked the lock?" he repeated.

"Yes, I picked the lock."

"With what exactly?"

"A hairpin." She lifted her chin, fully expecting him to rebuke her again for interfering. Instead, Malcolm turned his face away so suddenly that she thought he was trying not to smile. "Is something funny?" she demanded.

"Not at all. I only wish I had your investigative resources."

She glared at him, then plucked herself up from the chair, swatting out a few stubborn creases from her skirt. "You're absolutely *useless*, Malcolm Sinclair! You wouldn't believe what I've had to go through just to get here, and all because I thought you could help me. But if you're going to stand there and make jokes instead of—"

He caught her by the arm before she reached the door. "All right, all right," he said. "You want the truth? I'm impressed you picked the lock. Without the proper tools, most constables I know wouldn't have the wherewithal to do it. Yet again, you've always been prodigiously stubborn." He loosened his fingers, then slowly released her arm. "The problem is that your evidence, intriguing as it is, doesn't make matters look any better for Paul. In fact, it looks to be the case that he was blackmailing your uncle over some kind of affair. Perhaps Paul took the blackmail money, burned the abbey as a spiteful farewell to Wilbeth Green, and took off before your uncle could realize it was him."

"Or perhaps my uncle only made it *look* like he did."

Malcolm darted a glance at the door. "That's a dangerous accusation," he said, his voice harsh but hushed.

"Won't you at least question him about it?"

"You want me to accuse a wealthy, powerful man of having an affair without any proof that he's committed an actual crime?"

"Is that really so unreasonable?"

"I'd rather keep my position, thank you."

Louisa folded her arms across her chest. "As inconvenient

as it may be for you, he's the only suspect I have at the moment." She paused pointedly. "Unless, of course, there's someone *you'd* like to add to the list?"

"And just what do you mean by that?"

"David Ashworth. You've been questioning him, haven't you?"

He laughed. "Do you want to know so you can solve the thing, or so you can go out driving in his Bentley with a clear conscience?"

Furious, Louisa answered: "I only want to know if he's a suspect or if he isn't."

"I spoke with him because he and Paul were seen arguing at the party that night. A witness overheard David telling your brother to 'keep out of it or else.'"

"You mean he threatened him?" Louisa's voice had lost its sting, and she hoped that Malcolm hadn't noticed.

"Rest assured, your Mr. Ashworth has an alibi for the time of the fire. You really should ask him about it before you agree to go driving with him anywhere."

There was something ominous in those words. Although Louisa felt as though the ground was tipping sideways beneath her, she couldn't risk the conversation sliding off its track. "You don't really believe that Paul burned the abbey," she said quietly. "You can't believe it."

"What I believe doesn't matter. What matters is what I can *prove*. That empty pack of cigarettes there? My men found it yesterday morning beneath some rubble. They pulled a partial print off the back that puts Paul *inside* the abbey before it burned."

"Perhaps he was there," Louisa agreed, "but that doesn't mean he set the fire."

"Well, I'm running out of time to prove otherwise. Word just came down the pipe today—my superiors want this case put to bed, and the clearest way forward is to formally charge your brother."

"But you can't!" cried Louisa.

"And I haven't. Not yet. But if I'm going to make the leap to Scotland Yard—and I fully intend to—then I can't entertain half-baked theories without offering suitable proof to sustain them. I've requested three weeks to find a fresh lead, and it's been granted. It's not a lot of time, but the evidence you've brought breathes a bit of fresh air into the thing. I suppose I should be thanking you, though I do wish you hadn't been so devilishly tardy about it. Is there anything else you've failed to mention?"

"Well, I've spoken with the vicar. He said Paul was definitely wearing his boots at the party."

"That much I already knew."

Louisa nodded. It seemed as though they were at last falling in step with each other. "Who was your witness?"

"An affronted footman. The dreadful fellow complained to me for nearly a quarter of an hour about the dirt your brother left behind on the parlor rug. I almost paid to have it cleaned myself just to shut him up about it."

"Which means I was right!" chirped Louisa. "The timeline doesn't make sense."

"It . . . raises questions," Malcolm conceded.

Louisa slapped a hand on his desk. "Oh, stop being so cautious! You never were the sort to be, and it suits you badly now. I know I haven't been entirely upfront with you, and I've already said I'm sorry for it. But three weeks is a pittance of time, and neither of us has made much progress on our own.

If we work together, however, maybe we can piece this whole mess back together."

She thought for sure he'd refuse her help. After keeping him in the dark about the photograph, she even supposed she deserved it. To her surprise, he circled the desk again and rooted around the books and files. He slid a black book out from the bottom of the stack and handed it to her. "That's Paul's work ledger," he said. "We found it in his room."

With a grateful bob of her head, Louisa flipped open the cover and found a long list of names and dates jotted within, each marked in the right column with a particular repair. "Have you spoken with everyone on this list?" she asked.

"Everyone who would have seen him in the three months leading up to the fire. No one remembers anything significant. But maybe you'll notice something."

Louisa scanned the entries. In the days leading up to the fire, Paul had done a few odd jobs in the abbey and around the vicarage, fixing pipes and painting mostly. If nothing else, this reinforced the vicar's piece of the story, that Paul had tools he needed to fetch from the abbey on the night of the fire. Her finger traced a line down the margin. Her brother had torn down a shed that week, removed a few stumps, and, as Louisa had already heard through the usual channels of churchly scuttlebutt, patched Mrs. Shaw's roof.

"Hold on," she said, focusing on the last few entries. "The surgery isn't listed here."

"The surgery?"

"Yes." She flipped back a few pages in case she'd overlooked it. "I heard a bit of chin-wag about it. According to Mrs. Shaw, Paul painted Dr. Clarke's surgery a few days before the fire, but it's not listed here anywhere. Perhaps Paul forgot to write it down?"

"Probably so. Still, you wouldn't happen to know where the doctor was at the time of the fire?"

"Yes, actually. Dr. Fielding came round that night. He said Dr. Clarke was visiting with Mr. Hexam. Seeing to his gout." She paused. "You don't think the doctor is involved, do you?"

When Malcolm didn't answer straightaway, she looked up to find that he was already slipping into his jacket. "It's unlikely," he said, "but I suppose we should look into it just to be sure."

"We?" As Malcolm put on his hat, Louisa set down the ledger, slowly, so she wouldn't appear overeager. "You mean you want me to come with you?"

"Well, certainly. Suppose I need a lock picked while I'm there." He didn't quite smile, not exactly, but Louisa did when he tweaked one of the pins in her hair as he escorted her out of his office.

16

I don't see why you're bothering with the doctor," said Mrs. Watson, parking her sedan with a decisive bump outside the surgery. "As if the dear man is capable of murder. If I had money, which I don't, I'd put it all on that Fernsby fellow."

Louisa, who had been nodding off in the passenger seat, sat up abruptly.

"Fernsby!" she repeated, bewildered. "But what would his motive be?"

"Motive?" said Mrs. Watson. "Oh, I don't know, but he rather looks the sort who might murder someone."

Louisa shook her head, unable to decide if she should laugh off the idea or if she should take a moment to formally add the butler to her growing list of suspects. "I don't think it's fair to suspect a man of murder on the basis of looking surly," she decided at last.

"I suppose you're right, dear. Otherwise we might have to add Inspector Sinclair to our list of suspicious persons."

Louisa angled a penitent glance at Malcolm, who *was* looking surly in the back seat, and for good reason. The poor man hadn't realized until he was walking out of the station that joining forces with Louisa that day meant toting Mrs. Watson along with them as well. He'd resisted the idea initially, until Louisa explained how the older woman had valiantly conspired to get her out of Everly Hall.

When they met with Mrs. Watson in the street, Malcolm had greeted her cordially enough, while Mrs. Watson wasn't feeling particularly generous toward him. She distinctly remembered Malcolm as "the sort who never bothered to show up for choir practice," and she didn't even try to lower her voice when she told Louisa as much.

"I was fourteen years old!" protested Malcolm. "Blimey, I've never heard of a more farcical grudge."

"A missing tenor leaves a hole," replied Mrs. Watson, "and a haunting one at that. It's something a musical creature such as myself can't so easily forget."

After that, there was a fierce and momentary dispute between the two about whose car they should take to Wilbeth Green, which rose to a downright hullabaloo right there in the street. Mrs. Watson won by pointing out that they couldn't question anyone discreetly while gallivanting around in a police car. What's more, she insisted on driving.

And so Malcolm, perhaps too proud to forfeit by driving separately, was shut up in the back seat beside a heap of unsuitable checkered linens and various other tea accoutrements. He said very little on the way but was scribbling away in his notebook and flipping through pages. After several nights of patchy sleep, Louisa closed her eyes a time or two and listened to his pencil tip scraping quietly across the pages. There was something oddly comforting about the sound, rhythmic and steady, so that by the time they arrived at the surgery, she was slumped over against the window and nearly asleep in the passenger seat.

The doctor and his wife lived in a stone cottage that was quintessentially the same as every other cottage in Wilbeth Green with its arched doorways and window boxes and west-facing stones, partially concealed by a layer of flourishing English ivy. The door to the surgery was on the right side, at the end of a flagstone path that was skirted by a row of shrubs.

Before Malcolm got out of the car, he reminded Mrs. Watson that she was to remain where she was for the duration of the visit (to which she'd already agreed) and that there was to be "no listening in at doors" (which grossly offended her).

Louisa climbed out of the car and was joined by Malcolm on the curb. Straightening the lapels of his jacket, he stared at the doctor's house with a contemplative expression. "As much as I hate to admit it, Mrs. Watson is right in one respect. If the doctor is involved, we should mask the true nature of our visit. Suspects are more likely to let something slip if they don't realize you're onto them."

"You sound as though you already have a plan."

Malcolm smiled. Then, without warning, he slipped his arm around her waist and drew her in close to his side. "Try to look like you're about to faint."

Startled by his nearness, and by the fact that her head *had* gone a bit fuzzy, Louisa laughed nervously. "That's your plan? Fainting? Isn't that . . . well, it's a bit old-fashioned, don't you think?"

"It might be, but you can't argue with results. Look, we're already giving Mrs. Watson palpitations."

Louisa followed his glance and found that Mrs. Watson had removed her sunglasses and was squinting at them through the windshield with a sharp, shrewd, matronly frown. Malcolm's arm tightened marginally as he pulled Louisa more snugly against him. And though Louisa knew he was merely goading Mrs. Watson, she was also struck by the sudden and rather silly notion that she was growing entangled with the kind of boy who had sometimes skipped choir practice.

"I can't help wondering," she said, striving to sound casual, "if this is how you carry on with all your young ladies."

"It is. Though none of them go on about it like you're doing. Can you get to the fainting bit, please?"

Though Louisa wasn't exactly sure how to go about faking something like a fainting fit, she was nothing if not committed, and so she snapped her eyes shut and slumped against Malcolm's chest so that he was forced to catch her to keep her from hitting the curb. Louisa could only imagine what Mrs. Watson would be thinking about *that*, but she was far too busy waiting for Malcolm to inform her that her acting skills were deplorable. And perhaps they were, she thought, but Malcolm didn't move, and he wasn't saying anything either. Feeling like a limp fish in his arms, Louisa counted to five in her head and then slowly opened one eye.

She couldn't quite interpret the way Malcolm was looking at her. There was laughter in his eyes, most certainly, his lips curving upward in a wry, conspiratorial smile. And yet there was nothing laughable about the way he held her, his hands circling in closely around her waist so that she could hardly breathe.

"Shouldn't we be getting along?" she whispered, still trying to sound like all of this was quite normal.

He laughed under his breath. "I happen to think we're getting along famously," he answered, then swung her up into his arms and carried her the rest of the way up the stone path.

Louisa's head bounced against Malcolm's collarbone as he
knocked with urgency on the surgery door. There was a brief
lull, followed by the distinctive pattering of footsteps within.

"Louisa!" cried Mrs. Clarke as she opened the door. "Good
heavens! What's happened?"

Malcolm shouldered his way inside. "I came upon Miss
Everly and Mrs. Watson while they were out shopping," he explained. "Miss Everly had been feeling faint, and though Mrs.
Watson insisted on bringing her straight home, I didn't feel
right leaving her unattended. I thought she should be seen to."

"How gallant of you!" admired Mrs. Clarke. Louisa feigned
a sigh of discomfort and, cracking an eye, saw the doctor's
wife struggling to untie her apron strings as she ushered them
promptly down the hall. "You must bring her straight back,
Inspector. My husband has been out all morning delivering
the newest Bradford baby, but I'm expecting him back at any
time."

Malcolm thanked her and was shown into the surgery. The
room smelled of antiseptic, and the harsh, unforgiving odor
of iodine made Louisa's knees sting as she remembered the
many childhood scrapes she'd had cleaned after toppling from
her bicycle. Through slatted lids, she saw an ugly painting of a
seascape hung on the wall in a tawdry gold frame. Beneath it
was a couch, florals faded beyond recognition, and it was here
that Malcolm was encouraged to deposit "the poor invalid."
Malcolm laid Louisa down on the couch, then slid his hands,
very gently, out from under her back.

Though more than a bit embarrassed by his proximity,
Louisa forgot all about him when she opened her eyes more
fully. All around her, the surgery walls were covered with
a falsely cheery shade of robin's-egg blue. She pictured her

brother in his boots, brush in hand, working from one corner to the next and never knowing that he'd hardly live long enough for the paint on these very walls to dry.

"She looks peaky," said Mrs. Clarke in the kind of clinical tone that could only be inspired by surgical surroundings. "I'll fetch some water from the kitchen."

As soon as she was gone, Malcolm stood and crossed the room in two swift strides. He bent low over the doctor's desk and began peeling hurriedly through a stack of files and papers while Louisa propped herself up on her elbow to watch him. "Be sure to check the drawers," she whispered, directing him with her free hand.

Malcolm didn't look up. He dropped the file he was holding, then plucked up another. "You're supposed to be unconscious," he said.

"Yes," she agreed. "And *you're* supposed to be conducting a thorough search."

"This isn't my first time around a possible crime scene. But if you'd rather we switch places, then by all means. I certainly wouldn't mind lolling around on the couch and looking pretty."

Louisa sat up abruptly. "Do you really think I'm pretty?"

Malcolm glanced her way for a second, quietly assessing, then dropped his eyes. "Oh, I don't know," he muttered. "Stop trying to be smart and keep watch for me, won't you?"

Louisa did some muttering of her own but nevertheless did as she was told. From her place on the couch, she could see through the door and clear to the end of the hall. "I think I just heard the faucet," she reported. "You don't have much time."

Malcolm shook his head. "There's nothing here," he mumbled, his head disappearing from sight as he foraged to the bottom of a drawer. "Just some old reading glasses and empty prescription bottles. The doctor might not even be—"

"Here she comes!" Louisa hissed and slumped like a corpse on the hideous couch.

Without making a sound, Malcolm shut the drawer and wheeled around the desk, positioning himself at Louisa's side, but it wasn't Mrs. Clarke who strode through the door.

"I told you to stay in the car!" Malcolm whispered furiously as Mrs. Watson trotted into the room.

Mrs. Watson looked at him. And if looks could kill, Malcolm would have been six feet under the ground with the service already spoken last Tuesday. "Well!" was her stout reply. "I'm certainly not going to sit out in the street, waiting behind the wheel like some *getaway driver*! And don't you take that tone with *me*, Malcolm Sinclair! I can still write to your grandmother, you know!"

"Yes," he matched coolly. "And *I* can have *you* arrested."

Louisa might have enjoyed imagining the kind of rumors that would circulate if Malcolm ushered Mrs. Watson out of Dr. Clarke's office in handcuffs, but there wasn't that much time.

"She's coming!" Louisa shushed them, and this time she was right.

They all resumed more natural positions as Mrs. Clarke entered the room with a glass of water in one hand and a small vial of smelling salts in the other. "Hello, Mrs. Watson," said the doctor's wife, stopping short in the doorway. "I almost didn't see you there."

"Louisa left her handbag in the car." Mrs. Watson held up said bag theatrically, as though presenting evidence to a jury. "I thought she ought to have it."

"A woman should never be without her handbag," agreed Mrs. Clarke. With a smile, she popped open the vial of smelling salts. "Here we are, Miss Everly! These always help me when I'm having a fit of the vapors."

Louisa faked a groan even as she yanked herself up into a sitting position. She hadn't minded the fainting ruse, but she categorically refused to *ever* use smelling salts in Malcolm's presence. "I think I'm beginning to feel better," she said feebly. "I'm mortified to have caused such a fuss."

"Nonsense!" cried Mrs. Clarke, slipping the glass of water into Louisa's hand. "Why, it's to be expected, isn't it, after everything you've been through? With your brother, I mean. I can't say how sorry I am, Miss Everly. I never would have imagined him capable of such a thing."

"He painted the surgery, I think?" said Louisa, hoping she didn't sound too forced about it.

Mrs. Clarke lowered her eyes. "Well, yes. Yes, I suppose he did . . ."

Mrs. Clarke's words drifted away at the end, and Louisa and Malcolm exchanged quick glances. He gave Louisa a pushy sort of nod, after which she took a slow, thoughtful sip of water. "You don't sound like you were very pleased with his work," she said casually.

"Oh no!" protested Mrs. Clarke. "It isn't that! It's just . . . my husband never liked your brother very much, I'm sorry to say. He said he was a criminal, and I suppose he turned out to be right in the end. But when your brother came by that day, asking if we needed any work done—oh, I don't know. He was so quiet and polite, and I'd heard he'd been having a harder time than usual finding work. So I told him that the surgery had been needing a fresh coat of paint for some time.

It was so drab in here. And he did a fine job, too. Everyone's always going on about how rude and unpleasant he is, but he was only 'yes, ma'am' and 'thank you, ma'am,' and he even smiled a time or two, as polite as a boy could be . . ."

Again Mrs. Clarke's words drifted away. Louisa followed the woman's gaze to an unfinished spot in the corner, where the fresh coat of blue fell just short of fully concealing the former beige. "Did something happen?" she asked quietly.

"Yes. Well, no. Not really. My husband came home and was very upset. He said I'd welcomed a known criminal right into our home. He was only worried about me, you understand, but there was no talking him out of it. As soon as I told him Paul was in the surgery, he marched straight back and slammed the door. I heard them arguing for a few minutes, and then he sent your brother off without any pay. I felt so dreadfully awful about it that I sent our housekeeper by with a meal for him the next night. It was a trifle after what had happened—he'd done nothing wrong really."

Louisa frowned at Malcolm as she pondered Mrs. Clarke's account of things. So far her uncle had been heard arguing with her brother at the party. So had David Ashworth. Now the doctor was brawling with him as well? She wondered if they were all three caught up in the same grudge, or if the list of grievances against her brother was really so varied. "Did you hear what they were arguing about?" she asked.

"Nothing in particular. Oh, dear, I'm sorry for having gone on about it. Please understand, my husband is a good man. He's as even tempered as they come, and I suppose we all have our moods at one time or another. But I can't help worrying that maybe—" She stopped abruptly, lowering her chin.

"Yes?" Louisa pushed herself up from the couch. She was

so engrossed in Mrs. Clarke's story that she plum forgot she was supposed to be dizzy or even the slightest bit unsteady on her feet.

Mrs. Clarke didn't seem to notice. She swallowed hard, then shook her head. "I only wonder if being treated that way, like a criminal—was *that* why he went and burned down the abbey?" She fell quiet again, staring absently at the unpainted corner, but there was a sound at the other end of the house that brought her back to herself. "Oh!" she said. "I think I hear him now!" With a startling grip, she grabbed hold of Louisa's hand. "Please don't tell him what I've shared with you. He's a good man, you understand. A good husband. I only wanted you to know the truth of it. Paul's your brother, after all."

"I understand," said Louisa. "I promise not to say a word about it."

Mrs. Clarke squeezed her hand, then released it as Louisa sat back down on the couch.

A moment later, Dr. Clarke appeared in the surgery door, his black medical bag swinging at his side. "Hello, dearest!" he called toward the kitchen. "The Bradfords have welcomed a fine, healthy—" He stopped short when he spotted Malcolm, Louisa, and Mrs. Watson waiting in the room; they were as unlikely a trio as if the Stooges themselves had gathered for a meeting in the surgery. "What's this?" said the doctor, picking up the bottle of smelling salts from the table. "Not another fainting fit, Miss Everly?"

Louisa winced as Malcolm looked at her. Until that moment, she'd failed to realize that she hadn't actually told him about her collapse on the night of the fire. And though he didn't say anything, the angle of his arched brow demanded an explanation that would have to wait until later.

"It's my fault, I'm afraid," said Mrs. Watson. "Too much shopping is good for the heart but bad for the head, as my mother used to say. Miss Everly became dizzy while helping me sort through tea towels, and no wonder—the patterns were altogether garish!"

Mrs. Clarke set her hand on her husband's sleeve. "And they would have gone home, silly things, but Inspector Sinclair noticed something was amiss and insisted on bringing her to see you at once."

While Mrs. Clarke had praised Malcolm for his "gallantry," her husband only said that this was "very sensible" and knelt at Louisa's side. His wife took the cue and ushered Malcolm out into the hallway to wait until the exam was over. Mrs. Watson was not about to be ushered anywhere.

As the doctor drew close enough to examine her, Louisa narrowed her eyes and returned the courtesy. He wasn't at all like Fernsby, who looked the sort to murder someone. He was a lanky, middle-aged gentleman with gray eyes, spectacles, and thick hair, much of it white. The matrons of Wilbeth Green said he'd been a bit too dashing for a doctor in his younger years, but everyone praised him now for having a famously calm bedside manner. He and his wife had three sons and two daughters, all of whom were grown and married. His eyes lit up whenever he spoke of them.

At the end of Louisa's brief inspection, she could find nothing at all unsettling about the doctor's demeanor, nothing to suggest he had committed arson and homicide and then returned to seeing his patients like nothing had happened.

By now, Dr. Clarke had pulled a small instrument out of his bag and was in the process of examining Louisa's eyes. When this was done, he felt all around her neck and asked her to tilt her head this way and that. He instructed her to lie down and sit up again as quickly as she could. Then he lifted her eyelids, one at a time.

"Have you been drinking water?" he asked, peering briefly into her left eye, then her right. "And eating well?"

"I think so."

"Any difficulty sleeping?"

"A bit."

"Have you been feeling anxious lately?"

"I've had a lot on my mind."

He closed his bag and stood. "Well, that's to be expected. Nerves, I should say. Very common and easily fixed with lots of rest. I can prescribe something to help you sleep if you'd like."

"I'd rather not," said Louisa. Then, as she was growing rather fond of fictitious details: "I have a hard time swallowing pills."

"It's entirely your decision, Miss Everly. But should you change your mind, I can write a prescription for you. Something mild."

"Thank you, Dr. Clarke. You're a regular saint."

He patted her shoulder and smiled. "If you're feeling well enough to return home, my wife can ring up your aunt and uncle. I'm sure they wouldn't mind coming out to fetch you back home."

"There's no need for that," said Mrs. Watson. "I have my Catholic grandson's car."

Dr. Clarke smiled. "I'll wish you all a fine afternoon, then."

He opened the door to see them out, but Malcolm stepped forward before they could leave. "How is Mr. Hexam?" he asked the doctor.

Louisa's heart gave a nervous skip at the obvious reference to the doctor's alibi, and she wasn't the only one affected by it, for the doctor stiffened, his face coloring from his chin to the tips of his ears. "Mr. Hexam?" he echoed vaguely, and Louisa thought his voice sounded slightly off pitch.

Malcolm nodded. "Yes. I haven't seen the old fellow for years. When he came into the shop, he used to show me how to make hats out of newspapers. Said they weren't any good for anything else. I seem to remember the two of you were particular friends."

"Yes, yes!" The doctor laughed, nodding vigorously. "He's very well. Very well indeed!"

"He's had a touch of the gout, though, hasn't he?"

Louisa held her breath as Malcolm went on needling his suspect. When Dr. Clarke spoke again, he asserted himself with all the calmness of his usual bedside manner: "So he does. But he doesn't mind in the slightest. Says it gives him something to talk about."

"Ah," Malcolm said with a smile, "I must remember to ask him about it, then."

17

O f course he was with me!" Mr. Hexam barked a laugh. "For nearly half the night, and it shames me to have to admit it, particularly in the presence of ladies—how do you *do*, Miss Everly? Mrs. Watson?—but really it was all Dr. Clarke's fault. He never did learn to hold his whiskey, and I poured several glasses past his limit during the course of our conversation. Unintentionally, of course!" Another laugh as he gestured to his telephone. "After that, his legs didn't feel solid enough to drive home, so he used my telephone to ring up his poor little wife. He apologized and asked her to forward his calls to his intern while he slept off the effects of the evening on my couch over there."

"Well, shame on you!" huffed Mrs. Watson. She'd located a duster almost as soon as they'd arrived and was now busily brushing a dense patch of dust off the fireplace mantel. "What if he'd been needed at the surgery that night?"

"He said Dr. Fielding was up to the task. Which was why Mrs. Clarke sent for the intern just as soon as she received the call about your hand, Miss Everly. And a fine job the young fellow did, or so I'm told."

Louisa felt Malcolm's gaze but kept her eyes on Mr. Hexam, trying to decide if he was lying to them. He sat across from her in an oversized armchair, sunken like an old log into the wilted cushion. The chair was upholstered in a gaudy gold and ruby floral, and his robe was of a similar pattern and color palette. He wasn't much older than Uncle Archie, mid-fifties at the most.

If he thought her arrival with Malcolm was odd, he didn't say so. And she hadn't had to do any improvisational fainting this time, thank goodness, though Mrs. Watson had graciously offered to be the next victim should they ever need one. But no, Mr. Hexam was as gossipy as a goose and always eager to catch himself up on the newest scandal, and so she and Malcolm had decided that the best course was to march straight up to his door and tell him exactly what they were about, just to see how he would respond.

Indeed, he was most delighted to hear they were there about the fire, but not very helpful when it came to dismantling the doctor's alibi. Not only had Mr. Hexam supported the doctor's account of the evening without being prompted, but he'd added so many colorful details as to make Louisa feel rather sure he was speaking in earnest. Of course, Dr. Clarke might have telephoned him to straighten things up just as soon as they'd left the surgery.

"And the doctor couldn't have gone out to stretch his legs while you were sleeping?" asked Malcolm, who had been listening intently from a bench by the fire.

"Pshaw!" Mr. Hexam shook his head, then took a moment to adjust the position of his right leg, which was propped on a footstool. "Not unless he brewed three pots of strong coffee, and I'd have known if he had besides. I dozed off right here, you see, sitting up straight as a board just like this. It's the only position I can stand to sleep in with this infernal leg. I didn't move an inch all night."

"Nettle tea is what you need," said Mrs. Watson.

"I'm sure you're right, Mrs. Watson. You usually are."

"And cherries!" she added, inspired by his flattery. "An aunt of mine swore by cherries. And—"

"Are you a light sleeper?" interrupted Louisa, trying against all odds to keep things rolling along.

Mr. Hexam threw back his head and laughed again. "A leaf landing on the roof could wake me from the deadest of sleeps. An aftereffect of the war, I'm afraid." He nodded with special emphasis to the table beneath the window, where there was an arrangement of photographs from the war. Though the rest of the house was veiled in a layer of dust, which Mrs. Watson was still battling to remove, there wasn't a speck to be found on this table. The frames weren't at all expensive, yet they gleamed in the light streaming in from the window.

As Louisa scanned the shrine, one photograph caught her notice. "This picture," she said, surprised to once again see her father's hand raised in silent benediction. "I've seen it before. In my brother's room."

Malcolm came and stood at Louisa's side as Mr. Hexam craned his neck to see where she was pointing. "Ah, yes, I'm the good-looking chap. There on the bottom left."

"I didn't realize you'd served with my father."

"It was for a brief time. And right before his death, I'm sorry to say. Fine fellow he was, too. The very best sort. Never knew a vicar who could hold his whiskey so well."

Mrs. Watson clucked her tongue, but Louisa smiled. "May I?" she asked, her hand hovering over the frame. Mr. Hexam gave a careless wave, so she picked up the photograph and took a moment to consider each of the soldiers' downturned faces, until all at once she gave a start and grabbed for Malcolm's sleeve. "Good heavens! There's the doctor!"

She'd tried to whisper, but Mr. Hexam heard her. "Why, yes," he said, frowning as though perplexed by her reaction. "We were all in it together for a time. And would you believe that of all those men there, the doctor and I are the only ones left?" His blustery laugh turned bitter. "I sometimes think it would have been better if I'd gone up in a blast of bullets when I was still reasonably handsome. But here I sit in this chair, weighed down by this wretched leg, plagued by kidney stones of all the dull, dreadful things, and pray for the day to come when I can join the rest of them."

"Celery juice is what you need," said Mrs. Watson in a sympathetic tone, "and dandelion tea."

"I'm sure you're right again, Mrs. Watson."

"But you aren't afraid of death?" Louisa hadn't meant to ask this question, and she spoke it in a soft voice, thinking of Paul and how it must have been for him to realize that his time to perish had come. Had he been afraid, she wondered? Or had he been taken by surprise, as swift and silent as a scissors snip disconnecting body from soul?

What if her own words—her hideous, hateful words—had visited him in his final moments?

"Fear death!" laughed Mr. Hexam, oblivious to her distress. "Ha! I *respect* him! And after the chase I've given him, I have no doubt he respects me as well. Why, if he were to walk through that door over there, black cloak or not, I'd stand up from this chair and shake him by the hand and say, 'Why, you crafty old devil, well done!'"

Louisa wasn't sure how to respond to that. She'd never known a person who longed for death, and it was hard to imagine that a man such as Mr. Hexam, only in the middle of his life and who laughed so often, should feel it. But the war had aged him, made him seem as though he'd seen twice as much as should naturally fit into fifty-odd years of living.

And he had.

Most certainly he had.

A short while later, after Mrs. Watson had vowed to return with nettle tea and celery juice, the three of them saw themselves out of Mr. Hexam's house. Mrs. Watson went straight to the car, wicker handbag swinging from her arm, and got in. But speaking so frankly of death had made Louisa feel solemn and strange, and she would have stood by herself for a long while if Malcolm hadn't joined her on the curb.

"What did the doctor mean earlier?" he asked quietly. "About another fainting fit?"

She sighed and kicked a stone down the path. If she admitted to collapsing on the night of the fire, she feared it might not convince Malcolm that Paul was really dead. A more reasonable man might suspect that she was somehow off-kilter in the mind. Unreliable.

But they weren't likely to come within an inch of the truth if she couldn't trust him, and he hadn't exactly cast her off when she told him that she'd sensed Paul's death. "It was on the night of the fire," she began. "When I felt as though something terrible had happened to Paul, I sort of . . . well, I got all fuzzy in the head and collapsed."

"You kept this from me. Why?"

"I don't know. I suppose I didn't want you to think I was losing my mind."

"And your hand?"

"I caught myself on my teacup on the way down, but it's healed up nicely."

She held out her hand, palm side up, as proof and fought a flinch of surprise when Malcolm's hand not only brushed but curved around her own. As his eyes narrowed on the scar, Louisa prattled nervously: "Of course, my aunt sent straight for the doctor, and that's how I knew he was out seeing to Mr. Hexam's gout because he had to send Dr. Fielding in his place to stitch me up. When he was on his way out, we were on the front steps, and that's when we saw that the abbey was on fire. I suppose Mr. Hexam's story matches up, though the doctor *does* seem to be hiding something. But then why should Mr. Hexam lie for him? Do you think he could be involved as well? Or have we spent the whole morning chasing after the proverbial red herring?"

"It's hard to know." Idly, Malcolm's finger traced the scar from one end of Louisa's palm to the other. She was still trying to decide what else there was to say, and whether her voice would cooperate with her long enough to say it, when a car horn blasted directly behind them.

Like jumping awake from a dream, Louisa snatched her hand away from Malcolm's and whirled around. Mrs. Watson was looking cool and attentive behind the wheel of her Catholic grandson's green sedan. "Some getaway driver," said Louisa, laughing under her breath.

"I can arrest her," offered Malcolm, "if you'd like."

"You can't arrest Mrs. Watson. She'd never allow it."

As if sensing the general theme of their conversation, Mrs.

Watson smiled and lifted one of her white gloved hands from the steering wheel. Malcolm smiled and waved back. "Just see if I won't," he said.

❧

When Louisa returned to Everly Hall, she was hoping to slip in through the back of the house so that no one would think to question her about where she'd been that day, but this was not to be. They were only halfway up the drive when Louisa spotted her aunt standing on the topmost step of the front porch. She wore a smart gray suit-dress with a narrow pencil skirt, and she was so still and unmoving, all but the silvery hairs at the nape of her neck which fluttered in the wind, that any passing stranger might have thought she was a statue carved of stone.

"Oh, dear," said Louisa. "She looks annoyed, I think."

"Wealthy people always look annoyed," sighed Mrs. Watson. "Money's bad for the constitution." And she gripped the steering wheel and swung them the rest of the way up the drive.

At first, Louisa thought Mrs. Watson was handling the vehicle admirably well for a beginner, but then the woman lost herself somewhere in the middle of the turn; a topiary near the front steps, which couldn't very well jump out of the way to protect itself, nearly became a casualty.

Her aunt was descending the stairs when the two clambered out of the car. "Louisa, dear, are you all right? Mrs. Kittle rang to tell us she'd seen you leaving the surgery with the inspector."

Of course Mrs. Kittle had called. There wasn't much that happened in Wilbeth Green without *someone* knowing about

157

it. And though Louisa would have much rather downplayed their theatrics at the surgery, Mrs. Watson was still excited and entirely in character, and so she swept forward and told, in the most animated language and with plenty of embellishment, all about Louisa's fainting fit while shopping, the unexpected heroics of Inspector Sinclair, and how he'd seen her safely to the surgery.

"I was only a little dizzy, is all," said Louisa, dismissing her aunt's concern with a wave of her hand.

"And it was *entirely* my fault!" cried Mrs. Watson, still aflutter. "There were too many linens to consider in a single afternoon. I ought to have known as much. But all she needs really is a cup of ginger tea."

"Is that what the doctor said?" Aunt Agatha frowned, setting the back of her hand on Louisa's forehead as if checking her for a fever. "You look so pale, my dear."

Louisa cringed. She hadn't minded so much about lying to the doctor or even to his wife. She'd been helping Malcolm, after all. But she hadn't considered how she'd feel about her faux fainting when she returned home. As her aunt looked her over head to toe for any lingering signs of illness, Louisa stepped back, beyond the reach of her aunt's fretting hands. "I'm feeling much better," she insisted. "Honestly I am. Inspector Sinclair saw to it that I was looked after properly."

"How glad I am that he was there to assist you."

Aunt Agatha didn't sound very glad. She sounded downright dismayed. But then she paused, lips pinched, and decided: "We should invite him to dinner."

Louisa blanched as she imagined Malcolm sitting across the dinner table from Uncle Archie, who was never ruder or more insulting to guests than when he had a rich and heavy meal to digest. "That isn't necessary." Louisa tried to sound firm about it, but she was afraid she sounded panicked instead.

"Of course it is," said Aunt Agatha. "The poor fellow can't have many fine dinners in his circles, can he? And besides that, I insist that chivalry must always be rewarded."

"It wasn't chivalry," said Louisa, choking on a laugh. "I can assure you it wasn't that."

Her aunt turned, talking on as if she hadn't heard her. "I'll telephone him and settle a date just as soon as we have you tucked into bed." She glanced sharply at the footman, waiting for him to open the door, while Mrs. Watson shifted from one foot to the other as though waiting to be invited to dinner herself.

She was thanked for her assistance, but she certainly wasn't invited, and Louisa was ushered back to her room like a proper invalid and promptly put to bed.

18

On Friday morning, when Louisa descended for breakfast, the halls near the kitchen were bustling and busy, and Mrs. Bottle, the housekeeper, was stooped like a shadow over Biddy, who knelt miserably over the shattered remnants of a vase.

"You clumsy thing!" hissed Mrs. Bottle. "Get a broom and sweep it up at once! As if we don't already have a hundred other things to do! When you're done with that, go straight to the larder to fetch the butter for Mrs. Hobbs."

By this time, Biddy had scraped together a few of the largest fragments of the vase and seemed not to know what to do with her hands now that they were full. "I'm t-terribly sorry, Mrs. Bottle," she stammered. "Really, I am!"

"And just what are you still going on about it for? Silly girl, shoo!"

Biddy gasped and, dropping the debris on the floor with an unpleasant clatter, scarpered off down the hall.

Mrs. Bottle was still shaking her head when she spotted Louisa in the entryway. In a twinkling, her expression transformed from the scowl of an old crow to an unmistakably false and ingratiating smile. "Good morning, Miss Everly! Please, forgive the mess. These young things can't seem to put one foot in front of the other without inflicting chaos. Breakfast has been set out in the morning room, and your aunt is there now. Unless you'd like for me to send something up for you in your room?"

While Aunt Agatha had always appreciated Mrs. Bottle's no-nonsense approach to breaking in her domestic underlings, Louisa felt protective of Biddy, whose age and household rank made her a natural target for the much older housekeeper. "Don't trouble yourself," Louisa answered in her coldest, most contemptuous tone. "You are excused."

Nothing singular changed or shifted in the housekeeper's smile, but her cheeks turned crimson. "Yes, Miss Everly," she said, her starched black skirt swinging like the tolling of a silent bell as she turned and strode away.

Louisa lingered in the hall. She watched a whole host of servants come and go before Biddy returned a few minutes later. The girl's expression was more fortified now, as if she'd used the time away to prepare herself for battle, and she was suitably armed for the task with a broom and dustpan.

"What's all the fuss about this morning?" Louisa asked, helping to gather a few of the larger broken pieces into a pile.

Biddy swept in a busy little circle around herself. "Dinner," she said without lifting her chin. "Your aunt wants twelve courses."

"Twelve!" cried Louisa. "Good heavens, what for?"

"It's all beyond me, Miss Everly, but Mrs. Hobbs says it's unchristian to have more than six courses when we all learned we could do perfectly well with less during the war, and that people really ought not to be eating so many canapés in one sitting regardless." Biddy was sweeping and growing more animated by the moment. "I've known Mrs. Hobbs to be sneaking pear drops out of her handbag almost hourly, ever since the sweet ration went by the wayside, so I don't think she should make herself too much of a pharisee about the canapés. Of course, when it comes to deciding on twelve courses rather than six, I'm sure your aunt has her reasons."

"Yes," agreed Louisa, "I'm sure she does." But what those reasons might be, Louisa couldn't begin to guess. She had a hard time believing her aunt would go to any extra trouble for a guest like Malcolm or that she thought so much about the service he had rendered to Louisa. Now, if her aunt was hoping to highlight the disparity in their situations, well, she certainly didn't need twelve full courses to do it.

Louisa sidestepped the path of Biddy's broom, the uneasy feeling in her stomach beginning to grow. "Do you happen to know," she inquired, "how many people are coming to dinner tonight?"

"About six or so, I think."

Louisa's aunt, who had said nothing about inviting anyone else to dinner, was most certainly up to something. "Have you seen the guest list?"

Biddy shook her head and crouched down, brushing the mound of fragments neatly into the dustpan. "I don't know anything else about it, Miss Everly. I'd better finish seeing to this before Mrs. Bottle comes back."

"She seems to have it in for you," Louisa observed, following Biddy down the hall.

"She says I'm always 'one step short of put together,' and I suppose she's right. My dress is wrinkled no matter what I do, and she caught me with a rip in my sleeve on Boxing

Day. She read me the riot act right in front of everyone and then sent me off to sew it up in my room without letting me open my present. I don't know what she would have said if she knew I'd lost a button a few weeks ago."

Louisa straightened. "A button, you say?"

"Yes, miss. On my cuff."

Biddy jostled the broom to point to her wrist where the missing button had been replaced. There was nothing remarkable about it, and yet Louisa felt a flutter in her chest. It wasn't a hunch, really, not even an inkling. After all, buttons went missing all the time, and a black button was as nondescript as they came. But for the moment she imagined herself an inspector and quickly laid out a line of questioning: "Where did you end up finding it?"

"I didn't. But one of the other girls scrounged up a spare before Mrs. Bottle could notice, thank heaven."

"That *is* lucky," said Louisa. "And should you ever need another spare, I found a button just like that one and tucked it away in my drawer."

"Did you?"

"Yes. I found it on the stairs. Just outside my brother's flat."

Louisa had spoken calmly, hardly expecting this to lead to much of anything, for it would be only too easy for Biddy to pretend she knew nothing about it. Still, she squinted her eyes, hoping she might be able to pick up on some subtle twitch of guilt or anxiety in the housemaid's expression. There was no need to look so closely. Just as soon as Louisa mentioned her brother, Biddy's arms went limp at her sides. The porcelain contents of her dustpan clattered back to the floor as a small white dust cloud rolled over her black shoes.

"Oh, Miss Everly!" sobbed Biddy. "Please don't tell your aunt! Please don't tell Mrs. Bottle! *Please!*"

Louisa was too stunned by her own success to answer at first. A footman had just rounded the corner with a pair of lofty candelabras clutched in his gloved hands. He saw Biddy weeping, grimaced once, and changed course directly.

Biddy was shaking too hard to handle the broom properly. If they waited much longer, they'd have a full audience, and so Louisa took the situation in hand. She quickly brushed up the pieces of vase and deposited them into the nearest wastebasket. Then, carrying the broom and dustpan under her arm, she steered Biddy down the hall. Since she couldn't very well abscond with the housemaid altogether, not when the girl was expected to be fetching butter for Mrs. Hobbs, and especially since Biddy was already in boiling hot water with the housekeeper, Louisa escorted her to the larder when no one was looking and closed them both up inside.

The air was a welcome change, cool and dry. All around them were slabs of meat and crocks of cream, cheese, and butter. Yet the change of scenery did nothing to calm Biddy. She sat down on a barrel, crying into her skirt.

"It's all right," Louisa said, ducking a low-hanging arrangement of onions. "I'm not going to tell Mrs. Bottle anything about it. But you must be honest with me—when were you at my brother's flat?"

Biddy sniveled some more, then dried her eyes on her apron. "The night of the fire," she hiccupped.

Louisa thought back to the two water glasses she'd seen in Paul's sink. "So the two of you were, what, involved?"

She hadn't meant to sound so surprised about it and hoped that Biddy wasn't offended. But the truth of the matter was that the housemaid wasn't at all Paul's type. Through the years, he'd offended his aunt and uncle by flirting his way through a long list of dark-eyed, willowy, worldly women, the sort who would have sat quite comfortably on his knee at a place like The Blind Cat. Mousy-haired and doe-eyed, Biddy was beautiful, to be sure, but in a quiet, buttoned-up, nervous sort of way.

"We always met at his flat, but it isn't what it sounds like." Biddy blushed and lowered her eyes, speaking directly to a basketful of eggs next to her feet. "He was a good man, your brother, and I should know. I've been asked out by plenty of fine-seeming young men who turned out to be rats. Of course, I turned him down the first few times he asked me. His reputation, you know. But he was patient about it, always civil, and when I said he could take me dancing if he liked, he was just so perfectly normal. And perfectly grand."

Louisa had never heard anyone say that her brother was perfectly anything, except perhaps perfectly *despicable*. "Did you always meet in secret?"

Biddy laughed a bit through her tears. "He wasn't the sort to sneak around. We quarreled about it once, and he said if he was going to pluck up the courage to kiss a pretty girl, he didn't care two pence who saw him do it. But I'm support-ing my parents, you see, and my siblings, and I couldn't risk losing my position. Mrs. Bottle doesn't permit gentleman callers, and your aunt would have given me the sack if she found out I was seeing her nephew. Paul didn't like it, but he understood."

"Was it serious between you two?"

"I didn't know how serious it was—not until a few weeks before the fire when he gave me this." She stood and pulled a thin chain out from under the collar of her dress. Dangling at the end was a stunning silver ring with an angular arrangement of diamonds in the shape of a shield. Stricken by the sight of it, Louisa sank back against the shelf behind her, nearly knocking over an enormous tray of pastry dough.

The ring had belonged to Louisa's paternal grandmother. Aunt Agatha had been heartbroken when it was willed to Louisa's father and pleaded with Paul to let her buy it when it was later passed down to him. He'd informed her, carelessly, that he'd already gambled it off in some Oxford slum, said it so convincingly that even Louisa had believed him.

"He told me that he loved me." Biddy whispered the words mostly to herself, slipping the ring halfway over her slenderest finger. "He said he wanted us to run off together and get married. We'd made plans to slip away during the party when no one would notice. But when I got to his flat that night, something was wrong. At first I was afraid he was getting cold feet, but he assured me it wasn't that. He said there was something he had to see to first. Something important."

The gnawing ache in Louisa's heart strangled her words to a whisper: "Did he say what it was?"

"No. All I could get out of him was that he had a number of tools he needed to get from the abbey that night for a job he had to do early the next morning."

"What job?"

"A broken pipe, I think it was. Some woman I've never heard of way out in Thornhill. She had one of those color kind of names—White maybe? Or was it Green? Oh, it's no matter now, I suppose. When I saw the fire later that night, I knew that something terrible had happened to Paul." She lifted the corner of her apron to her eyes and began crying again. "And then when I overheard you arguing with your uncle about what had happened—"

Louisa seized Biddy's hand. "It was you who slipped the note under my door!"

"Yes . . ." Biddy sniffled, her shoulders shaking as she again attempted to compose herself. "It w-was me."

"But why didn't you go to the police?"

"I never thought it might have been murder until I heard you say it out loud. But then it all made sense. Your brother had his faults, but he was a good man, Miss Everly. He wouldn't have done it. He *couldn't* have done it. But I was too afraid to go to the police after that. I couldn't lose my position, certainly not without a reference to see me settled elsewhere. Too many people depend on me, and I've already bungled things up for them enough times already. But I thought maybe if you knew that you weren't alone in your suspicions, that you'd keep at it and find the truth."

"And a bang-up job I'm doing of it," groaned Louisa. She plopped herself down on a barrel and began to sort through things again from the very beginning. "I've heard that a number of people argued with Paul on the night of the fire," she began. "When you saw him that night, did he seem out of sorts at all?"

"He seemed nervous, I suppose. Agitated. He kept looking out the window and forgetting what time it was. Once, there was a pair of headlights coming up the road, and I actually thought he was going to force me to hide under the bed! But whoever it was drove off. After that, he insisted that I leave. I offered to cook him something before I went—on account of his looking so pale—but he said his stomach was bothering him, and so I left."

"His stomach?"

"Yes. He told me he didn't feel as though he could keep anything down."

Louisa thought of the empty prescription bottles Malcolm had spotted in Dr. Clarke's desk. If the doctor had wanted to get Paul out of the way, poison would have been the easiest method at his disposal. He had the means certainly, but what exactly was the motive? Mrs. Clarke had said her husband didn't like Paul because he thought he was trouble, but Louisa didn't suppose most people, even vigilantes, went about knocking off the odd hooligan for sport.

Perhaps she was getting ahead of herself. Paul might just as easily have eaten a bit of fish that didn't agree with him.

There was no time to think it through any further than that. Someone was advancing, very rapidly, down the short stairwell that led from the kitchen to the larder. Gasping, Biddy unhooked the ring from the silver chain and held it out to Louisa. "Take it," she said quickly. "Please. I know it was your grandmother's ring. I don't suppose so fine a thing belongs with one such as me."

Shaking her head, Louisa pressed the ring back into Biddy's palm and curled the housemaid's fingers around it. "Paul wanted you to have it," she said. "That makes you practically my sister."

They both smiled tearfully as Biddy slipped the ring back under her dress. The doorknob behind them was turning now, but Louisa had enough of her wits about her to turn and snatch a glass jar of dried ginger down from the shelf above her. She was turning it over carelessly in her hand when the door to the larder swung open and Mrs. Bottle appeared.

"Miss Everly!" the housekeeper exclaimed, her eyes darting

suspiciously from Louisa to Biddy and back again. "What on earth are you doing in here?"

Louisa held up the jar of ginger. "I've been feeling a bit light-headed lately, and Mrs. Watson recommended some ginger in my tea. And as Biddy was on her way to fetch the butter for Mrs. Hobbs, she kindly offered to show me where I could find some."

Mrs. Bottle's smile was as stiff as her starched collar. "When it comes to dizzy spells, peppermint is *far* superior to ginger."

She said it in a way that would have offended Mrs. Watson to an incredible degree had she been there. And what Louisa wouldn't have given at that moment to have heard Mrs. Watson's reply.

19

Though Mrs. Hobbs was morally opposed to overindulgence, which was perhaps an odd trait for a cook, she never could have shown her face if it was said that she had prepared anything less than what the mistress of the house had asked of her. As far as cooks went—and Louisa's aunt had engaged many—the woman was remarkably talented and nothing if not dutiful, and so there was, along with several trays of other hors d'oeuvres, an outrageous number of cheese and crab canapés laid out in the parlor.

In agony, Louisa sat herself down by the deviled chestnuts to wait. After talking to Biddy, she'd tried to ring up Malcolm to warn him that he was likely walking into an ambush that evening. But it was to no avail, for every time she reached for the telephone, someone came and fairly pounced upon her.

First it was her uncle, who demanded to know why the devil he had to share his best brandy with an upstart inspector who likely knew more about cabbages than catching criminals. Then it was Fernsby, as expressive as a tombstone, to inform her that her aunt was looking for her. And Aunt Agatha had kept Louisa busy, and entirely chaperoned, for the remainder of the day so that she didn't dare reach for the telephone again. She did venture to ask her aunt who else was coming to dinner, and her aunt had answered elusively, *"We needed a few guests to round out the table."*

Wesley Barrows was the first to arrive. Only his parents called him Wesley; the rest either called him Barrows or "that poor fellow who can't find his handkerchief" because he never seemed to remember which pocket he'd slipped it into. Indeed, he was the vaguest of young men, but when it came to mixing martinis, he was a regular chemist, and he set himself to work in this regard just as soon as he was through the sitting room door.

He was followed by Hugh Wentworth, who called everyone "old chap," and Hugh's younger sister, Viola, who was engaged to an earl. Next came Lionel, known to all his friends as "Old Lionheart" on account of his prowess on the rugby field, and Lionel's newest darling, a young heiress in gaudy red who didn't look the slightest bit impressed by the number of crab canapés. Louisa had met her once at a cricket game, but for the life of her she couldn't remember the woman's name.

She was still trying to recall it when Lionel crossed the room. "Smashing to see you again, old girl," he said, pressing a kiss to Louisa's cheek. Then to Barrows: "Make one of those for me, will you? I got fleeced at cards last night and need consoling."

"Anyone else need consoling?" asked Barrows.

"I'll take one," sighed Hugh. "Last night gave me the worst kind of headache, and I'm still fighting it off today."

"Why?" said Viola. "What were you doing?"

"Fleecing Old Lionheart at cards, of course," he said, sniggering. "You want one too, Sibyl?"

"I don't care for martinis," answered the heiress, her painted red lips pursing in distaste.

Barrows couldn't have looked more personally affronted if he'd been the one to invent martinis in the first place. "Well, why not?" he demanded.

"It's as Mother says, why drink gin when you can drink champagne?"

"Your mother is a woman of enormously good sense," observed Viola. She laughed and flounced down on the couch. "I think I shall apply that logic even further, and so no more drinking water for me—only *champagne!*"

Louisa stared out the window as the conversation moved on in the background without her. In general, she'd always gotten on well with her friends, but the usual nonsense, which often made her laugh, sounded hollower than it normally did. She could only imagine what Malcolm would have said, or how he would have looked at her, if he'd arrived early enough to hear it.

"Bad luck about your brother," said Hugh, coming over to stand beside her. "How are you holding up, old chap?"

"Well enough, thank you."

"Have you heard from him?"

A gust of wind blew a stray leaf, flat like a veiny green hand, against the window. Louisa stared at it a moment, then answered: "I don't really expect to."

"Bad luck," he said again, then reached for a mushroom roll. Viola got up from the couch before he could take a bite and elbowed him hard in the ribs. "Ow!" he howled. "What the devil are you—? Ah, yes! Yes, of course." He cleared his throat and kneaded the wounded rib. "Here's the thing. We've been talking—all of us together, I mean—about taking you away for a bit of a holiday."

"A holiday?" repeated Louisa.

Barrows had abandoned the bar and was now shuffling absently through a nearby stack of records, which Louisa's aunt had told her to bring down for the party. "You could use it, don't you think," he encouraged, "after everything that's happened?"

"Something modest," put in Viola. "Paris maybe?"

"I can't stand Paris this time of year," sighed Sybil. "But I'll go if Lionel is."

The wind was blowing harder now, as though it was trying to force its way into the house, but no one other than Louisa seemed to notice. Viola laughed and snatched a vinyl out from the pile Barrows was still shuffling through. She slipped it into the record player and lowered the needle. "Tilly's already said she'll go," she said, tapping her foot to the music. "David too, of course. And my parents have agreed to come, to keep everything proper, since we all know you're still a vicar's daughter, poor thing, and must be mindful about such things. So you see, it's all quite settled."

Not long ago, Louisa would have jumped at the chance for a holiday in Paris, especially if David was going as well. But her priorities were no longer what they had been. Her brother was dead, and there was no holiday long enough or fine enough to make her forget that he was gone and that she and Malcolm hadn't yet found the person or persons responsible.

She looked back from the window and realized that her friends were all staring at her. "I'm grateful to you all for thinking of me," she said. "Truly, I am. But I doubt very much if my aunt and uncle can spare me."

"Nonsense!" cried Aunt Agatha, strolling into the room in a mauve gown with matching stole. "We think it's a marvelous idea, don't we, Archie, dear? We'll have to settle on dates just as soon as we can. Now, who still needs a drink?"

After that, someone turned up the volume on the record player. Canapés began vanishing from trays. Uncle Archie planted himself behind the heavily stocked beverage cart, where he would no doubt remain until dinner. The revelry was well under way with laughter and the sound of glasses clinking when Tilly entered the room a moment later. She was as skinny as a maypole in her blue swing dress, which made her look even taller and leggier than normal, and her blond curls were pulled back in her usual high ponytail, with an abundance of bangs rolled in a tall, elegant curl above her brow.

Though Louisa was relieved to see her friend, she didn't rush to Tilly's side as she usually might have done. The two hadn't spoken since the Chitwell incident, and Louisa wasn't sure if her friend would have forgiven her for leaving her in such a terrible lurch. But then Tilly raced across the carpet, stopping only long enough to fetch a stuffed grape from a footman's platter, and took a fiendishly strong hold of Louisa's hand.

"Don't look behind me, Louisa," said Tilly, her cheeks flushed, "but *look!*"

With a tactful turn of her head, Louisa looked. Malcolm stood in the hall. His usual gray suit had been swapped for a dark blue three-piece, and even if his hair wasn't quite as wild as it had been when a lad, his eyes were twice as defiant.

David stood beside him, whispering furiously. He was dressed to the nines in a black, double-breasted suit, a white carnation peeking out from his winged lapel. His blond hair was parted and slicked to one side, gleaming faintly in the glow from the chandelier overhead. Louisa doubted if anyone had ever walked away from David in the middle of a conversation, but Malcolm cut him off with a cynical laugh, then strolled idly away.

"What were they arguing about?" whispered Louisa.

"Beats me," said Tilly. "But I just heard the inspector call David the sort of name I couldn't imagine repeating to a vicar's daughter." And then she leaned close and whispered it in Louisa's ear anyway.

And Louisa really was very shocked.

"Ah, here he is!" said Barrows, smirking as Malcolm strode into the room. "The guest of honor!"

It was unlikely that Barrows thought much of Malcolm, or even remembered him, but he found any gathering an occasion to drink, and so he lifted his glass in a silent, one-sided toast. Beyond that, no one moved, and only Tilly smiled, which made Louisa decide that the girl was easily worth all the rest of them put together.

Given the setting, Louisa wasn't sure if Malcolm would rather she address him by his first name or as Inspector Sinclair, and so she made up her mind to call him neither as she crossed the room and said: "How serious you look this evening! I do hope you haven't arrested Mrs. Watson or something so terrible as that."

Viola giggled before he could answer. "Arrest Mrs. Watson!" she echoed. "Whatever do you mean, Louisa?"

"Miss Everly likes to tease me," answered Malcolm. "It shames me to admit that Mrs. Watson and I quarreled this week."

"Poor fellow!" sympathized Tilly. "But you mustn't take it too much to heart. The woman quarrels with everyone—even the vicar!"

Aunt Agatha chose that moment to sail across the floor and usher Malcolm into the room. "We're so glad you were able to tear yourself away from policing," she said, "and from quarreling with our aged church ladies."

"One must always make time for leisure," acknowledged Malcolm.

"Certainly! One must. And I hope you don't mind that I've taken the liberty of inviting a number of Louisa's friends this evening. It's been an age since you lived in the neighborhood, and I wanted to help you feel more settled with the young people. Of course, you'll remember Miss Harbrook, whom you interrogated so competently when Louisa was in Oxford. The Wentworths, I believe, were here during your time, for their cook always complimented your parents on having a fine selection of turnips. You can't have forgotten Mr. Barrows and Mr. Croft—they were always so famous at rugby. However, you likely haven't met Miss Sybil Shaw, who is visiting from London."

"I haven't had the privilege," said Malcolm. "How do you do, Miss Shaw?"

"You speak very well," the heiress replied, "for a policeman."

Louisa's stomach turned to gravy when she heard David laugh snidely behind her. "Well, of course he speaks well!" he sneered. "Haven't you heard that Inspector Sinclair is a *hero*?" A second later, stiff footsteps disturbed the silence as he slowly crossed the room. "First you bring Louisa back from that slum in Chitwell. Now you're there to catch her when she swoons?" He drew up alongside Louisa, resting a hand tenderly on her shoulder. "How glad we are for your interference, Inspector, for we couldn't begin to imagine if anything were to ever happen to our dear Louisa."

Malcolm smiled tensely, as did the rest of the assembly, but Louisa didn't even try to smile. She was sure that David had already been drinking that evening, and so she reached out and confiscated the martini that Barrows was about to hand to him.

"Stop this nonsense," she said, "and have a mushroom roll."

"Yes!" added Tilly, shoving a plate of hors d'oeuvres at David, who only just managed to catch the plate, the food rolling within a hair's breadth from soiling his crisp white shirt. "And the walnut sablés are *divine!*"

Louisa wasn't sure what might have happened if Aunt Agatha hadn't stepped in and taken the situation in hand. With a cheerful smile, she shooed David toward the fireplace and encouraged him to sit with Lionel and Hugh, inquiring about a celebrated rugby game from their time together at Harrow. As soon as this conversation took hold, she steered Malcolm to the drink cart on the other side of the room, where she instructed her husband to offer him something he might not be able to afford on a policeman's salary.

By now Louisa's aunt was in her element. She sought out champagne for Sybil. She had Uncle Archie fix a sidecar for Viola with good, strong cognac and a coil of lemon peel. She found something for Malcolm and the heiress to talk about and even managed to corral Barrows into the discussion. Aunt Agatha had always excelled at organizing guests without their ever realizing they were being organized. She moved deftly among the group, laughing and fueling conversations and making sure the record player never fell silent—and that Louisa and Malcolm remained on opposite sides of the room.

20

There were those who believed that drinking cocktails before a meal dulled the palate, but the guests that evening were in no danger of that. The feast began in proper form with blinis topped with caviar and soused herring salad, followed by a luscious almond soup, stuffed brussels sprouts, and a curled endive salad with French dressing. Then there was the usual procession of more formidable dishes: grilled stuffed mackerel, partridges cooked in vine leaves, and Mrs. Hobbs's specialty, ragoût of beef with herb dumplings. All was served on a tablecloth so white and so skillfully starched that Mrs. Watson might have swooned if she'd been there to see it.

Louisa thought the meal itself might have been a success if Aunt Agatha wasn't as transparent as a picture window when it came to scheming. She hadn't "rounded out the table" that evening. Not in the slightest. Barrows and Tilly were seated next to each other, as were Lionel and Sybil—and, of course, David and Louisa. Though siblings, even Hugh and Viola made up a pair of sorts. But Malcolm's presence as the so-called guest of honor made the table an odd number, an impossible oversight for someone who valued balance and dinner party etiquette as much as Aunt Agatha did. And he, poor fellow, was grilled more thoroughly than the stuffed mackerel.

"How are your parents?" Aunt Agatha inquired during the first course.

It was a harmless enough question. Polite even.

"My mother died some years ago now," Malcolm answered, "but my father does very well."

Louisa stared down at her caviar, but she couldn't find her appetite, let alone her voice to offer her sympathies. She hadn't heard anything about Malcolm's family. Certainly not that his mother had died. And though there was no excessive or even outward hurt in Malcolm's voice, she felt dreadful that during all of their interactions, she'd never bothered to ask about his family—while they were rushing around trying to sort out her own.

"Does he still sell turnips?" Uncle Archie couldn't help that his voice was gruff. Even when he wasn't smoking, his lips were pressed together as if trying to hold a phantom pipe in place, and so it just came out that way.

"He has a corner shop in Oxford."

"Do your siblings still help him?" asked Aunt Agatha. "I seem to remember there was an inordinate number of you."

That was not quite as polite, but Malcolm, who had nine older siblings in all, smiled as though there had been no irony in the question. "They're all married now and settled on their own. But my sisters drop in a great deal to make sure he's all right."

"Your father must be very proud of you," said Tilly, "for becoming an inspector."

For the first time that evening, Malcolm's forced smile

relaxed into a more genuine expression. "He is, Miss Harbrook. Thank you for saying so."

Under normal circumstances, Viola would have cared far more about hats than homicide when it came to dinner conversation, but she must have decided that Malcolm was handsome enough to make his profession seem a good deal less unsophisticated than she'd earlier thought, and so she was leaning toward his side of the table. "Have you arrested many people?" she asked, her eyes wide.

"Yes," he said. "Many."

"How thrilling!"

"Not especially. I'm afraid I've nearly arrested Miss Everly on any number of occasions, and she never looked very thrilled about it."

His timing was terrible. Louisa was mid-drink when he chose to say this. She sputtered for a second and looked, appallingly, like a drowning victim. When at last she recovered herself, she considered kicking his shin under the table for saying such an outrageous thing, but then she saw him cover his grin by taking a bite of herring and very nearly burst out laughing herself.

"Even so," said Hugh, "aside from Louisa here, there can't be very many criminals for you to apprehend. Wilbeth Green's as dull as tombstones, if you'll forgive the tired idiom. Not many criminals need rounding up, do they?"

"You'd be surprised," Malcolm said without looking at anyone in particular, and yet Louisa saw several people stiffen.

"There are rumors that you've been tapped for a position with the Yard," said David. "Is that true?"

"I couldn't really say," said Malcolm. "They keep such things fairly quiet."

"But you're hopeful?"

"I'd be honored if my superiors decided I was fit for such a position."

"With *your* background?" Uncle Archie snorted into his soup, which had only just arrived to be snorted upon. "I suppose I shouldn't be surprised."

Though Malcolm smiled, his voice hardened. "How do you mean, sir?"

"Well, no one puts any value on a man's rank anymore, do they? Seniority means nothing. Good standing means even less. I shouldn't be surprised when nearly anyone with more than two pence to rub together can be called a gentleman and admitted to the finest clubs."

"Hear, hear!" cried Hugh.

Barrows's first and only contribution to the conversation was an ill-timed sneeze. He searched four pockets before locating his handkerchief, then sullenly blew his nose.

"You know," Viola went on, speaking in a low voice, "I crossed paths with a coarse fellow at a tennis match in London. He milled about with all the fashionables, was said to be a splendid tennis player and an altogether promising young man, and yet I watched him with my own two eyes as he submerged a scone into his tea!"

Sibyl inhaled sharply, while Aunt Agatha was more subdued in her displeasure. Dabbing her mouth with her napkin, she inquired if perhaps the man was an American? This was cutting criticism indeed, for the only American Louisa's aunt showed the slightest tolerance for was Grace Kelly, which had more to do with the actress's wardrobe and royal marriage than anything else.

"Really now," said Louisa scornfully, "I don't think any of you are being fair."

"Aren't we?" Uncle Archie's left brow rose so high she half expected it to jump ship into the bowl of soup below. "Why should a man who has put in years of work—and who has a princely amount of patience, I'd imagine—be passed over for a position, only to see it granted to a man of inferior status and few, if any, social connections?"

Malcolm didn't move, didn't speak, but his jaw was tight on one side, like he was trying to grind his words into a powdery silence. Louisa didn't wonder that he didn't speak a word in his own defence. After all, he was the guest of honor that evening. And perhaps he had few social connections, while Uncle Archie had plenty. It would be only too easy for him to ruin the inspector's career with a single telephone call, and all before dessert was served.

"And why," Louisa challenged, "should a man of good sense and moral standing be passed over because his so-called superior, with far less sense, has been at it for decades and happens to play bridge with the chief of police?"

Her speech was punctuated by a terrible silence, which was only interrupted by a squeaky, nervous laugh from Viola's end of the table. To make matters worse, the footmen had arrived to exchange the empty soup bowls for brussels sprouts, only to realize this was not the best time. Aunt Agatha's lips were tightening and twitching by turns, yet she gestured for the brussels sprouts to be carried forward, perhaps hoping that the shifting of dinnerware would offer a necessary distraction.

Uncle Archie was not distracted. As his bowl vanished at the hand of a footman, he drew himself up and shoved a candelabra a few inches to the side, centering his sights on Louisa. Before he could start in on her, however, David flung himself rather jauntily into the conversation: "You know," he said, "I think Louisa's onto something."

Uncle Archie's harsh guffaw turned into a gape of disbelief when he realized David was speaking in earnest. "You do?"

"Certainly. If the police force is looking to advance men with integrity and high standards of honesty, then I say they ought to do it. A man's connections shouldn't matter. Neither should his background. Just so long as he has nothing to hide."

He stared at Malcolm. Malcolm stared back. Louisa could see that her aunt's trick of shuffling them to opposite sides of the room wasn't likely to work at any future dinner parties, not unless she could shuffle the two men to opposite sides of the continent.

"Good sense and moral standing, you say?" Hugh considered the words with an indolent yawn. "Sounds like a rather obnoxious existence, if you ask me."

At the far side of the table, Lionel burst out laughing, nodding in agreement. Then he started choking on a pickle.

21

Dinner ended in a far quieter manner, with tea cake and praline ice. When at last the group drifted out of the dining room, it was with a sense of listlessness and a strange spirit of camaraderie, which Louisa supposed was only natural after the harrowing experience of consuming twelve consecutive courses in one another's company. And even if the lull in quarreling was brought about by nothing more than a mutual state of indigestion, well, she thought, then Mrs. Hobbs's talents had not been spent in vain. Even the heiress had set aside her apathy to observe that the guava jelly, which had been served with the cheese platter, was "rather nice." And the evening, it seemed, was far from over.

"Into the parlor!" said Aunt Agatha, sallying forth in that direction. "I wouldn't think of sending you off into the dreary night without an after-dinner drink."

The group followed eagerly, while Malcolm begged the excuse of an early morning schedule, which none of the other guests seemed to comprehend, though they took turns offering forced words of sympathy and regret. Louisa's aunt made Uncle Archie promise to send round a box of cigars for him, attempting to make up for the horrifying display at dinner. Louisa had never seen Malcolm smoke a cigar, but he thanked them both anyway, collected his hat, and off he went.

Ignoring several scowls and stares, Louisa hurried out after him, catching him up just before he reached his car. "I'm sorry about tonight," she blurted, then gestured lamely toward the house. "I tried to ring you up this morning, to warn you that they were coming, but my aunt is impossible. She wouldn't—"

Malcolm put up his hand. There was an iron lamppost to the right of them, but his eyes were in shadow beneath the brim of his gray fedora. "It's all right," he assured her. "It's good for one's constitution to be treated like a peasant every now and then. Not that I'd like to make a habit of it, of course."

"Really, Malcolm, you have the forbearance of a saint."

He laughed, tipping his hat so it sat back on his head at a more casual angle. "Well now, I never thought I'd see the day when Louisa Everly said I was a saint."

"I most certainly did *not* say you were a saint!" She felt her cheeks go warm. "Nor would I ever!"

He laughed again as he searched her face. "I'd forgotten how easy it was to make you blush." Before she could answer snappishly, as they both knew she was very likely to do, he hooked a finger in the sash at her waist and drew her into the lamplight beside him. "But I never forgot, not for a moment, how stubborn you were." He brushed his thumb in a light curve across her temple.

Louisa had a scar there. At ten years old, she'd stood too close to the batsman during a schoolyard game of cricket and received an accidental blow from the backward swing of the bat. It had hurt like the dickens, bled terribly, and then, much to her mother's chagrin and her father's good humor, faded into a splendid scar. She parted and curled her hair so as to hide the scar, but the wind was playing tricks that night and had blown the curls back from her face.

Louisa's flush deepened as they both remembered, but she was spared from speaking when the wind kicked up again, knocking Malcolm's hat askew. With comical abruptness, he clamped a hand to his head to hold it in place, but the wind had already lifted it up and carried off with it. It rolled a few times, just out of reach, then scuttled like a startled cat up the drive. Louisa laughed as Malcolm lunged after it. After two unsuccessful grabs, he caught the hat before it rolled into the hydrangea bushes.

When he returned to her side, he was still laughing, the brim of his hat clutched now in his fist. His dark hair blew wildly, and the moment brought his youth back into his eyes. Despite the smart lines of his fine suit, he had the sudden look of a boy who had once flown over back roads on his bicycle, delivering groceries for his father.

Feeling as though she had blinked herself into the past, Louisa shook her head and shivered in her strapless gown as the evening wind grew cooler.

Malcolm noticed. "It's getting cold," he said. "Perhaps you ought to go back inside."

"Perhaps. But you ought to know, before I go in, that I've been speaking with our housemaid, Biddy. It turns out she and my brother were engaged."

Malcolm's eyes widened. "Really? How'd you figure that out?"

"A missing button, if you can believe it," said Louisa with a coy smile. "Anyway, she saw him on the night of the fire. They were supposed to elope, but he said that he had something he had to see to first. And he wasn't feeling very well. He told her he didn't think he could keep anything down. Do you think it's possible that Paul could have been poisoned?"

Malcolm frowned. "It's possible, yes, although I'm not sure how to follow it up without a . . . well, without a body, I'm sorry to say. Did the housemaid say anything else?"

Louisa nodded, her voice still struggling. "Paul had an appointment early the next morning."

"With whom?"

The front door creaked open before she could answer, and Aunt Agatha stepped out from the house, waiting on the top step with an impatient pinch of her lips. Malcolm glanced at her once, a bit coolly, then back at Louisa. "Can you meet me tomorrow?" he asked in a lowered voice. "Around two?"

"I think so. We'll have to meet at the vicarage, I'm afraid."

"I'll see you tomorrow, then."

Louisa smiled, then turned back toward the house. As she mounted the stairs, she heard Malcolm's car door open and close, followed by the groan of the engine as his car glided up the drive. She would have gone inside without speaking a word, but Aunt Agatha blocked the way. "My dear," she sighed, and for the first time that night, she looked tired and spent and nothing at all like a hostess. "You must at least try to be careful."

"Careful? How do you mean?"

"Oh, Louisa, there's no need to pretend with me. The heart is a torturous thing, is it not? We see a pair of fine gray eyes, and we fall before ever realizing we were tripping."

Louisa stared at her aunt, unnerved by the rush of emotion that had entered her usually mannerly voice. "What are you talking about?" she asked.

"I'm talking about *men*, Louisa." Aunt Agatha laughed bitterly at the word. "They aren't all of the same quality, but we must make allowances where we can. Your uncle, for instance—I married him because I knew that doing so was the best and only course. My family had certain expectations of me, and I had expectations for myself. Your uncle was the obvious choice. He came from a well-connected family with the right lineage. He had money and influence, and I wanted to be influential in my own way. We suited each other. And yet . . . and yet I was very much in love with someone else when I married him."

"Someone else!" cried Louisa. Her aunt rebuked her with a glare, and so she lowered her voice to a tremulous whisper: "But . . . who?"

"Don't you see? That doesn't matter. What matters is that he was unsuitable. As the better ones often are."

"But—"

"But nothing. Inspector Sinclair is a fine enough man, I'm sure, and he will no doubt make someone a fine enough husband. I'm not blind to what you see in him, but you must recognize, especially when seated with company such as we've had this evening, that he is *not* for you."

Louisa gaped at her aunt, furious but also astonished. She'd known all along that the dinner party that night was a cunning pretext, but she couldn't believe her aunt was actually admitting to it. "You mean to say that you've belittled him on purpose just to prove a point?"

"On the contrary. I invited him to thank him for a service rendered, which was a good deal more than I was obliged to do. After all, he was only doing his job. But now that is done, and he is gone, and we must get back to the way things are. Your guests are waiting for you inside."

"Well, they're going to wait a good deal longer," bit out Louisa. With that, she turned hard on her heel, and with an undignified curse on her lips marched straight back down the steps.

Louisa walked until she found herself in the farthest corner of the garden. She picked up a stick and, without thinking, knocked a scattering of dogwood petals from nearby branches. She knew this was petulant—childish even—but she couldn't help it. She felt as though there were more versions of herself than could reasonably fit in her own skin, and so perhaps she had to rail against something.

She missed her parents. There wasn't a soul living who would have been deemed "unsuitable" to sit at their table. Certainly not Malcolm. She missed the worn scratches on the vicarage floor, left there after the frequent pulling together of tables and a menagerie of mismatched chairs. Though her feet were planted in her aunt's garden, in her heart she could still hear her mother's voice calling her to supper. The low drone of the old radio as she and Paul carried the dishes to the sink. She would have given anything to curl up beside her father on the sofa and be called Lou by him.

He always knew what to say, knew what was to be done. Like the time Paul had broken her new roller skates on purpose because he was tired of her always trailing after him. She'd wept inconsolably, far more from the rejection than from the broken skates themselves, and Paul had felt truly awful about it. He'd apologized for nearly an hour and even offered his own skates to make up for it and pleaded with her to, pretty please, open her door so he could tell her how very sorry he was. When she refused to let him in, her father had rapped on her door quietly, then sat beside her on the bed. *"I can't help thinking about Joseph and his brothers,"* he'd said after a time of silence.

"How they lobbed him into that pit, you mean?" sniveled Louisa, still fuming.

Her father's cheeks puckered like he was trying not to laugh. *"Well, yes,"* he said slowly, *"but also how he wept and wanted to see them again. How he forgave them and spoke kindly to them. And so it is for us when we see our sins and cry to God for mercy. I know you're hurting, but withholding forgiveness hurts both you and your brother. Forgive him, Lou, and speak kindly to him."*

As Louisa remembered her father's words, she dropped the stick from her hand and lifted her eyes to the house. The windows were brightly lit, music and laughter pouring out through the open French doors onto the back terrace. Her brother had thought she was a traitor for how easily she'd settled into life at Everly Hall, and now, for the first time, as she thought about those skates while standing there in her high-priced heels, she feared that he might have been right about her. It had been hard to forgive her brother that day, but it was infinitely harder to forgive herself for everything that had happened since.

"So this is where you're hiding."

She flinched, turning just in time to see David's shadow edging forward through the trees. As he moved closer, a patch of moonlight revealed the cigarette dangling idly from his hand.

"What are you doing here?" Louisa demanded.

He frowned at her tone but kept on walking, a curl of smoke

lingering in the air behind him. "Your aunt said I ought to check on you. She told me you weren't feeling well, that you came out for some fresh air."

Louisa didn't answer.

"Well?" he pressed. "Are you feeling better?"

"I suppose."

He smiled, reaching for her hand. "In that case, how about that drive we'd planned? I can pick you up first thing in the morning."

"I'd rather not," said Louisa, shaking her fingers from his.

"Rather not!" he blasted back. "Say, what's the matter with you tonight? You've been stiff as starch since I got here. It's as if I didn't step in and get you off the hook with your uncle during dinner. Unpleasant little display, wasn't it? And he'd still be shouting at you, I'd reckon, if I hadn't spoken up and saved you."

"Well, well!" she scoffed. "Far be it from me to sound ungrateful."

He caught her by the arm when she tried to walk away. "I know what this is about," he said sharply. "This is about him, isn't it? The *inspector.* I suppose it is hard to look quite so chivalrous by comparison with him skulking around."

She yanked her arm out of his grip. "This has nothing to do with him."

"Doesn't it? Well, why don't you tell me what this *is* about so we can stop sneering at each other?"

"Very well. You argued with my brother on the night of the fire, didn't you? At your family's party."

"Yes," he agreed irritably. "So did your uncle. So did the footman. So did half a dozen other people. He was in a terrible mood that night."

"And yet you told me you hadn't seen him at the party. Why did you lie?"

"Oh, I don't know." He dropped his cigarette and ground it out with the heel of his shoe. "I didn't think it was important. I'm entitled to some privacy, aren't I? Besides, I thought it might upset you, and it turns out I was right. Can we go in now? It's cold out here."

"And what about after?"

"After *what?*"

"After the two of you fought."

David paused. "Are you asking me what I was doing during the fire?"

"Well?"

"I can guess who told you to ask me about that. Well, I don't feel obliged to answer, nor am I inclined to finish this conversation. You're in a terrible mood, you know, and you're deluding yourself if you believe your brother wasn't troubled enough to have burned the abbey."

Louisa balled her hands into fists. "I think you should leave."

"And *that*," he snarled, "is the first sensible thing you've said all night!"

22

For nearly two hours, Louisa sat in the vicarage kitchen paging through the telephone directory. Thanks to the vicar's ecclesiastical connections, she was able to check the Thornhill church records as well, searching for anyone with one of those "color kind of names." There were eleven families by the name of Brown living in Thornhill, nine Greens, six Whites, and two families listed under the surname Black. Malcolm had suggested, cheekily, that she check the listings for anyone called Mr. Taupe or Mrs. Silver. There wasn't any, but there was one funny young man named Roger Beige, who shouted "jolly good!" and "right-o!" to nearly everything Louisa said.

The process of ringing up the rest of the families was not the least bit encouraging. No one had heard of Paul, and two people even went so far as to hang up on Louisa while she was still explaining her predicament.

She stretched her aching back and glanced at the clock above the stove. Her aunt had made her promise to be home at a reasonable hour in case David called, but Louisa didn't expect him to. He'd left the dinner party in a sour mood, dispensing a stiff peck on Louisa's cheek after a hasty fare-well. Her aunt had witnessed the moment. Naturally it made her anxious, and naturally that made her insist on ordering three new gowns and two new hats for Louisa. This wasn't very likely to help, but at least it kept her aunt busy and out of the way.

Since Louisa couldn't risk being overheard at Everly Hall, she'd called on Mrs. Watson for assistance again. The older woman had arrived in her usual fashion to inform Aunt Agatha that there was a mountain of silver in need of polishing for the upcoming tea tent. It wasn't entirely a lie. For the last two hours, Mrs. Watson had indeed been polishing silver in the vicarage kitchen while Louisa worked diligently, with telephone in hand, through the lengthy list of names.

It didn't help that Mrs. Watson was forever halting things to scold Malcolm in the background.

The poor fellow had arrived with notebook and pencil in hand, ready to settle in with Louisa. But Mrs. Watson was not yet finished exacting penance for a childhood of skipped choir practice; she put him to work polishing spoons, which he did in an intentionally apathetic fashion, missing spots and blemishes left and right.

"Who's next?" asked the vicar, circling the room with a steaming teacup perched in his hand.

Louisa crossed the last name off her list with a violent stroke of her pen. "There's no one else. That's the end of the list."

"Perhaps Biddy was mistaken?" suggested Mrs. Watson.

"Or someone on the list is lying," said Malcolm. Louisa felt twice as hopeless at the thought.

With a studious frown, the vicar put on his glasses and ran a knobby finger over the names on Louisa's list, looking very much like a tutor checking his pupil's Latin or arithmetic. "Hmm, was there really no one in Thornhill by the name of Gray?"

Louisa stared at the list until the names blurred together, then laughed and rubbed her eyes. "Good heavens," she cried. "I *am* tired! I've forgotten to search the Grays!"

Mrs. Watson nodded stoutly. "And a fine name it is, too!"

"It's Norman," the vicar informed her, sipping his tea.

"Is it really?" Mrs. Watson lowered the spoon in her hand and seemed to reconsider her own stance. "Well, I've always favored Anglo-Saxon names myself. Far more traditional, you know."

"I thought your maiden name was German?"

"Oh, Vicar, do hush and drink your tea."

Looking physically pained by the prattle, Malcolm tossed a spoon into the drawer, unpolished, and Louisa flapped an impatient hand, gesturing for everyone in the room to be silent as she flipped back a few pages in the directory. There were three listings for Gray. The first didn't answer the telephone. The second seemed to think Louisa was playing with a few cards short of a full deck and darted off before she could finish explaining herself. She was already crossing the third name off her list as she dialed the number, fully supposing she'd come up empty—

"Hello?" The voice on the other end of the line was soft and surprisingly pleasant.

"Yes, hello!" Louisa did her utmost to sound cheerful and not at all imbalanced. "I'm trying to track down some information about my brother. He's gone missing, you see, and the last I heard he was going to be fixing a broken pipe for someone in Thornhill."

"What's his name?"

"Paul—Paul Everly."

"I've never heard of anyone by that name," said the woman. There was a pause, followed by a single burst of static. "But there was a young man, not long ago, who was supposed to come by to look at my kitchen plumbing. He never came. But his name wasn't Paul. It was . . . Johnny, I think. Yes, Johnny Brimfield."

Louisa shot up out of her chair, nearly bowling Mrs. Watson into the vicar. "Yes! I mean, yes, of course. So sorry for shouting at you. That's him."

"Are you sure?" asked the woman. "I thought you said his name was Paul."

"I know," said Louisa, "and this all must sound so strange, but it's also frightfully important. Would you mind if I paid you a visit?"

"What, today?"

"Yes, if it isn't too inconvenient."

"This is not the best time . . ."

Louisa was about to be hung up on. She could practically hear the handset lowering through the air toward the cradle. "Please! I promise not to stay long, and I assure you, I'm not as ridiculous as I sound." She heard Malcolm snort in the background and flung her pencil at him. "At least not in person," she amended.

"Well," said the woman, "I suppose it would be all right. Just make sure you don't upset the cat."

◦⌒◦

The woman on the telephone turned out to have a name as long and lovely as a string of pearls: Miss Elsie Ann Gwendolyn

Gray. She lived in homey quarters above a fish-and-chips shop, which made her front room smell of vinegar, even with the windows cracked. As Louisa, Malcolm, and Mrs. Watson approached the storefront, a few children playing football in the street, when questioned about the occupant upstairs, said that Miss Gray was "awfully nice for a spinster." But then an older child came tromping along and added that the woman wasn't yet forty, so she hadn't really been a spinster for all that long; he said to come back again in twenty years or so and they'd say how Miss Gray had turned out. (Mrs. Watson wasted no breath in telling him that this was an impertinent suggestion.)

Miss Gray worked out of her home as a seamstress. Her flat was clean but cluttered, a puzzling maze of faded damask furniture and iron-footed mannequins. Several chairs were piled with parcels of lace and other fabrics, and there was an ancient Singer sewing machine hogging the window light near an assortment of wilting plants. The only other notable fixture in the room was a scraggly and opinionated tabby cat named Miss Mabel, who watched the newcomers with sharp eyes from her dusty domain beneath the sofa.

"I'm not sure I'll be of much help," sighed Miss Gray.

She was a tall woman, pencil straight, with an impressive length of reddish-brown hair pulled back tightly at the temples. She was pretty without a doubt, but frightfully austere. She set a chipped tea service down on the table, then gathered up old issues of *Pins and Needles* magazine from a chair beside the fireplace. "I wish I could offer you something more," she said, gesturing vaguely. "I've had a few large orders come in this week—the spring weddings are popping up like crocus blossoms—and I tend to run myself to the bottom of the biscuit tin when I'm busy."

From her place beneath the couch, Miss Mabel mewed crossly.

"You've been more than generous," Louisa assured her hostess. "Anything you can remember from that day would be helpful."

"There's really not much to remember." Miss Gray shook her head and began straightening a tin of buttons as the others drank their tea. "Your brother said he'd just moved to the area and was looking for work. He seemed a nice sort of fellow, and so I told him the sink pipe's been leaking, but he'd have to come back in a few days. I was finishing a large order, as I said before, and couldn't be troubled to let him in."

"And then what?" prompted Malcolm, thumbing through his notebook.

"That was all. He never came back. I did ask around town about him, but no one had heard of him, and the vicar said there was no one new to the neighborhood. I figured he was a con man—what, with a name like Johnny Brimfield—and thought it was so much the better that he never returned. You can be sure I locked my doors for a week or so after."

"One can't be too careful," agreed Mrs. Watson. She was shifting a good deal in her seat and hoisting her teacup higher and higher as Miss Mabel, deprived too long of biscuits and subjected to the unthinkable torture of living above a fish-and-chips shop, unfolded herself from beneath the couch and began sniffing in the direction of Mrs. Watson's saucer.

"You're sure you never saw my brother before that day?" Louisa asked Miss Gray after a moment's consideration.

"Never before. Never since. He was like a ghost."

"And you've never heard of our family? Never known anyone by the last name of Everly?"

"No, never. I mean, I did read about the fire in the papers—such a dreadful thing—but I didn't put it together right away when you were on the telephone, and I certainly had no idea that the man who came around was the one who is thought to have done it. I'd have called the police straightaway if I'd known."

By this point in the conversation, Miss Mabel had curled up on Mrs. Watson's handbag and didn't look likely to give it up. Trying to dislodge the feline with the toe of her shoe, Mrs. Watson forced a smile and struggled to maintain the expected formalities. "You have a lovely home," she said unconvincingly. "Have you lived here long?"

"Yes, my whole life. My mother moved in shortly after I was born. She'd worked in a number of houses as a laundress and settled here as a seamstress shortly before marrying my father. She did fine work and taught me everything she knew. She died many years ago now, my father as well, but the flat was owned by that time and left to me. I can see that you are disappointed that I don't have more to share with you, Miss Everly, and I really do wish I could be of more help. But it's all quite beyond me, you see."

"That's all right," said Louisa, setting down her teacup. "I know you are very busy at the moment, and so we thank you for letting us visit on such short notice. Good day to you, Miss Gray."

"You might as well call me Elsie Ann. Everyone else does."

"Gladly," agreed Louisa, following her to the door. "And if I may say so, I think you have a rather magnificent name. When you first said it, I thought it sounded just grand. Like a character in a children's fairy tale or a musical."

For the first time, Elsie Ann smiled, and though Louisa

knew very little about her, she could see that the gentleness of the expression fit her features quite naturally.

"Thank you," she said. "I'm partial to it, though I wasn't when I was a girl. It was a chore to learn to write it all out, and the other children liked to make fun. But my parents couldn't help it. They had a trial of sorts in trying to decide who to name me after, so I was named after my mother's sister, my father's grandmother, and a passing gypsy woman who told them I was sure to be a girl."

"A gypsy!" gasped Mrs. Watson, still struggling to shoo away the persistent feline. "Surely they could have left that one off."

"A name for every day of the week. That's what my brother always said when he wanted to tease me." Elsie Ann laughed wistfully. "Then again, he was named for an encyclopedia salesman who came along while our parents were still dithering over what to call him. I told him it served him right for teasing, for I'd never heard a name so dour and drear as Joseph Fernsby!"

23

Fernsby!" Louisa turned so fast that her foot got caught in the rug by the door. She staggered sideways and, insensibly, uttered an apology to the mannequin behind her, which she'd nearly knocked through the window. Though Mrs. Watson kept her head enough to remain seated, she did let loose a magnificent gasp of horror, which succeeded in displacing Miss Mabel from the top of her handbag.

Elsie Ann was the quietest of the group. She sat down slowly and gave a hesitant smile. "Well now," she said, "I may not know your brother, Miss Everly, but it seems you know a good deal about mine."

Louisa drifted back to her seat, but she wasn't sure where or how to begin. She believed what Elsie Ann had said about having never heard of the Everly family. And this meant that Fernsby had been lying to his sister about where he'd been and what he'd been up to for more than fifteen years. "But your last name is Gray," she said at last.

"Yes, and so is my brother's. Joseph Fernsby Gray. He started using Fernsby as his surname when he set out looking for work in some of the grand houses. Said it would make him sound more like a butler."

Louisa choked on a laugh. "I suppose he was right about that. Your brother's been our family's butler for the last fifteen years."

"Goodness me." Elsie Ann's head tipped inquisitively. "Has he really?"

"Yes, and he buttles *extremely* well!" put in Mrs. Watson with nervous energy. "He scowls *very* stiffly, and when he takes my hat, he's always *so* careful not to crush the flowers."

Steam hovered in a haze over their cups as Elsie Ann refilled their tea. "How glad I am to know he's been such a credit to our family."

"You don't sound surprised about any of this," observed Malcolm, scratching his eyebrow thoughtfully with the end of his pencil.

"I don't think I am. Not really."

"And where did you suppose he was all this time?"

"Oh, here and there. Joseph got into a good amount of trouble when our mother was sick, and he took it very hard when she died. He made enough enemies of the locals back then that it wasn't safe for him to stay. But he sends me letters every so often. And money. Always with a different story about a new job, each sent from a different address."

"I'd like to see those letters," said Malcolm.

"Of course." She sighed and shook her head. "I thought being named after an encyclopedia salesman had just brought out the drifter in him, but I suppose he had good reasons for not wanting to be found."

Louisa leaned forward. "What sort of trouble was he in, if I may ask?"

"He was good at digging up secrets. Sold a few to local papers. Things were at their worst for him when he destroyed a highly respected judge's reputation, and the poor man was forced to resign. That's when he left."

"Blackmail, you mean?" Louisa's heartbeat bounded.

"You can call it that if you'd like."

At last! Louisa had uncovered the source of the blackmail photograph. She wanted nothing more than to be off so she could question Fernsby, but Malcolm gripped her by the arm when she tried to stand and yanked her back down. "And you haven't seen your brother?" he asked Elsie Ann. "Not once in all these years?"

"He always said he wanted to see me, but then he was just as quick with an excuse."

"He might not have been making excuses," said Mrs. Watson in a consoling voice. "I've heard that Mrs. Everly is a bit of a dragon about giving days off to staff, if you'll forgive me for saying as much, Louisa, dear."

Elsie Ann answered in a plaintive voice: "I'm sure he would have come if he thought it was safe and wise to do so. Now, I've answered your questions, Miss Everly, as many as I can bear to answer. But I would have you return the favor, and so answer me this if you can: do you think my brother had something to do with that fire?"

Louisa considered. "I think our brothers have a good deal more in common than I ever could have guessed," she replied soberly. "And so, for now, I'll do the sisterly thing and grant him the benefit of the doubt."

⟨~⟩

"I *knew* it!" hissed Mrs. Watson as they made their way back down the stairs. "I *knew* there was something about that Fernsby. There's something suspicious, isn't there, about a man who buttles so well? A little *too* well, as it turns out. I can hardly imagine what the vicar will say when we tell him! You know he wanted nothing more than to come along and play detective, but he'd already promised to oversee the Quarterly Quilters. They've been quarreling *terribly* at their meetings, ever since Mrs. Kittle and Mrs. Simpson debated whip stitches and ladder stitches. Oh, but it's all just as well he had to stay behind as an intermediary because I happen to know he's more allergic to cats than he is to quarreling."

"We shouldn't get so far ahead of ourselves," cautioned Louisa, even as she tried to bring her own galloping suspicions to heel. "Fernsby might be our blackmailer, but that doesn't mean he had anything to do with what happened to Paul on the night of the fire."

"You can't mean to say we have a blackmailer *and* an arsonist scampering about at the same time!" cried Mrs. Watson.

"I'm sure they aren't scampering, whoever they are," Malcolm put in. He carried the thick stack of letters that Elsie Ann had brought down from her bedroom.

"Even so." Mrs. Watson shuddered once, then straightened her little straw hat, which was not the slightest bit askew.

The boys were still playing football in the street, plowing into each other as they struggled to kick the ball into the crate they'd turned sideways for a goal. One of them kicked the ball much too wide. It came barreling like a cannonball in Mrs. Watson's direction.

She shrieked and lurched sideways, but Malcolm hardly looked up. Still perusing one of the letters in his hand, he straightened, then punted the ball with a conclusive *bang* into the crate at the far end of the street, hard enough that the crate turned over twice and landed in the gutter.

The boys cheered and went scampering off to set it up again, while Malcolm, looking a little smug, went on walking. "We should question Fernsby straightaway," he said. "Miss Gray was very helpful, and I'll see if I can shake anything loose from these letters, but I have a feeling she might try to warn him in the meantime."

"Why do you think she would?" asked Louisa.

"You'd have warned Paul, wouldn't you?"

"Fair enough," she sighed. "Still, we can't very well return to Everly Hall at the same moment to ask questions. My uncle will realize I've been investigating."

"So?"

"So he's already revoked my driving privileges and threatened to disinherit me if I don't knock it off."

"And those dresses don't pay for themselves, I'd imagine." He gave her a once-over. "What is that, anyway—taffeta? A bit formal for the morning, don't you think?"

Louisa lifted her chin as they reached the sedan and yanked hard on her door handle to open it. "You won't make me feel silly just because I have a healthy appreciation for taffeta. People have developed a fondness for much sillier things, haven't they?"

Malcolm looked at her, digging his hand into his pocket like he used to do when he was called on in school for a question he didn't know the answer to. "You have a point about that" was his grudging reply.

                                                      ∽

For the first time in fifteen years of service, Joseph Fernsby was not at his post by the front door when Louisa returned home. She stopped Mrs. Bottle, who was passing through the hall, to inquire about the missing butler.

"He's gone," Mrs. Bottle answered in an anxious huff.

"What do you mean?" said Louisa. "Where's he gone to?"

"Well, that's the thing. No one knows exactly where he's gone. He left a note an hour ago saying he was done. Then he cleared out his room—everything but the dust, of course, and *plenty* of it!"

"Did anyone see him go?"

"Not that I know of."

"And he didn't say where he was going?"

"Oh, something about his sister being sick. I never knew he had a sister, let alone a sick one, but then he's always kept to himself. I suppose it's only proper, after all, to keep things like sisters and such to yourself when there are doors to be answered and maids always breaking things without the slightest bit of warning. Why, I have two sisters myself, but I'm sure *I've* never mentioned them. Not that anyone's ever cared to ask me."

Louisa was too stunned to ask about Mrs. Bottle's sisters. Instead, she went straight to Fernsby's room, hoping he might have been obliging enough to leave some clues behind. She found plain white walls, hardwood floors, and little else. The bed had already been stripped, the closet emptied. As Mrs. Bottle had said, there was only a thin layer of dust on the bedside table, surrounding the smooth, shiny places where his personal things had so recently been.

Louisa might have taken Fernsby's departure as a sign of guilt, but Paul had seemed to vanish under equally abrupt circumstances, and so she felt a crushing terror that the same person might have been behind both disappearances.

Though it was entirely possible that Fernsby had realized Louisa was closing in on him and had bolted to protect himself; as Malcolm had feared, his sister might have called the house ahead of their return to warn him.

She sat down on the bed to think, the springs creaking like old bones beneath her weight.

Why had Joseph Fernsby left Everly Hall? It wasn't yet safe to hazard a guess, but Louisa was determined to get to the bottom of this.

24

After a week, David sent flowers. It was an impressive bouquet of roses in varying shades of pink and red, tied with twine and rolled up in a long, smooth sheet of lacy white paper. The note inside was simple and to the point: *Sorry. I'm a cad.*

"You see?" said Aunt Agatha, arranging the flowers in a vase on Louisa's bedside table. "The boy's crazy about you."

And changes course more often than a weather vane, thought Louisa. "Perhaps I'll call him tomorrow," she said, tossing his note onto the table beside her. She sank back into the window seat cushions. She'd pinned her hair again that evening and began securing the curls beneath a white linen scarf that had been resting on her knee. "Though I'm not sure what we have left to say to each other."

"Well, that's easy enough. You say that you forgive him for being a cad, and how could you do otherwise? To hear his father speak, one would think it was a hereditary trait, so it really isn't the poor boy's fault. He's always been so courteous. There's no reason you shouldn't forgive him when you've been stubborn yourself. And besides . . . Oh, dear, let me help you with that."

Louisa had been struggling to tie off the scarf and now slipped down from her perch in the window. Her aunt stepped behind her, tying things off with a neat little tug, then patted the top of Louisa's head to make sure the pins were snug. "There!" she said cheerfully. "Ready for another day! Oh, and by the way, you should wear your navy dress tomorrow. The collared one. For when you ring up David, I mean."

Louisa laughed. "I could call him dressed like this"—she gestured to her oversized, blue-and-white-striped pajamas— "and it wouldn't make a bit of difference. He can't very well see me through the telephone."

"True. But we must always look our best—especially for the sort of man who takes the time to send us flowers."

Louisa shook her head and snatched her book off the nightstand. "Good night, Aunt Agatha."

Smiling still, Aunt Agatha closed the curtains with a swish of her slender wrists. "Good night, dear."

As soon as she was gone, Louisa tucked herself up in the armchair, trying against all odds to convince herself to read. She hadn't yet made it to the end of the first paragraph when she was interrupted by a soft *tink* on the other side of the room. She thought it might have been an acorn hitting the window ledge, but she lowered her book to her lap and tilted her head, listening.

There it was again!

Dropping her book with a carpeted thud, Louisa flew up from the chair and darted across the room, pushing aside the curtain as a pebble struck the glass in front of her nose.

She pressed her face against the window, squinting down at the lawn, and saw a shadow dashing off into the bushes. At first she wondered if it was David coming to see if his peace offering had softened her, but she couldn't imagine why he would run away as soon as she appeared in the window.

Half a second before the man disappeared from sight, the moon caught him in its pale, silver light. He was tall and thin and wore a familiar tweed flat cap pulled down over his brow.

Louisa recognized the hat; she thought she even recognized the man. Though she'd ceased to breathe, she had just enough wind left in her lungs to whisper his name: "Paul . . ."

The hope in her voice hurt more than grief ever had, for she knew it was false, knew that Paul was dead despite what she saw, but she hoped nonetheless. Turning wildly, she fished a torch out of her closet and hurried downstairs in her bare feet, bursting out of the house and into the foggy night.

"Paul!" As she spoke his name again, she wondered if the grief had finally fractured her mind, if she was now seeing things she only hoped to see. She fumbled along the path as bits of gravel gathered and stuck between her toes. A pair of branches swayed to the right of her, stirring the fog, but there was a scuffling sound to the left. Her torch beam swung like a pendulum from one side of the path to the other. "Paul?" she whispered uneasily. "Is it . . . is it you?"

She heard a low laugh, the kind that lingered in the air, as a man's hand slipped over her mouth, smothering the beginnings of a scream. She tried to swing around, but her torch fell to the ground and blinked out on impact as she was wrenched backward into the darkness.

Louisa thrashed and clawed, but her arms were pinioned from behind, the balls of her feet dragging ditches in the dirt as she was pulled through the bushes. She tried again to scream, to bite down on the hand that held her, but her body was uprooted from its own senses. She could no longer make heads or tails of the darkness or where she was within it. Stricken stiff with terror, she wondered if she was about to disappear like Paul, like Joseph Fernsby.

If she was about to *die.*

As soon as she thought it, she was wrestled back against the outer wall of the house, and a familiar voice murmured against her ear, "Take it easy, sweetheart."

He loosened his hold, and Louisa collapsed against the wall behind her, her nails scraping on stone as she scrabbled to remain upright. She couldn't see her captor's face clearly in the darkness, but she brought up her hands and shoved him back a step.

"You!" she growled.

Thomas Sykes laughed again. "This isn't the kind of greeting I expected. Not when I've come all this way to offer you so friendly a warning."

"Friendly!" Louisa scoffed, straightening her buttons and collar. "You nearly scared me out of my wits! And what were you doing luring me into the bushes? I thought I was about to be murdered! I thought you were . . . Hang on. Where's my torch?"

Still laughing, Thomas went back to the path and found it. As he slid back into the bushes, he clicked it on and pointed it at himself. Louisa inhaled sharply at what she saw in the harsh light. Thomas Sykes's right eye was swollen purple as a plum, and there was a nasty gash on his temple still sticky with blood.

She gasped. "Good gracious! What happened to you?"

"That's what I came here to tell you. I was at your brother's flat tonight—"

"What? Breaking into a crime scene is against the law, you know," said Louisa righteously. She quite conveniently forgot to mention that she'd already done as much herself.

"Your brother owes me a lot of money. I thought if I had a look around, I could rattle something loose, maybe figure out where he's gone, if he's still alive, or if he had money stuffed anywhere."

"I take it you didn't find anything?"

"No, but I wasn't the only one looking. The door was already open when I got there, and someone was hiding in the room."

Louisa was horrified, but also eager for another clue. "Who was it?"

"No idea. He came up behind me, the coward, and clipped me on the back of the head with a metal shoehorn. Beaned myself on the corner of the desk going down, and they peeled off, but not before I sent a rather loud farewell." He lifted his shirt, revealing the handle of a pistol tucked into the top of his trousers.

Louisa leaned back against the wall again, her voice fainter. "You *shot* him?"

"Of course I shot him. Somewhere on his left arm. I wasn't sure if I got him at first, but I saw blood on the landing when I was leaving. He's a dead man, whoever he is, and make no mistake about it. But until I catch up to him, there's someone out there who doesn't want folks poking their noses into your brother's business. Which made me think of you, Miss Everly, since you have such a pretty nose, and you seem pretty keen on poking it around."

Louisa pondered all of this in silence. Whoever had assaulted Thomas Sykes was likely the person who had burned the abbey; they had a similar, if rudimentary, style of sneaking up and bashing people on the back of their heads. But what had they been looking for in Paul's room? There must have been something she and the police had overlooked, and she could only hope the man in Paul's apartment had been scared off before he could find it.

"And what about this?" She slipped her brother's hat off Thomas's head and refused to let on just how hopeful, how *desperately* hopeful she'd been to think her brother might have yet been alive.

Thomas shrugged. "Nicked it from your brother's place on my way out. I figured you might not be so eager to come out if you knew it was me waiting, but maybe if you thought I was your brother or even his ghost? Oh, don't look so miffed. It worked, didn't it? Though I must say, I didn't expect you to come down in those fetching pajamas."

The beam of light followed the path of his eyes to Louisa's shapeless striped pajamas. Face flushing, she stepped forward and seized the torch from his hand. "Enough of this," she snapped. "You said you'd come to warn me, and you've done as much. Now I think you'd better leave before I scream for help."

"And who's awake, I wonder, to come outside to your rescue?"

"My uncle," she bluffed. "He's always smoking in the study this time of night."

"I happen to know that rich old fool finished with his pipe and went to bed an hour ago, but I appreciate the effort—you lie pretty well, sweetheart."

"Not as well as you do, I'd imagine," she said, unnerved that he'd been watching the house for so long.

"No," said Thomas. "Not as well as me." And then he slipped his hands in his pockets and ambled casually into the night.

25

The next morning, Louisa's aunt burst into her room a full hour before breakfast, without knocking. She flipped the light switch dramatically and stood framed in the doorway, her panicked face a near match in shade to her billowing fuchsia robe.

"What is it?" grumbled Louisa fuzzily. After her interlude with Sykes, she hadn't managed to sleep for more than an hour that night altogether. Whenever she closed her eyes, she imagined that someone was about to force their way into her room and bludgeon her. At one point, she'd dozed off just enough to dream that Everly Hall had been set on fire and she was trapped inside alone.

"Get up, Louisa!" whispered her aunt. "Get up at once!"

Louisa levered up on an arm, rubbing her eyes with the corner of her sleeve. "What is it? What's the matter?"

"It's David Ashworth!"

Instantly awake, Louisa sat bolt upright in bed. She'd spent so many hours consumed with her brother's disappearance, with making things right, that the investigation was her first and only thought. She was sure this was to be the grand reveal, that her aunt was about to announce that David had done it, that he'd set fire to the abbey and been arrested for her brother's murder.

A few weeks ago, Louisa would have been shattered by the news. She'd have wrung her hands and wept. She'd have been heartsick over David as well as anguished over the loss of her brother, and she might have grabbed ahold of David's shirt and demanded to know how the man she loved, who she hoped to marry someday, could have done such an evil thing. Instead, she felt empty. Wholeheartedly so. With a sense of resignation, she thought that David really might have done it. After all, he'd been lying to her about that night all along. And though she wanted to know the truth—to put her brother to rest—her heart didn't pitch at the idea of David being a murderer or being gone from her life forever.

She stared absently as her aunt bustled over to the wardrobe, threw open the door, and began sliding hangers left and right. "You must wear something arresting," she said.

"Arresting?" echoed Louisa, fully aware of the pun but not entirely sure if it was meant intentionally.

"Something chic," her aunt modified, tossing three perfectly lovely dresses aside with a distasteful shake of her head. "Something unforgettable!"

"I don't understand."

Her aunt looked sharply over her shoulder. "There's no *time* to understand!" she hissed, jerking Louisa's covers back. "That poor boy has planted himself in our front hall and refuses to leave until he can see you. And that's what comes, my dear, of refusing to answer or return a gentleman's calls. Still, I suppose I can't criticize you for it, not when the result is standing down at the bottom of the stairs and looking perfectly miserable."

Louisa was feeling pretty miserable herself. She dropped back on the bed with a grunt, battling the urge to pull the sheets and covers up over her head. "Perhaps I don't wish to see him."

Her aunt's lips puckered. "Enough of this shilly-shallying!" she snapped. "I don't care to know whatever it is the two of you have been quarreling about. All couples have their tiffs, and there's nothing at all remarkable about it. Call it a storm in a teacup and put it behind you."

"It's a bit more than that, I think."

"Even so. David has something he wants to say to you, and he's not going to leave until he's said it. If you hear what he has to say and still feel compelled to reject him, very well. That's your prerogative. But this is my house, Louisa Everly, and I will not permit you to be petty."

Louisa got up, but it took an age for her to start moving in any forward direction. She wasn't sure she could justify the ethics of entertaining overtures from a young man she suspected of murdering her brother. Still, if it brought about the answers she so desperately needed, then she owed it to Paul to at least give it a try. Choosing what to wear for the mission, however . . . well, that presented a unique sort of crisis.

If David was in any way involved in her brother's death, then she would have very much liked to look like an avenging angel, with dark red lipstick and a dress that was marvelously bold and black. If he was innocent, then she would have preferred the dreamy green organza, which Aunt Agatha was in the process of considering even now. She settled for a pale yellow shirtdress, which was long in the skirt and high at the collar. To her aunt's dismay, Louisa skipped the usual coat of red lipstick on her way out the door.

She paused once on the landing to peer over the banister. David was pacing a path of checkered tile at the bottom of the stairs, looking like a rook who couldn't remember his position on the chessboard. Louisa was more than halfway down the stairs when he popped out of his head to notice her. "What took you so long?" he demanded, which didn't sound particularly rosy or romantic, but at least it got things started.

"I was sleeping," Louisa answered in an equally abrupt tone.

"Your aunt said you'd go for a drive with me."

"Did she?"

David surrendered with a sigh. He pulled a cigarette case from the breast pocket of his coat, then opened and snapped it shut several times with agitated fingers. "I don't care anymore," he muttered. "Do you understand? Come along or don't, but let's not play this game anymore."

And with that, he turned and strode through the door without even waiting to see if Louisa would follow.

Of course, she followed.

She held no scrap of the earlier hopes she'd harbored, but if there was even the slightest chance that David knew what had happened to her brother, then she would do her best to wring it out of him.

His wine red Bentley was waiting outside the front door, freshly polished and engine idling. Grudgingly gallant, David circled to the other side of the car. He held her door open like usual, then slammed her shut inside while she was still tugging the corner of her skirt clear of the door.

Eyes gritty from lack of sleep, she stared ahead as he trudged around the back of the car. The morning was crisp and misty, the sky streaked with purple and everything covered with dew. A quick burst of cool, fresh air followed David into the cab, which he effectively smothered by lighting a cigarette. He took a slow drag as he revved the engine, and neither of them spoke a word until he pulled out onto the main road.

Not wishing to prolong the drive if she could help it, Louisa folded her arms and ended the stalemate: "All right. What's this about?"

David squinted at the road ahead, drumming his fingers on the steering wheel. "Here it is. I'm crazy about you, Louisa. You know I am. I wasn't sure what that meant or what I ought to do about it, but I'm ready to lay all my cards on the table, if that's what you want, so we can have done with it and get on with things the way they used to be."

"What do you mean by that?"

"You don't trust me. I can understand that, and I respect you for holding me to account. But you have to believe me now when I say I'm done lying to you, and I'm done keeping secrets. If there's a question you want to ask me, then ask it now."

Louisa stared forward again as the nose of the car swooped elegantly around a shadowy bend. "Why did you argue with my brother at your family's party?"

"He wanted me to stay away from you."

"Did he give any particular reason for that?"

"Did he have to? You said yourself he hates anyone with money. And he was in an awful mood. I told him he could stay and have a drink if he wanted, and all he said was that if I didn't stay away from you, he'd knock my head in."

"Knock your head in?" Louisa scrambled up straighter in

the seat, her heartbeat accelerating right along with the Bentley's engine. "He really said that?"

"It's not the kind of exaggeration I'd add for effect."

Louisa closed her eyes and thought of Thomas Sykes and the vicar, both of whom had received blows to the head. The phrasing couldn't be a coincidence, could it? "And where were you later?" she went on. "During the fire?"

He was driving faster now, the engine snarling like a crazed creature on the otherwise silent street. They blew past the high street of Wilbeth Green in a blink. "It's like this," he said. "Sometimes things happen when we don't mean for them to. And we realize, after the fact, that it was a mistake. Do you know what I mean?" He darted a glance at her and then sighed when she shook her head no. "Are you really going to make me spell it out? I have an alibi for that evening, but I didn't want to tell you about it. And that is because I was in a . . . well, in a compromising position, and it doesn't just concern me. I was trying to be sensitive to the fact that your family's been hopeful for an engagement between us."

"Who?" Louisa demanded, her face as red as a phone box. "Who were you with?"

"Does it matter?"

"Of course it matters!"

"Take it easy, will you? I was with Viola."

He kept the car steady on the road, barreling straight ahead, but Louisa felt as though everything around her were spinning. "With Viola!" she cried, her voice hitching in the slight gap between hurt and horror. "But she's engaged!"

David didn't look at her but lifted one shoulder in an apathetic shrug. "She and the earl have a fairly modern understanding of things. But you and I weren't engaged, were we? I mean, we aren't—not yet anyway."

And was *this* the proposal her aunt had been hoping for? A rasping laugh climbed its way up Louisa's throat. "Nor are we very likely to be," she added, gripping the side of her seat as he steered them roughly around a curve.

"Viola said you'd feel this way about it," he muttered. "That's why we didn't tell you. But you really needn't worry. Once things are settled between you and I, it won't happen again. I've already told Viola as much."

"Oh, well, that's *very* reassuring."

He glared at her without bothering to look at the road for an unnerving length of time. "You know, I'm trying to be open with you. I'm trying to be honest." He struck a pothole and had to swerve so abruptly that Louisa nearly skidded off the seat. "There wasn't even a formal understanding between us at the time. But if you're going to punish me for it and hold it against me—"

"How did you think I'd react? You lied to me! And I may not be particularly used to the *modern* way of things. But even you have to admit that your attitude about it, though open, is still somewhat less than penitent."

"Penitent!" he sneered, laughing at the road. "Shall I go to confession before I dare to make any formal declarations toward you?"

"You can keep your formal declarations to yourself," she shot back.

He laughed again and went on as if she hadn't spoken. "I'm sure the vicar will be happy to absolve me if you won't. But that's not what you really want, is it? Once absolved, you wouldn't have anything to hold against me."

"I think I'd like to walk from here."

"Walk where?" He shrugged impatiently. "We're miles from anything."

"I don't care. Let me out."

If anything, he drove faster. "So this is what I get for telling the truth, is it? Well, if this is how you feel about things, then you might bother to ask Inspector Sinclair if he'll be nearly as forthcoming."

Louisa had been staring out her side window, feeling almost stubborn enough to throw open her door and try the old tuck-and-roll, but her limbs all turned to dead weight as David's words registered. "The inspector?"

"Oh, don't sound so surprised." He cranked down his window and flicked the stub of his cigarette sideways into the ditch. "Your inspector friend isn't nearly as righteous as he makes himself out to be. If you'd like to put him through the same wringer you've put me, you can start by asking him what he bought with all that money he stole."

"What on earth are you talking about?"

"I saw him, Louisa. I saw him do it with my own two eyes. I saw Inspector Sinclair break into the school that night, and I saw him with the school roof money. So did Paul."

"You're lying."

"You know I'm not. Why else should you sound so afraid?"

David was going so fast now that he nearly sideswiped a fence post. Louisa remained focused on the road ahead, unblinking. She would never have admitted it, but she was afraid. Dreadfully so. She knew that David was jealous. It was in his own best interests to lie.

But what if he wasn't lying? She'd wondered earlier if her uncle might have charged past the reach of his own temper and killed Paul without meaning to. Now she closed her eyes and recast the roles just as a film director might do.

And it was frighteningly easy to do.

Where her uncle had previously stood, she now saw Malcolm. He and Paul were arguing, Paul laughing in that nasty way he sometimes did. He brought up the roof money and called Malcolm a hypocrite. Said he'd never make it to Scotland Yard, not when Paul was finished telling everyone that he was nothing more than a gutter-class thief and the sort of man who let his friend shoulder the blame. Paul was laughing again. Malcolm took a swing to shut him up, just one, and caught his friend off guard. Louisa squeezed her eyes tighter and tighter, but she couldn't help but see it all. Like paging through a flip-book, she watched in halting motions as her brother tripped back and struck his head on the abbey steps. How easy it would have been for a police officer to have covered it up in a way that discredited his victim and ensured that no one would wonder, or care, where he'd gone.

Don't be daft! Louisa scolded herself, tussling defiantly with her own suspicions. It couldn't have been Malcolm. He'd been helping her every step of the way, hadn't he? He'd invited her to come along with him to question the doctor when he might have easily left her behind. He'd shared evidence with her when he might have kept it a secret. She couldn't have possibly misread him so terribly. And yet . . .

She opened her eyes. Malcolm himself had warned her that she couldn't trust anyone, not even those who were closest to her. It had seemed like sound advice at the time. Friendly even. But then she'd made that silly quip, asking what his motive might have been for the crime.

He hadn't answered that question, she realized, not even in his customarily caustic way.

Then there was the morning when she first told Malcolm that she had felt Paul die. Only now did it strike her as odd that he'd believed her about Paul's death without question, demanding to know how she knew.

"When?" had been Malcolm's next question, as if he had no doubt at all what she'd felt. And then more ominously, he'd asked her: *"Who else have you told?"*

26

Louisa didn't share any of her suspicions with David, but she did renew, in more animated language, her earlier demand to walk the rest of the way home alone. By that point, David was annoyed enough that he readily agreed. He pulled off to the side of the road, depositing her without any sort of farewell beside a stubby field of freshly planted turnips.

Dirt shot like mortar off his tires as he sped off. As Louisa watched him go, she recollected one of her father's old sermons. It was about the ancient practice of shaking the dust from one's feet. As it turned out, this was a far less pious gesture when one was gunning it up the road in a Bentley. Thankfully, she'd learned from past mistakes and worn a pair of flats that morning, which spared her from blisters and the indignity of tottering along the roadside in heels. And she might have made it all the way home without incident were it not for the arrival of the oldest of old British walking companions: rain.

It sprang up a few minutes before Louisa approached the high street of Wilbeth Green and turned into a steady squall by the time she'd reached the first storefront. There were only a handful of shops on the main drag, and as a general rule, they opened when the owners jolly well felt like it. Louisa tried Bridge's first, the corner store where she and Paul had bought candy cigarettes and other sweets as children. Closed. So was the butcher shop next door and the hardware store, which had the most ridiculous sign Louisa had ever seen taped on its front door: CLOSED DUE TO RAIN.

Closed due to rain indeed! Well, she thought, if every establishment in Wilbeth Green closed because of inclement weather, the villagers would be left without basic provisions on at least three hundred days out of the year.

She bunched her shoulders, cringing as the cool rain slipped past her collar, and sprinted for The Three Foxes. There was no need to check if the lights were on; the pub stood as constant as a lighthouse at the end of the street. Come hell or high water, it opened every day, and had even had the riot act read for serving a round during the queen's Christmas address a few years back.

By the time Louisa reached the front door, which was propped open with a brick, her feet were throbbing, her curls sopping wet, and the aroma of frying kippers wafting from the kitchen, though not her favorite, made her keenly aware that she hadn't eaten breakfast that morning.

The floorboards in the entryway were slick. Louisa slipped on her way in and, like a broom toppling out of a cupboard, fell halfway through the door. Without trying to, she caught herself on a passing gentleman's arm. "Steady on," the man said, chuckling as he released her.

The air within the pub was stale, clouded by tangling curls of cigarette smoke. Yet Louisa knew better than to pull a face at the stench, for she had no intention of being heckled any more than she'd already been that morning. Drawing herself up as best as she could, she trooped ahead.

She'd never been inside The Three Foxes, but she knew her brother had spent a considerable amount of time here. Aside from a few muddy floorboards, it was a notably clean establishment. Crossing the room, Louisa looked from table to table and group to group, wondering which chair was Paul's usual spot and which of these men were his friends. Half the room's occupants were local shop owners, including the indolent Mr. Willis who had closed up the hardware store on account of the rain.

Wet from hair to hem, Louisa ignored the stares and sideways glances as she stepped up to the bar. The pub was run by a man named Josiah Miller, who had moved from London to Wilbeth Green with his wife and ailing daughter shortly before the war. He was well liked, but his business hadn't taken off until he, like many German families at that time, had anglicized his name, changing it from Mueller to Miller.

He laughed when he saw Louisa and tossed a bar towel into her hands. "If you are looking for ein tea party, das Fräulein, you are in zee vrong parlor."

"I'm looking for a telephone," she answered, using the towel to pat the water out of the ends of her flattened curls. "Have you got one?"

Mr. Miller rubbed his stubbly chin and reached under the bar. He clanked down an old rotary with half the numbers rubbed off. Smiling her thanks, Louisa picked up the receiver and thought for a moment before ringing up Mrs. Watson at the vicarage; it was pruning day.

The vicar answered first. He spoke empathetically when

Louisa explained to him how things were, then summoned Mrs. Watson from the other room.

"Hullo!" said Louisa once the older woman had come to the telephone. "Mrs. Watson, I wonder if you could . . . what's that? Ironing, you say? Well, no, I'm not interested in seeing the new tea linens at the moment. Yes, I'm sure they're marvelous. Of course, I'm *highly* appreciative of a nice bit of lace, but listen. I'm at The Three Foxes. Of course the pub! I haven't the time to explain, but everything's gone sideways, and I need somebody to come and pick me up. Would you be a dear and—oh, drat. You don't have the car anymore? No, I wasn't swearing, I said 'drat.' And there's no need to tell on me to the vicar, for I'm sure he'd agree with me. Anyway, about the car . . . Yes, I'm sure your grandson had a reasonable need for it. Oh no, please don't send him over! I'm sure he's a lovely chap . . . No, I'm not against being driven around by a Catholic! It's just my hair is all wet, you see, and I'm standing in a pub without any lipstick on, so I'm not ready to meet anyone at the moment, Catholic or otherwise. Well, you don't have to get chuffy. I'm the one up the creek, so to speak, and . . . Oh, very well, go and see to your lace! I'm sure it requires *far* more attention than I do!"

As she dropped the receiver back into its cradle, Louisa craned her neck and stared hopelessly out the front window. The rain was pelting harder now. She could hardly see the oversized *Gibbs Dentifrice* advertisement in the chemist's shop window across the street. And though she refused to admit that David had been even the slightest bit right about the foolishness of walking, she could see that there was nothing else for it now—she'd have to ring up her aunt.

"You need to eat something," said Mr. Miller, "so you can think."

Louisa sighed, then laughed tiredly. "I would love nothing more, but I haven't got any money with me."

"You really are, how dit you zay, 'up ein creek'?"

"Yes. Haven't got a paddle beneath that bar, have you?"

Mr. Miller jabbed a thumb in the direction of the nearest open table. "Zit," he commanded. "You vill eat."

Louisa straightened, her mood brightening at the thought. "Thanks," she said. "You're a real brick."

Mr. Miller nodded, grousing under his breath about the clumsiness of the English vernacular as Louisa moved to one of the benches nearest the fireplace. Three men at the table across from her were having beer for breakfast and quarreling about how much it would cost to tear down the old shed behind the cemetery versus letting it fall naturally in its own good time. They still hadn't reached a consensus when a plate of kippers and eggs was pushed across the table in front of her, followed by a hot cup of strong German coffee.

Louisa snatched up her fork, twirling it in her fingers. "Cheers!" she said, then jolted when she looked up and realized it wasn't Mr. Miller who had brought her breakfast.

It was Malcolm.

"What are you doing here?" Louisa sounded far more panicked than she wanted to let on, but she couldn't decide if she was imagining the sharpness in his eyes.

"My father and Mr. Miller were friends," he answered, taking a nip from the steaming cup in his own hand. "He has a spare room upstairs and has graciously rented it out to me. Never seen you here before, though. What's the occasion?"

Louisa squirmed in her seat, too tired, wet, and out of sorts to think up a decent lie. Thus defeated, she dropped her eyes to her plate. The kippers stared back at her. They were no help.

"Did you . . . walk here?"

Louisa bristled at his incredulous tone, as angry with David for getting her into this mess as she was with Malcolm for having the nerve to find her in it. But then she lifted her eyes despite his disbelief and answered as frankly as she could: "Yes."

"What for?"

"For breakfast."

"And you didn't think to bring an umbrella with you?"

"Really, Malcolm, I should think the answer to that question is rather obvious."

She hoped this sounded dismissive enough, but he plunked his cup on the table as if she'd sent him a written invitation and dragged out the chair across from her. Before he sat, he shrugged out of his jacket and tossed it over the back of the chair. The inside of his white shirtsleeve, near the crook of his left arm, was marked with a splotch of red. Louisa stared at it absently, like studying a doctor's inkblot test, but then the fork fell from her hand and clattered against her plate when her mind caught up to what her eyes were seeing.

There was blood on Malcolm's sleeve. Her thoughts were no longer sluggish, no longer mired. She knew that whoever had attacked Thomas Sykes had struck him on the head, and it was the same method used in the vicar's assault on the night of the fire. She also knew that Thomas had shot his assailant—shot him in the left arm.

She took a second to still the tremor in her voice, like tamping her thumb down on a thrumming cello string. "What's happened to your arm?"

Malcolm glanced down. "Blast," he said. "It's bleeding again, is it?" Gingerly, he rolled up the sleeve, revealing a thick bandage that had been wrapped several times and secured just beneath his elbow. "Devil dog in Sutherby got off its leash. Like an idiot I tried coaxing it out of an alley—doing the police bit, you know—and it sank its teeth into me. Well, I don't care if the dog's a female or not, whoever named that wretched thing *Lulu* was *way* off the mark."

He'd rattled all of this off quite naturally, like nothing in the world was wrong, like he wasn't lying to her, and how would she ever be able to tell if he was? She was beginning to feel light-headed; the sudden rush of panic was now making the edges of the room seem less defined in her peripheral vision. Yet this might have been fatigue or even hunger. She had skipped breakfast, after all.

"I haven't poisoned it."

Louisa froze, her heartbeat tripping over itself. "What do you mean?"

"Your breakfast. You aren't eating it."

Louisa followed his gaze to her plate. She thought of what Biddy had told her, how Paul had felt ill on the night of the fire, like he couldn't keep anything down. She imagined a dose of strychnine being slipped into her coffee by an assassin's hand. An invisible garnish of arsenic sprinkled over the top of her eggs.

Malcolm tipped his head to one side. "What's the matter? Something wrong with your food?"

He was goading her. She had the sudden, distinct sense of a mouse darting hopelessly between two large paws. "I'm not hungry," she decided, pushing her plate away.

"And yet you walked all this way for breakfast."

"I'm too cold to eat."

"Well, at least take a few bites. Mr. Miller is a proud man. He'll be peeved if you leave behind a full plate."

Louisa was already scooting off the bench. "I'll have to risk it," she said. "I just remembered there's something I need to do."

"Are you going to walk the whole way back in the rain, alone?"

She didn't think she was imagining the threatening emphasis he'd put on the word *alone*. "It just so happens that Mrs. Watson is on her way to get me. She'll be here any minute."

Malcolm laughed, and Louisa saw the humor even if she wasn't in a position to properly appreciate it—as if the arrival of a petite, moralizing octogenarian in reading glasses was likely to thwart any plans he might have had at the moment. "Will she really?" he said dryly.

"Yes," said Louisa, "so you needn't wait around. You can get back to catching stray dogs just as soon as you'd like."

She stood up quickly, but Malcolm's fingers grasped her wrist before she could get away. "What's the matter with you?" he demanded.

"Let go of me!"

He stared at her coolly, then relaxed his grip, releasing her. "I happen to know that Mrs. Watson isn't on her way. Neither is her grandson, though you might have given the poor bloke a chance, even if he is a Catholic."

Louisa flushed. "You mean you were listening? The whole time?"

"Everyone was listening," he said with a derisive snort. "Your voice bounces off the rafters when you're angry."

"And you just let me go on lying to you!"

"Yes. Though I can't begin to imagine why you'd lie about

232

Mrs. Watson. Or about being hungry, for that matter. Why, the way you're acting you'd think the food really was . . ."

He met her eyes, and his words cut away, guillotine quick. For as long as Louisa lived, she would never forget the slack-jawed look of frozen horror that came upon him. In a twinkling, she recognized her own idiocy for what it was and reached instinctively for Malcolm's hand on the table. But he shook himself as if awakening from a stupor and pushed back in his chair. He grabbed his jacket before she could stop him, forgot his hat, and made his way to the door. He wasn't rushing, yet his stride was such that Louisa struggled to keep up with him.

"Malcolm!" she cried. "Wait!"

The door banged shut on her plea, but she shoved it open and pushed forward into the driving rain. She caught him by the elbow just before he reached his car. His skin felt uncommonly cold beneath his damp cotton shirtsleeve. "Wait!" she panted miserably, yanking back on his arm to slow his steps. "Please let me explain!"

He turned viciously, his face streaked with rain. Before she could squeak out a sound, he'd crowded her back a few steps, into the alley that ran between the pub and the butcher shop. While the passage was no wider than the set of a man's shoulders, he took her hand and towed her through without bothering to sidestep the leaky gutters and grimy puddles. Louisa was twice as drenched and miserable by the time they made it to the other end of the alley. Looking up, she saw a narrow metal stairway that zigzagged up the back of the building, leading to the second floor of The Three Foxes.

There was no time for Louisa to protest. She was marshaled up the stairs, through a door, and into living quarters that could only belong to a police inspector. The room was marked by the balance of order and chaos: suits pressed, bed neatly made, and yet there were photographs, newspapers, and case files stacked and scattered all around the space. Before she could register what was happening, Louisa heard the door slam shut behind her.

Malcolm placed his hands on her shoulders and turned her to face him. "So," he said in a deceptively soft voice, his gaze fastened on hers, "you think I killed him, do you?"

"No!" she answered hurriedly. "No, I don't."

"But you *did* think it, didn't you? You thought I may have killed him. That I may have tried to . . ." His fingers tightened on her shoulders. She thought he wanted to shake some sense into her, but he released her with a shudder and turned away.

"I was tired," she said in a quieter voice, and would have laid a reassuring hand on his arm if she thought he would allow it. "I know that's no excuse, but it's the truth. I haven't been sleeping well, and then when I saw the blood on your arm, I became afraid."

"Afraid? Why?"

There was no easy way to explain any of this delicately, and so she lifted her chin and came out with it: "I spoke with Thomas Sykes last night."

"Thomas Sykes!" Malcolm flinched, then shouted, "I told you, Louisa, he's dangerous!"

"Yes, yes, I know. But it wasn't my fault. He lured me down into the bushes, you see, and—"

Malcolm made a sound, and Louisa broke off when she saw how pale he'd become. When he spoke again, his voice was deep, dangerously low: "What do you mean he *lured* you into the bushes?"

He sounded like he might have been coming around to the idea of murder, at least where Thomas Sykes was concerned, so Louisa waved a flippant hand and tried to laugh it off. "It was nothing, just a bit of dramatics. You needn't look so livid about it. He came to warn me, which was very nice of him. If you see him, you should try to remember to thank him."

"I'll remember something," Malcolm muttered, tugging some slack into his tie knot. "And what exactly did he warn you about?"

"He went to Paul's flat yesterday, poking around, and someone came up behind him and coshed him on the back of the head with a shoehorn. He's all black and blue and dreadful looking from the fall, but he said he shot the man in the left arm as he ran off. So when I saw your arm—"

"You made the very stupid assumption that I was about to murder you."

Louisa glared at him. She thought she'd explained the basis for her suspicions fairly well, yet he was going out of his way to be difficult. "Well, it wasn't only that. David also said—"

"Oh, well, if *David* said it!" He laughed brutally under his breath and went over to his wardrobe, yanking a clean button-up shirt off its hanger. He disappeared through a narrow door in the corner, which Louisa took to be the washroom, and was gone for a few moments.

She lifted her voice so he'd be sure to hear her through the door: "It isn't entirely my fault, you know—*you're* the one who told me I had to consider everyone a suspect!"

"Obviously I didn't mean you should suspect me!" was his muffled reply.

"And I didn't! Well, not at first anyway." There were a few discarded ties and a stack of Fats Domino records piled on the table beside her, and she busied her nervous hands by straightening them. "But then I thought about what you said and wondered if you were just being cryptic. Some murderers are, or at least I thought they might be. You know, like they are in books, always dropping little hints—"

The door swung open, cutting her off, and when Malcolm stepped back into the room, she was dismayed to find that he resembled the younger Malcolm she remembered. The rain had snarled his hair, curling it at the nape and all across his brow, and he was still buttoning his shirt, which made Louisa recall him as the delinquent student often caught out of uniform.

"How's this for clarity?" he said coolly. "Next time you fling yourself into a murder investigation, if I turn out to be the killer, I'll *tell* you so, all right?"

Louisa knew she ought to stand down, but the feeling of embarrassment only fueled her anger. "And why would I think you'd be honest with me? You never told me what you spent all that money on, did you?"

He left off with his buttons to glare at her. "What are you banging on about now?"

"The school roof money. You stole it, didn't you? And you let Paul take the fall for it." She studied him carefully for his reaction. She wasn't sure what she expected really. At first she thought he might deny it, but then she thought it was more likely he'd be furious with her for discovering the truth.

To her astonishment, he tipped his head back and laughed. "So *that's* what he said to you, is it?"

"You aren't even going to deny it?"

He brushed past her. "On the contrary. I'll go down to the station and turn myself in. Make a full written confession. I'm sure the constables will care a great deal to know the kinds of mischief I got into when I was thirteen years old."

Louisa stabbed a finger at him. "Don't you dare make it sound like that."

"Like what?"

"Like it was nothing. How could you do that to Paul? You were his closest friend—his *only* friend—and you let him suffer your blame for years. Everyone thought of him as a criminal after that."

"Paul never needed any help from me when it came to being thought of as a criminal."

"But you were supposed to be his friend!"

"I *was* his friend!" he bellowed. "Do you think this is easy for me? In case you haven't noticed, there's no winning here, Louisa. Paul was like a brother to me. Now I either have to chase him down like a miserable dog if he did it, or I have to find his murdered body. I've already peeled through every inch of that rubble, half expecting to have to dig him out."

Louisa recoiled, hot tears stinging her eyes at the image his words had conjured. "I'm so sorry," she choked out, stricken and shamed in equal measure and wishing that she could take back everything she'd said. "I'm sorry for all of it." She was no longer sure if she was apologizing to Malcolm alone or if Paul was haunting her after all—for all the ways she hadn't been a good sister to him.

Malcolm went on as if he hadn't heard her. "And it might interest you to know that I *was* going to turn myself in when he got pegged for the missing roof money. But Paul made me swear not to do it."

Louisa nodded and swiped at the few traitorous tears that had slipped her guard.

Malcolm drew closer and brushed one of them away with his thumb. In a quieter voice, he said, "I didn't steal it on a lark, by the way. I needed the money—my family needed the money. Paul knew how hard things were back then. And when my parents realized what I'd done . . . well, they were furious with me, but they were too afraid to give it back in case I was arrested."

Louisa stared up at him, stunned by his candor and humbled by her suspicions. "I'm sorry," she said again. "I know this can't have been any easier for you than it's been for me, and . . . Oh, I suppose I should leave now. If we keep quarreling like this, we're going to start giving each other gray hairs."

She expected him to say something cutting. Instead, he nearly smiled. "I'd pay right handsomely to see you with a few gray hairs."

If Louisa blushed again, Malcolm was courteous enough not to comment on it. "Perhaps I'll see you at the fete next week?" she said, trying to make amends. "You really ought to come after polishing all of that silver for Mrs. Watson like an indentured servant."

There was a pause. A fairly uncomfortable one, if Louisa was any judge of pauses. "I'm going with Dorothy Simms," he admitted after a moment. "To the fete, I mean."

"Oh!" Louisa was unprepared for the way her stomach pitched at this development. Though she tried to sound cheerful about it, her voice emerged in a nervous squeak: "She's a pretty girl, isn't she?"

"Er—yes," agreed Malcolm.

"Well, good." She swabbed the last few tears from her cheek. "Good for you, I mean. And for her! You'll still have to come round the tent for a cup of tea. No charge, of course.

I've said I'll make scones as well, but you really shouldn't try them, and neither should Dorothy—I'm rubbish at baking. Always overdone or underdone, my mother used to say, and never in between. I'm not sure why I told Mrs. Watson I'd make them to begin with, except that she was in a fearsome mood that day, and I always say far too many things in general when I'm flustered—"

"Yes," Malcolm said again.

He scrubbed a hand through his hair and glanced at the door. His shirt was still untucked, half unbuttoned, and the ends of his hair were damp and curled. All of it made Louisa feel nervous and embarrassed. And so she said a bit too much for a good while longer before she forced out a blathering sort of goodbye and saw herself out.

27

The rain relented, and this was the finest, if not the first, bit of good fortune Louisa had received in some time. Still, she didn't walk home as she'd previously planned, which was sure to cause a kerfuffle at Everly Hall when her aunt and uncle realized she was missing—again.

But it couldn't be helped, not really, for she'd passed the road home without meaning to and found herself bound instead for the road to Rosemont Abbey.

Thus far it had been fairly easy for her to avoid going there, as the Rosemont congregation had been gathering for worship at St. Stephen's. Even when Louisa visited the vicarage, she always averted her gaze when she passed the ruins, as if there were a dead body sprawled somewhere nearby, and so she caught only swift, fragmentary glimpses of tower and stone out of the corner of her eye.

But that morning was different. It was as if she was a regular Odysseus, and the ruins had called to her, wrenching her off course. She couldn't say why exactly, but she *had* to go to the abbey. She had to look.

Since she was already thoroughly wet and uncomfortable

from her walk to the pub, she didn't bother looking for a dry spot. She plopped herself down on the first patch of soggy moss she found and stared upward at the wasted remains. Wherever her eyes fell, the stones were blackened, crumbling at the tops like a row of bared, rotten teeth, and the casements, once resplendent with their stained glass, now framed a grave-yard of blackened pews and fallen ceiling beams. The prover-bial bats had settled into the gutted belfry and were screeching and swooping endlessly overhead while dense clouds prowled low on the horizon, threatening another blitz of rain.

"Miss Everly!" a voice called from behind her.

Though surprised by the intrusion, Louisa was too ex-hausted to flinch. Footsteps hastened as she stared drearily forward, waiting for the vicar to come nearer.

As he drew up beside her, he asked if she was all right, to which she mused very softly: "He wasn't ever any worse than me."

Reverend Hughes looked at her a moment. Then, using his hat, he brushed a dusting of soil from a nearby boulder and sat himself down. "Paul, you mean?"

"Yes. I've spent years, nearly my whole life, being talked about like I was the good egg and Paul the rotten one. I sup-pose I even started to believe it myself, which is really the worst sin of all, isn't it? Thinking ourselves rather too good? But Paul knew the truth about me—I'm proud, wretchedly vain, and devilishly slow when it comes to forgiving. My father was always reminding me of such."

"None of us are better than any other," the vicar agreed. He opened his mouth to say something else, but Louisa cut him off.

"All of this sleuthing business has turned everything on

its head," she admitted, burying her face in her hands. "All I ever wanted was to find out what happened to Paul, to find out who had killed him, but then I find that he cared for someone. Cared enough to give her a priceless ring that he had told everyone, quite cruelly, he'd gambled away. They were going to get married. And he was looking out for me, you know, and doing all kinds of other perfectly nice things while I was going to parties and buying new gowns in taffeta—and caring a bit too much about taffeta in general, I suppose. Oh, dear, is any of this making sense?"

"I understand what you are saying, Louisa, and you need look no further than your own baptism for the answer. Perhaps it's true that you and Paul have been compared to each other all your lives. And yet, as you've said, your brother was no more a sinner than you are—than any of us are. You may thank God for using these painful circumstances to remind you of this, but do not get so caught up in looking at your own shortcomings that you forget that you and Paul were baptized into the same Jesus. You both belong to Christ, and *that* is the only comparison that truly matters."

Louisa bent her head down. For a moment, the tears choked her. Then, after sniffling for a long while, she blew her nose with a handkerchief he'd offered. "Forgive me for blubbering," she said. "Death has been a dreadful companion."

"He's a proud beast, to be sure, but you needn't worry—he hasn't got any teeth."

She smiled faintly at this image. "I wish I could make things right for Paul, insofar as I am able. If only I could uncover the truth—if only I could bring his body home . . ."

The vicar considered this. "Please forgive me for this rather hackneyed comparison," he began. "I lost my reading glasses a few weeks ago. Tried to get them replaced, but the doctor keeps giving me the wrong prescription. Ever since, delivering sermons has been a trifle painful for all involved, as I'm sure you've noticed—saying *acrimony* when I've written *matrimony*, that sort of thing. Well, I've checked in all the most unlikely of places, but Mrs. Watson told me that all I needed to do was retrace my steps. It's the kind of advice we give to children, and yet how easily we forget."

"I ought to retrace Paul's steps, you mean?"

"Or your own if you'd like. You might notice something you didn't before."

Louisa nodded, her head still thick from crying as she heaved herself up onto her feet. She supposed she ought to start where she'd started to begin with, in Paul's flat. After all, Thomas Sykes had been there just the day before, and he'd obviously unsettled someone with his search. Before she left, she thanked the vicar and handed back his handkerchief. "Out of curiosity," she said, "where did you end up finding your reading glasses?"

His ears turned pink, and he chuckled. "Well, I haven't found them. Not yet anyway. That's actually why I'm here. I trot down the path a few times a week and sit on this very boulder to pray." He cast a hopeless glance around. "I don't see them, though."

Louisa laughed. "I'll retrace my steps again, but only if you keep retracing yours. We can't very well have you saying *concession* in your sermon when you really meant to say *confession*, can we?"

"Right you are!" laughed the vicar.

Together, he and Louisa hiked up to the gravel path that led to the main road. Louisa turned back at the last moment, a stitch in her side and an ache in her chest as she stared at the blank expanse of gray sky where the steeple had once been. "It really was like a fortress, wasn't it?" she whispered. "How terrible it is, knowing that such a mighty structure can fall so easily . . ." She shivered, her words trailing off.

The vicar smiled gently. "God's Word still stands, Miss Everly, and that's enough."

28

Louisa could match anything to a shade of lipstick, and so the spatters of blood on the steps to her brother's flat weren't much of a challenge; they were "Sundown" by Lenthéric, a dark and dramatic shade.

She wasn't the only one taking stock of the surroundings.

A cluster of police officers was already milling about by the time she arrived, as well as a number of other important-looking figures, including a man with a medical bag and a scrawny, stooped-over fellow who was snapping photographs with a camera.

Louisa slipped past two constables rather easily and ducked behind a police car, but she still only made it as far as the bottom step. "Stop there, you!" a stern voice shouted behind her. Louisa halted as ordered, and a man in a sergeant's uniform came shuffling around to stand in front of her, scratching his brow with his finger as though perplexed she'd made it so far. "This here is police business," he said.

"But it's my brother's flat." She stood on her tiptoes and peered past his hulking shoulders, trying to survey as much of the scene as she could in case she was sent away. "I'm Louisa—Louisa Everly."

The sergeant considered her muddy dress and her bedraggled hair. "Not very likely," he chortled.

Louisa glowered at him. Even if she didn't look like a well-bred young lady at the moment, she certainly sounded the part when she spoke again: "If you would ring up Inspector Sinclair, I'm sure we can clear this up."

"Listen, girl, I don't care who you are or who you say you are. The only clearing you can do is to clear out of here!"

He grabbed her arm to drag her away, but Louisa gripped the stairwell railing and clung on for all she was worth. "I'm not going *anywhere*!" she vowed imperiously. "Not until you've at least *tried* to contact the inspector. I can be very stubborn, a point which I'm sure the inspector will corroborate if you only ask him!"

"Stubborn, you say?" The sergeant grunted. "More like a pain in the—"

"Let her come up, Billings."

Louisa blinked and followed the path of the sergeant's astonished eyes up the stairs. Malcolm was leaning out from Paul's room, looking infinitely dryer and more put together than when she'd left his place a mere two hours before. She had no doubt he'd overheard the entire confrontation, and after his sergeant had snorted at her appearance, Louisa felt like a dowdy commoner in his presence. Sergeant Billings had already released her, and so Malcolm waved her up when she found herself too stunned to move.

"Watch your step," he instructed, nodding to a few tiny spatters of blood, which Louisa had already noticed on the stairs.

Making an unsuccessful effort to straighten her hair, she brushed past the disgruntled Billings, obediently sidestepped the spatters, and came face-to-face with Malcolm, who snickered when she drew even with him in the doorway. "About time you caught up with the rest of us," he said.

"When did you call in the cavalry?"

"Just as soon as you'd gone."

"And you didn't invite me to come along?" She tried, unsuccessfully, to hide the disappointment in her voice.

"Well, I might have done, but I had a feeling you'd still be nattering incoherently on account of my date with Dorothy Simms."

Though mortified by that remark, Louisa pivoted topics like a true diplomat. "Well," she said, "I *am* glad you're looking into Sykes's story at least."

"And it checks out," Malcolm admitted, sobering. "At least as far as we can tell. There's blood on the stairs, as you've seen, and obvious signs of a struggle inside." He pressed a hand to the small of her back, ushering her into the room. "The table was shoved back a few inches there. Chair knocked over. Watch your step again—the trail of blood starts just there."

"Where's the shoehorn?"

"On the bed. No prints. Of course, the intruder must have left in a hurry, what with the bullet in his arm."

"Which means he planned ahead enough to wear gloves."

Malcolm lifted a brow. "Well, yes."

"Paul wouldn't have had any reason to wear gloves, even if he'd come back to his room for something. His prints would have been all over everything anyway." She held her breath. "Does this mean he's been cleared of arson?"

"The investigation is moving in that direction, yes."

The relief was so swift that Louisa dizzied, feeling as though the room had slipped sideways as soon as the truth had been set straight. And though she thought she'd masked her reaction well enough by smiling, Malcolm seized her hand as if to steady her. "It's not settled, of course," he said. "A skeptic might suggest he had an accomplice. Someone he sent back because it was too dangerous for him to come himself."

Louisa pulled back from Malcolm. "What about Fernsby?" she asked. "If he's been up to his usual blackmail schemes, I suppose he'd have a thumping good reason not to want to be sighted."

"I've combed through the letters from his sister," said Malcolm. "A few days ago, I thought I tracked him down in Oxford, but the room was empty when my men and I got there."

"Really? You might have mentioned."

"I might have," he agreed. "And you might not have suspected me of murder. We all have little lapses in judgment, don't we?"

"Oh, come off it. I've already said I'm sorry."

"And as a peace offering for that, I'll share the following: we've collected samples for your poison theory, but there wasn't much food in the place, just a handful of biscuits and some canned goods."

"And the scotch," she added quickly.

"Yes," he said with a smile. "We've taken care of the scotch."

Louisa nodded. She tried strolling the room to steady her nerves, but it wasn't working. There was something about this space. Something didn't feel right, didn't fit. Was something missing, she wondered, or was something there that didn't belong? As she pondered, she slid her fingertips along the desk and the bedside table, finding that a layer of dust had already settled in the wake of her brother's absence. There was the record player; the now empty bottle of scotch holding vigil beside an empty ashtray; the water glasses in the sink; the photograph of her father from the war . . .

"Sir." Billings was crouched near a vent on the other side of the room, pinching a tiny object between a pair of tweezers. As he held it up, Louisa's thoughts flashed back to the night of the fire, when Dr. Fielding had removed the shard of china from the palm of her hand. Only this was no piece of floral china. This object was small, metallic.

A bullet.

Frowning, Malcolm went over, tugging a handkerchief out of his pocket. He crouched beside Billings, who dropped the bullet, very gently, in the center of the handkerchief. "We dug it out just there," he said. "There's blood on it. It must have gone straight through his arm, whoever he was."

"Send someone down to the pharmacy," said Malcolm without looking up. "Have them draw up a list of names, anyone coming in to buy bandages or disinfectant in the last twenty-four hours." He spoke dully, as if he were throwing a net but didn't expect to catch a single fish for his trouble.

He was still staring at the bullet when Louisa came and stood beside him. "There's something about this room," she said, peering all around. "Something is missing, I think, or else something has been moved—I can't work out what it could be."

Malcolm didn't seem to be listening. He was still staring down at the bloodstained bullet in his hand.

"Malcolm?" She poked him in the shoulder. "Malcolm, did you hear me?"

He straightened and, enfolding the bullet within the hand-kerchief, abruptly shook his head. "It's time for you to step back from this, Louisa."

"Step back? You can't be serious!"

"I've let things go too far. Until now, it was easy enough to think of this case as a puzzle. But someone's fired bullets in this room, and I'd just as soon keep you out of it. You're a frightfully easy target."

"Because I'm Paul's sister, you mean?"

"It's because of your dresses, if you must know."

"My dresses!"

"Just look at that yellow skirt you've got on. The 'new look,' isn't it? Well, if I were a sniper, I could pick you off in a rainstorm from three miles away."

Louisa scowled. "What would you have me do? I'm not exactly the sort to sit at home and twiddle my thumbs."

"I'm aware. Which is why Sergeant Billings will be escorting you home just to make sure you don't take any detours on the way." He flagged down the sergeant and explained to him how things were to be, then caught Louisa when she would have stomped off without a farewell. "And don't go trying to give him the slip either," he murmured, his fingers brushing her wrist, "because we both know you will. Billings there, he's a good chap. Family at home, lots of adorable kids. It would be a shame to have to write him up for losing track of you."

"That's blackmail."

"True, but it's for the greater good. And I think you ought to take this with you—just in case."

He was speaking in a closer whisper now, and so the dramatic part of Louisa's brain expected him to slip her a gun or some other sleek-looking weapon with which to defend herself. Instead, he grabbed a long, black umbrella, which had been propped in the corner behind the door. When he held it out to her, Louisa was too surprised to refuse. Her fingers curled instinctively around the curve of the wooden handle.

Malcolm stepped back and appraised her with a sharp eye. "You sure you know how to use that thing? It's just occurred to me that I've never actually seen you use an umbrella before, and that's my only one. Shall I give you some instructions before you go?"

If Louisa said what she *wanted* to say at the moment, she had a feeling she might have gotten herself arrested, after all. Instead, she tucked his umbrella tightly under her arm, saluted him once, and marched out the door. Sergeant Billings rushed to catch up with her.

29

The only thing worse than being escorted home by an inspector was being escorted home by a sergeant. The way Louisa's aunt and uncle looked at her—well, it felt as though she had been demoted.

"Louisa!" cried Aunt Agatha. "Where have you been? You aren't hurt, are you?" Louisa was still clutching Malcolm's umbrella as her aunt shepherded her across the room and pressed her down to sit in an armchair. The Chesterfield couch was more comfortable, but it was also new, and so Aunt Agatha changed course just as soon as she noticed the muddy state of Louisa's nylons.

"Caught her sniffing around a crime scene," grumbled the sergeant by way of introductions. "Inspector Sinclair asked me to deliver her back home." Then in a more petulant tone, he added, "Though nowhere in my job description does it say I'm responsible for delivering *baggage*."

"Crime scene?" Aunt Agatha's voice was shrill, while Uncle Archie's was not:

"What are you muttering about?" he demanded. "Speak up, man!"

"We found her at her brother's flat," explained the sergeant, straightening his uniform. "It appears that someone was shot there last night. Your niece was—well, she was poking around the place and being very *in the way*, going on about poison and blackmail. It sounds to me like she's been reading too many novels."

Louisa could have expertly argued each of the sergeant's remarks, but she knew when to keep her mouth shut. Whenever Uncle Archie was aghast, he had the look of a man delivering a speech in parliament who had just swallowed a magnificent sneeze. She watched him warily now, wondering how much more Sergeant Billings could reasonably share before his head downright imploded.

The sergeant plowed ahead, heedless of any such danger: "It seems she knew about the attack after speaking with a man by the name of Sykes. Dodgy fellow, runs a boxing club in Oxford."

Her aunt wheeled around. "Louisa, *really*! Not these boxing clubs again!"

For once, Uncle Archie was first to reach the point: "You said there was a shooting." If Louisa didn't know any better, she'd have thought his skin was paler than usual behind his mustache.

"Yes, sir."

"My nephew—was he involved?"

The sergeant removed his hat and squinted, looking as though he was auditioning, very poorly, for the role of inspector. "Why do you ask that, Mr. Everly?"

"Well, the shooting. You said it was in his room, didn't you?"

"And?"

"And I'd like to know which side of the gun my nephew was standing on!" That time, her uncle's voice made it all the way up to the rafters and echoed clear into the hall. There was a bead of sweat on his brow, which he mopped away impatiently with his handkerchief.

"We aren't sure yet who was there exactly," answered the sergeant. "Or who was shot, or what they were after . . . or even why—"

"All right!" barked Uncle Archie. "You've delivered your 'baggage,' as you've called her, and proven yourself less than useless in every other regard. You may go now."

Despite everything that had happened to sour her against him, Louisa almost felt sorry for Sergeant Billings. The poor fellow's neck turned scarlet beneath his shirt collar, and he looked thoroughly cut down at the knees as he saw himself out.

As soon as he was gone, Aunt Agatha sat down beside Louisa. "Now," she said, "what happened with David?"

Louisa was so tired that she couldn't help but laugh. Her aunt had just been informed that someone had been shot in her nephew's flat. That her niece had been caught poking around the crime scene and had to be escorted home by the police. And yet her drive with David was more urgent to her aunt than even the pressing matter of boxing clubs!

"What's so funny?" trilled Aunt Agatha.

"We quarreled," Louisa answered flatly. "David and I quarreled, and I asked to be let out of the car."

"And he really let you out to walk? In the *rain*?" When Louisa nodded, Aunt Agatha stood in a rush. She pursed her lips and paced the room, but then she waved her hand airily and forced a smile. "Well," she said, "that's quite all right."

Louisa couldn't keep her mouth from popping open. "Quite all right?" she repeated.

"Of course. You can ring him up first thing tomorrow morning and tell him you're sorry for whatever it was you quarreled about. Be sure to wear the blue dress this time—it brings out your eyes. And where on earth did you get that hideous black umbrella? You look like an undertaker holding that thing!"

Louisa had forgotten about the umbrella. She felt as though she'd lived three years in the last three hours and was having a hard time keeping up. "I won't be wearing the blue dress," she replied, "and I won't be calling him either. Not tomorrow, nor ever again."

Her aunt rang the bell. "All you need is a bath—with lavender, I think. My mother always said there's no quarrel that can't be settled once you've had a plate of finger sandwiches and a nice long soak."

"Don't you understand?" snapped Louisa. "It's over. It's done. I have no wish to settle anything with David Ashworth. He's not at all the sort of man he seems to be."

"Oh, nonsense! You young ladies are always so dramatic. I blame the cinema for that. Whatever it is you're quarreling over is nothing more than a storm in a—"

"Agatha." Uncle Archie set his pipe down on the desk. "Leave the girl alone."

The room fell silent, and no wonder, for this was an unprecedented interference, at least where courtship matters were concerned. "Leave her alone, indeed!" hissed Aunt Agatha, turning on her husband. "We're talking about David Ashworth, aren't we?"

Uncle Archie rubbed his eyes and lowered himself into his

desk chair. "Louisa, if you are going to make your escape, I suggest you do it now."

Feeling like a cornered animal, Louisa remained seated, her muddy shoes streaking the carpet and the hideous umbrella still clutched in her hands. She blinked rapidly and looked between her aunt and uncle. It was as if they'd somehow traded bodies when she wasn't looking.

Uncle Archie lifted a brow. "Or would you rather stay where you are?"

His question prompted as swift a retreat as Louisa had ever made in her entire life. Before retiring to her room, though, she stopped for a quick rummage through the kitchen because she couldn't stop thinking about what her aunt had proposed: sandwiches and a nice long soak.

The woman was wrong about everything else, of course, yet Louisa made up a plate of food nonetheless. She knew better than anyone that a person could speak a lot of pishposh, as Mrs. Watson called it, and still be right from time to time.

30

The fete was on a Friday, and it was fine timing too, for it seemed as though summer had pounced on them overnight. The rain had cleared at last, leaving everything a bit soggy around the edges, but the air smelled like honeysuckle, and the skies were a ravishing blue.

Louisa's aunt rose with the sun and saw to it that everyone else in Everly Hall did, too. The flower arrangements—sprays and garlands of peony, rose, and hyacinth—were fretted over one last time before they were packed off with the servants to be delivered to St. Stephen's. Not wishing to be pulled into the whirlpool, Louisa rang for tea and toast in her room and stayed in bed for as long as possible, admiring a vase of pink-and-purple flowers that had appeared on her dresser early that morning. A peace offering, she presumed, from her aunt.

Once breakfast was done, she wiggled into a voluminous tea-length dress, which rested slightly off the shoulders and was covered from bust to hem in flashy pink-and-yellow chrysanthemums. *And let Malcolm say of that what he will!* she thought, nodding determinedly to herself in the mirror.

Three strands of pearls and two coats of lipstick later and

she was slipping on her prim, white gloves and hurrying down the stairs to where Mrs. Watson was waiting behind the wheel of her grandson's sedan with the last of the tea things. They'd spent the whole day prior readying their tent for the festivities, and even Louisa had admitted, when pressed, that the lace table coverings were worth most of the anxiety they'd caused.

"Your driving has improved tremendously," Louisa lied once they were on the road—and then clung to her seat for dear life as they nose-dived over the crest of a hill.

"I'm thinking of buying one for myself," said Mrs. Watson, patting the dash affectionately, "and naming it Anthony, after the prime minister."

"I didn't realize you were so fond of the prime minister."

"I'm not. Not really. But everyone wants to talk politics, don't they, even if they don't say so? And yet no one seems to know how to jump in properly these days. But if I refer to my car as Anthony, people might ask me why I named it Anthony, and it doesn't matter whether they like the prime minister or whether they hate him, only that it would be a natural conversation starter, don't you think?"

Louisa didn't think many people would go out of their way to ask why Mrs. Watson had named her car Anthony. Most would be too afraid to even let her get behind the wheel. But she still smiled and nodded, and when Mrs. Watson missed the turn to St. Stephen's, she swiveled in her seat to check the road sign and asked where they were going.

"I have a thermos of nettle tea I need to deliver to Mr. Hexam. I brought him some after our last visit, and he said it helped his leg tremendously. And perhaps—well, not to sound too *transactional*, but perhaps we could ask if he'd like to be the first to contribute to our money box for the tea tent."

Louisa laughed. "Pump him for a donation, you mean?"

The marigolds in Mrs. Watson's hat wobbled as she looked sideways at Louisa. "It's not *pumping*," she declared in her saintliest voice, "if it's for the *church*."

⌒〜〜

"Mrs. Watson, you are a national treasure!" cried Mr. Hexam when they arrived in his sitting room. His leg was propped on a stool as before, but Louisa could see at once that the swelling, particularly around his knee, was much, *much* worse.

Mrs. Watson tutted and yanked an enormous thermos out of her wicker handbag. "It seems I've come just in time!" she said.

Louisa felt a good deal less confident in Mrs. Watson's healing powers, and so she tried a more practical approach. "Has the doctor been around to see this?" she asked him.

"Yesterday, as a matter of fact. He brought my prescription. Feel bad for the fellow. I'm rather a hopeless case. It's this leg of mine. He had to prescribe something for the swelling— which, would you believe it, has to do with my heart? The girls in school always said there was something wrong with it!" He laughed until he was red in the face, then coughed himself to a stop. "Anyway, I'm supposed to take it for the swelling, but the medicine gives me gout."

Mrs. Watson shook her head. "Doctors!" Then, tucking the thermos under her arm, she went to the kitchen in search of a suitable teacup.

As soon as she was gone, Mr. Hexam turned his face away from Louisa, masking a grimace as he shifted his weight in his chair.

"It must be terribly painful," she observed with a sympathetic shudder. "Perhaps I ought to call the doctor now?"

259

She reached for the telephone, which was sitting on a stack of old newspapers behind her, but Mr. Hexam flapped his hand to stop her. "You won't be able to call anyone," he said. "Not with that thing. It's the most impressive-looking paperweight I've ever had. Blasted phone hasn't worked in months."

"That doesn't seem safe. How do you send for the doctor when you need him?"

"We have our usual appointments. I also have a tenant who lives upstairs. The stingy chap lets me use his phone when I'm in a pinch, but he charges me a quid per call. Gross extortion, isn't it? Still, he's my only nephew, so I can't in good conscience evict him." Mr. Hexam squirmed once more as he struggled to achieve a more comfortable position.

"Are you sure there isn't anything I can get for you?" asked Louisa, reaching forward to help straighten the cushions behind him. "Anything I can do? Have you already taken your medicine?" She took up the bottle, squinting at the label, but a belated realization made her set it back down at once. "Hang on," she said. "How exactly did the doctor call his wife?"

"Eh?" said Mr. Hexam. "What was that?"

"On the night of the fire. You said he'd had too much to drink and telephoned his wife. That's how she knew to send Dr. Fielding over to see to my hand. But how could he use your telephone if it's been broken for months?"

Mr. Hexam stared at her, then released a blustery laugh. "I suppose he must have gone upstairs and used my nephew's telephone."

"But that's not what you said. You said he used *your* telephone." Louisa closed her eyes for a second, recalling their conversation. "Yes, that's right. You even pointed to it, didn't you?"

"Oh, what does it matter what I said? Perhaps I misspoke. Or perhaps you aren't remembering correctly. It was a good number of evenings ago, wasn't it? Now, where is dear old Mrs. Watson with that tea?"

They both looked to the doorway and jumped when they realized Mrs. Watson was already standing there. Her scowl was perhaps the most inspiring thing Louisa had ever seen. Even with a thermos in one hand and a cup of steaming tea in the other, she managed to look like an avenging angel in periwinkle rayon. "Albert Hexam," she shrilled, "I remember that day *distinctly*! You pointed to that telephone, the one you now say is broken, and said the doctor had used it to call his wife!"

Mr. Hexam's mouth popped open, but Louisa spoke for him when no sound came out: "The doctor never was here that night, was he?"

"B-balderdash!" stuttered Mr. Hexam, his gaze swinging nervously between the women. "Of course he was here! He slept right there on that couch and . . ."

As he spoke, he reached hopefully for the cup of nettle tea in Mrs. Watson's hand, but she stepped back at the last moment, threatening to pour it out into an already miserable-looking fern behind her.

With a cantankerous sigh, Mr. Hexam sank back into his cushions. "You women really are relentless, aren't you? Well, you've dragged it out of me, but don't say I folded like a house of cards over a cup of nettle tea. But no, the doctor wasn't here that night. He came to me early the next morning and asked me to say, if anyone came asking, that he was here with me all night."

"Where was he really?" asked Louisa.

"He said he'd spent the night with a . . . well, hang it all, he was with a woman, if you really must know, and he didn't want his wife finding out."

Mrs. Watson clutched her thermos like a prayer book. "A *woman!*" she shrieked.

"Who was it?" gasped Louisa. "Who was the woman?"

"He never did say, but the poor fella looked grotesquely hungover and smelled of cigarettes. I didn't want to lie to you, Miss Everly. Please, believe me. But we're brothers of a kind—those of us who served together—and I didn't want to plunge him into hot water with his wife if I could help it."

Louisa thought for a moment. "The doctor doesn't smoke, though, does he?"

"Truthfully, he doesn't do much of anything, which is why I was so surprised about the affair. But his female friend, whoever she is, must be a pretty heavy smoker for him to have smelled as much like an ashtray as he did. He would have had to take a bath and burn the clothes for his wife not to have noticed—" He broke off abruptly, holding up his hands in supplication. "Now, Mrs. Watson, don't you look at me like that. I did my very best to convince him it was all more bother than it would be worth in the end."

"Well, that's the very *least* of what you ought to have said!" she snapped, but she did finally hand him the hostage teacup.

While the elders in the room went on bickering about morals and what ought to have been said, Louisa sat rubbing her eyes and pondering. There was something that Mr. Hexam had said, something that made her think of something else, but no matter how many times she rehashed the conversation in her mind, she couldn't figure out what either of those *somethings* were.

Mr. Hexam had talked about the telephone, yes, and the war, and the medicine from the doctor that gave him gout. And there was still the matter of the blackmail photograph and the locket, the recent attack in her brother's flat, and, of course, the assailant now strolling about Wilbeth Green with an unseen bullet hole beneath his left sleeve.

She went over the pieces again and again in her mind, like a child wiggling a loose tooth, but all she got for her trouble was a throbbing, ill-timed headache.

31

Before leaving the house, Louisa asked to use the upstairs telephone to call the station in Sutherby. Mr. Hexam's nephew was a tall, sallow-looking young man named Beauregard. He charged her half a crown for the call, which Louisa argued was highway robbery, and Mrs. Watson added that he'd never move out of his uncle's attic if he went on treating lovely young ladies like that.

Louisa reluctantly paid the toll, only to learn that Malcolm was off for the day. She was therefore passed off to Sergeant Billings, who came on the line sounding like he had the beginnings of a headache, too. "Miss Everly, I *really* haven't got time for—"

"I haven't got time either," she groused in return. "I'm *supposed* to be at the fete serving scones and milk to sticky little children, but there's this one thing that is *slightly* more pressing at the moment. I've just been speaking with Mr. Hexam, and he's admitted to the fact that Dr. Clarke lied about his alibi on the night of the fire."

"His what?"

"His alibi!"

Sergeant Billings didn't respond further. Louisa closed her eyes and listened through the static to make sure she could still hear sounds of life on the other end of the line. "If you hang up on me," she warned, "Mrs. Watson and I will come straight over and set up all of our tea things in your office!"

That got a sigh out of him at least.

"Well?" he said, defeated. "What do you want me to do?"

"I wouldn't dream of telling you how to do your job, Sergeant, but you might start by writing it down in a file somewhere and perhaps asking the doctor about it?"

"You're welcome to ask him yourself," he said. "He'll be at the fete this afternoon."

"How do you know that?"

"Not by poking my nose where it isn't wanted, I can assure you." He didn't seem apt to elaborate, but perhaps he knew he'd never be rid of Louisa if he didn't. "My wife's in charge of the games," he added gruffly, "and I've heard of little else for the last three days. Dr. Clarke and Dr. Fielding will be handing out ribbons for the three-legged races."

"Oh, I see!" Louisa tried to sound pleasant so as to stay on the sergeant's good side. "In that case, I wonder if you and I should—"

Sergeant Billings hung up the telephone.

Staggered by his nerve, Louisa stared at the silent receiver a moment before hanging up. "Half a crown sure didn't get us very far," she muttered, glaring at Beauregard Hexam as she shoved the telephone back to his end of the table.

"I, for one, am not the least bit surprised that Mr. Sinclair has taken the day off at such a critical time," stated Mrs. Watson. Moments before, she had delicately appealed to Mr. Hexam for his tea-tent donation, which she now slipped neatly into her white lace glove. "Though I do wonder if we should try to track him down. He would want to know that the doctor's been spreading stories."

"There's no need," sighed Louisa. "I know exactly where Malcolm will be this afternoon."

"Up to some sort of mischief, no doubt?"

"Very likely, yes. He'll be at the fete—paying court to Dorothy Simms."

The village band was warming up beneath a banner of colorful bunting when Louisa and Mrs. Watson arrived at the grassy knoll outside St. Stephen's Church. Mr. Miller was on the accordion, the pharmacist on the dulcimer, while Elias Tuft, an eleven-year-old lad who worked for his father at the post office, was trying his best to keep up with them on a bulbous tuba that was twice his size. All the noise did nothing for Louisa's headache, but she pushed through the gathering crowds, her arms laden with platters of pastries.

"Set them just there," said Mrs. Watson, pushing a squeaky cart piled with hot-water kettles. "And then off you go to find the inspector."

"We're a bit behind the starting time." Louisa began unloading the kettles. "I wouldn't dream of leaving without seeing things settled here."

"Nonsense!" protested Mrs. Watson, shooing her away with a tea towel. "Dorothy Simms is a lovely girl. She has a fetching smile, as all the young men say, and a fine sense of humor. She plays the piano beautifully, far more beautifully than you, I'm sorry to admit, but I should know—after all, I taught you both! But if the inspector thinks he's going to spend the entire afternoon paying compliments to Miss Simms, why, it's . . ." She cast about briefly for something else to say before ripping a page out of Mr. Hexam's book and declaring, "It's balderdash!"

Though Louisa hated to abandon her post, she knew when to follow Mrs. Watson's orders, and so off she went. She started her search for Malcolm near the duck pond, past the crockery smash, where children were hurling balls at towering vases, then past a group of Morris dancers with bells on their ankles and knees. Next was the cake tent, where four Victoria sponge cakes would be vying for crown and glory. The competition was a pretext. While the lesser cakes underwent a somewhat fair scoring, Mrs. Kittle had won Best Victoria Sponge every year for as long as anyone could remember, and no judge would dare vote against her now.

Louisa found no sign of Malcolm anywhere, nor of Dorothy Simms, and so to keep her spirits up, she nipped in at the Mothers' Union tent for one of their famous sugared apple fritters. To her surprise, Malcolm was leaving the tent as she was entering, and they nearly collided in the entrance.

She blinked up at him. Gone was the suit that made him look so much like a detective. Gone was the fedora. Instead, he wore an olive-green sports shirt loose over a white T-shirt. And denim trousers. Louisa could hardly believe it, but Malcolm was wearing jeans. He held two apple fritters wrapped in crisp white paper, one in each hand.

"There you are!" she wailed in flustered haste. "I've been looking for you everywhere! Mrs. Watson and I—"

"I can't talk right now," he cut in brusquely.

Louisa's mouth was still open when he shouldered past her and strode away, but he walked at an unhurried pace, which was all the encouragement she needed to follow him. "Why can't you talk?" she asked.

"Because I'm undercover."

"Undercover!" She bobbed a look over her shoulder to make sure they weren't being followed, then lowered her voice. "As what exactly?"

"As someone who's trying to have a good time."

She colored at the jab but kept up with him, hovering like a persistent mosquito near his elbow. "Malcolm, this is serious! Mrs. Watson and I have just been to see Mr. Hexam. There was something funny about the telephone. It gave me an inkling. He told me it was broken, but then I remembered that he'd said the doctor rang up his wife that night. I was right—Mr. Hexam lied about where the doctor was on the night of the fire."

Finally, she watched Malcolm stiffen and stop beside her, but his voice, when he finally took the bait, was unaffected. "Where does Mr. Hexam think he was?"

"With a woman. All night."

"Hm." Malcolm sidestepped a few unruly youths, who went tearing past with mammoth clouds of candy floss. "A story like that could be as hard to discredit as it could be to corroborate. He might easily clam up and claim he's protecting the woman's honor."

"You're going to talk to him, though, aren't you?"

He shuffled the fritters to rub his eyes with his free hand. "This is the first proper day I've had off in over a month," he grumbled. "Why'd you have to go and have an inkling today?"

"An inkling about what?"

Louisa and Malcolm turned in tandem as Dorothy Simms approached. She was wearing a simple blue sundress covered in miniature white roses, and her blond curls fell naturally beneath the dainty perch of a pale straw hat. She touched Malcolm's arm when she came to his side, and he, finding a smile, handed her one of the fritters.

Cringing inwardly, Louisa slipped back a step. Malcolm and Dorothy looked perfectly familiar with each other, an attractive couple without the need for finery or frills. Louisa never would have pictured Malcolm courting anyone like Dorothy. If pressed, she might have imagined him in one of those shadowy sorts of clubs, tie loose at the end of a long day while dancing with pretty girls to the music of Fats Domino. And yet, as he and Dorothy stood together in the sunny church courtyard, they both seemed so . . .

She was still searching for the right word when Malcolm spoke: "Louisa's been inquiring about the status of her brother's case," he said to Dorothy, and ignored the way Louisa was now glowering at him. *Inquiring?* she thought, raising her brow. *Ha!*

"I'm so sorry, Louisa," said Dorothy, catching her hand. "I've been praying that Malcolm and his men are able to bring him home soon." As usual, the girl was gracious, composed, and impossibly kind. No reasonable person could have found a single fault with her.

But Louisa still had a headache and was not feeling particularly reasonable. "If Malcolm follows the clues as enthusiastically as he pursues apple fritters, I'm sure all will be solved in no time at all."

"Look!" said Malcolm, clearing his throat. "They're about to announce the cake competition winners. Think you'll get a ribbon, Dorothy?"

"I haven't a prayer," she laughed. "I don't know what came

over me when I decided to enter the Best Victoria Sponge contest. Mrs. Kittle would never forgive me if I won."

"For all our sakes, I hope you do. If the woman wins another ribbon, she'll be on the inevitable road to dictatorship."

When Dorothy laughed and swatted his arm, Louisa realized, at perhaps the most inopportune moment, that her aunt might have been right all those years ago. It seemed Malcolm had indeed had an influence on Louisa, after all.

The three of them made their way toward the cake tent, where Mr. Shaw, the sexton at St. Stephen's, had taken his position behind the podium. "Gather around!" he hollered, proving to the entire assembly that he never should have been trusted with a gavel. "Gather around, please!"

The cakes had already been cut, divvied among the judges, and cheerfully consumed. Now all twelve judges sat in a straight line behind their little card tables with all the silence and solemnity of a real jury. The crowd pressed in tightly beneath the canopy as the results were handed down on tiny slips of folded paper.

There were two surprising upsets that day. The first was that Mrs. O'Malley lost to her sister, Miss Willoughby, in the seed cake category, and after holding the title for the last three years. The other was that Miss Rice took the ribbon for the finest Battenburg, though the woman had never baked anything edible in all her life. This caused everyone to speculate, in not quite so delicate whispers, that her mother, world-class talent that she was, had baked the Battenburg for her!

By the time they came to the Victoria Sponge category, Mr. Shaw had to use his gavel liberally to quiet things down, and Mrs. Kittle had been holding her breath for so long that her face matched her cobalt cardigan, and she looked ready to keel over from lack of oxygen.

Without looking at anyone in particular, one of the judges got up and handed off the last slip of paper to Mr. Shaw, who proceeded to open it with a melodramatic flourish. "And the winner for Best Victoria Sponge is . . ."

He lifted the paper to his eyes and slowly wet his lips. As Dorothy Simms clutched Malcolm's hand for support, Louisa closed her eyes and stopped herself one second short of committing gross sacrilege by praying for Mrs. Kittle to win.

". . . Mrs. Eustace Kittle!" Mr. Shaw finished.

Mrs. Kittle's face resumed its usual color as she sallied forth to claim her ribbon. Yet the smattering of perfunctory applause was cut short as a petite figure in purple rayon came dashing through the crowd, nearly knocking Mrs. Kittle off the platform.

"Mrs. Watson!" scolded Mr. Shaw, banging the gavel again. "You must control yourself! I'm sure your year will come!"

Mrs. Watson scowled. "You look as silly as a mongoose with that gavel!" she informed him. "I haven't come here about cake—although I've always thought your sponges were a bit on the *denser* side, if you'll forgive me for saying so, dear Eustace. But no, I haven't come about that. I've come about the doctor. Dr. Clarke, that is."

"Dr. Clarke?" Mr. Shaw looked as though he wasn't sure if he ought to bang the gavel again. "If the doctor wishes to speak to the assembly, I'm sure we don't mind waiting for him to arrive."

"Well, you'll be waiting quite a long time for that," Mrs. Watson answered tartly. "The man's dead!"

32

The glory of the Victoria sponge had been somewhat dampened by the discovery of the doctor's body, but Mrs. Kittle still made sure she had her first-place ribbon in her possession before everyone went rushing off.

Mrs. Watson had been the one to find the body. She'd left the tea tent only long enough to say "How do you do?" to Mrs. Sawyer, who was serving lemonade across the path, and the doctor's body was lying there, right in front of the strawberry scones, when she returned. Dr. Fielding, the unfortunate intern, was getting himself a glass of lemonade when he heard Mrs. Watson's shrill cry for help, and he reached his comrade's body before anyone else. Seconds later, Malcolm elbowed his way through the crowd to join him, Louisa following close at his heels. Dorothy, she realized with some satisfaction, hadn't managed to keep up with him.

"His sleeve," Malcolm said urgently to Dr. Fielding, sinking to a crouch beside the body. "Roll it up. The left one."

Though Dr. Fielding looked puzzled by this request, he complied. Louisa followed Malcolm's gaze to the skin beneath Dr. Clarke's sleeve. It was clammy and pale but entirely unmarked. They checked the other arm to be sure. Neither man noticed the dab of red on the doctor's collar just beneath his jaw.

"Pippin Red," Louisa whispered, pointing.

Malcolm's eyes sharpened. "What is that?" he asked, leaning closer. "Is it blood?"

"No," she said. "It's lipstick."

Malcolm's notebook made a sudden appearance, and Dr. Fielding fetched one of the new lace tablecloths to cover the body. Louisa sagged with relief as the cloth was pulled up to shroud the doctor's face. She'd always assumed that people looked like they were sleeping when they died, but Dr. Clarke's eyes were glassy and open, his jaw sagging and lips parted as though he'd glimpsed eternity when no one else was looking. She clamped her own eyes closed until she saw starbursts behind her lids, but there was no banishing the ghastly image.

"He likely died of a heart attack," she heard Dr. Fielding murmur behind her. "I spoke with Dr. Clarke's wife recently, and she said he was anxious, not sleeping well either. He was taking something to help him along."

"Was he anxious about anything in particular?" asked Malcolm.

"If he was, she didn't know what. And I don't believe she's here today. She'll need to be told straightaway."

"I'll do it," Malcolm muttered gravely, "just as soon as my men can set up a perimeter here. We need to keep the crowds away."

His voice was more muffled as he turned away to dole out orders, and Louisa lost herself to the drone of low-speaking voices, some of whom wept and grieved, others who were swept up in gossiping, who couldn't seem to help themselves from being fascinated by the grotesque. These were the same sort of murmurs Louisa had heard after the fire, after Paul had disappeared, and now she felt as though it might have easily been her brother's corpse instead of the doctor's lying prostrate at their feet with that look of frozen surprise.

She didn't realize that she wasn't breathing or that her head was beginning to swim until she felt a hand brush her elbow. Malcolm's voice was near her ear. "Come away," he said. "Here, take my hand."

His fingers were firm around hers as he tugged her out through the back of the tent. The sunlight helped to warm her trembling shoulders, but the brightness of it hurt her eyes and cast a strange, glowing halo around everything she looked at. Summer flies buzzing near her ear made her think of a rotting carcass.

She felt like she might throw up.

Malcolm slid his knuckle beneath her chin, lifting her gaze to his. She squinted up to find his lips were pressed in a thin, worried line.

"Stop looking at me like that," she snapped, stepping back out of his reach. "I've never seen anyone like that, is all. Dead bodies may be part and parcel for you, but they certainly aren't for me. But that doesn't mean you need to spend yourself on heroics. We both know I'm not the sort to faint—at least not real fainting. The pretend fainting did come naturally enough, I suppose, but that was *your* idea, and you—"

"Would you stop talking for two seconds, please? You'll pass out if you don't take a breath."

Though Louisa scowled at him, she was secretly grateful for that remark. "I'm fine," she insisted again, though less touchily, and dragged in a few lungfuls of air for extra emphasis. "See? And anyway, if you don't mind getting down to business, you can't believe that the doctor had a heart attack. It's far too coincidental."

"I don't know what to think," Malcolm admitted, rubbing his eyes again. "Only that there's nothing at all connecting him to your brother or to the fire."

"He argued with Paul."

"So did you," he said pointedly. "It doesn't mean you murdered him, does it?"

"But the doctor lied about where he was on the night of the fire."

"It's entirely possible that he really was having an affair. The lipstick on his collar rather suggests it. I've never seen the doctor's wife wearing red lipstick, have you?"

This time, Louisa's scowl was genuine. "Do you enjoy being disagreeable, or do you have to work at it in your spare time?"

His lips quirked like he had a know-it-all answer for her, but Dorothy had just ducked through the tent flap, her eyes shimmering with tears. "Oh, Malcolm," she said hoarsely, reaching for his hand. "Dr. Clarke . . . the poor man, I can hardly believe it!"

Malcolm stepped to Dorothy's side, but Louisa thought—or rather she hoped—that his eyes didn't fully meet Dorothy's. "I'm sorry to leave so abruptly," he said quietly, "but I have to tell his wife."

"Of course!" agreed Dorothy, nodding vigorously and swiping a hand across her damp cheek. "Yes, I understand."

At this point, Louisa couldn't decide if it was more awkward to linger or to disappear from the conversation without a proper farewell. She settled for a nervous, backward shuffle and made it as far as the tent flap without either of them taking notice of her.

"I can drop you off at home on the way, if you'd like," Malcolm was saying to Dorothy. "Or perhaps you'd rather stay?"

"I couldn't possibly stay. Not after what's happened." Then in a much lower voice: "We really should offer to bring Louisa home as well. Poor thing looks peaky. Don't you think she looks peaky, Malcolm?"

Louisa froze as Malcolm lifted his head and looked at her. He winced, then asked, "Can we drive you home, Miss Everly?"

And just like that, Louisa was transformed from a basket case to a charity case, and she couldn't possibly have said which was worse. "I can't abandon Mrs. Watson," she answered, speaking very fast but somehow managing not to stammer. "But thank you for offering."

"Are you sure?" Dorothy asked. "You're pale as a ghost."

It was terrible that Dorothy had to be so awfully nice when all Louisa wanted to do was say something cutting. "I appreciate that you're both looking out for me, but Mrs. Watson has her grandson's car. I won't have to walk."

Malcolm frowned, his eyes steely and suspicious. *Just stay put,* he seemed to be thinking. *And don't do anything stupid.*

Fat chance of that, thought Louisa as she walked away. The tea tent had already been cordoned off when she returned, keeping the crowds at bay, and a number of officers who had been in attendance and enjoying the fete were now stationed there.

Mrs. Watson stood on the civilian side of the rope with an annoyed expression. "They've all refused to buy anything," she said, glaring at a red-faced young constable who had been charged with making sure no one touched or moved the body.

"It's probably just as well," Louisa said. "My scones really were inedible."

33

Though Louisa wanted nothing more than to go home, Mrs. Watson wouldn't hear of it. She echoed Dorothy's sentiments that Louisa looked rather pale, then went and bought sandwiches for them to share as well as glasses of lemonade, which was a bit too tart but still refreshing. The first table they found had been recently vacated by a group of "hooligans," as Mrs. Watson called them. They'd been using an old coffee tin as an ashtray. Before tucking in to eat, Mrs. Watson insisted on carrying it off to the nearest trash bin to be emptied.

Louisa watched her, vaguely at first, but then a memory flashed in her worn-out brain . . . and ignited. All at once she realized what had been missing from her brother's room, what Mr. Hexam's story about the doctor had triggered in her memory. "The *ashtray*," she whispered. Standing quickly, she knocked over her glass of lemonade.

Mrs. Watson was at her side in an instant. "What's the matter?" she asked urgently. "Are you ill?"

There was no time to explain, no time even to mop up

the lemonade, which Mrs. Watson was hurrying to do when Louisa wheeled around and went rushing off to the tea tent. By now the crowds had dispersed, the horror of death overshadowed by the promise of frivolity. Sergeant Billings had arrived with a band of constables. He looked up from his notebook and said something uncouth under his breath when he saw Louisa approaching.

"Sergeant Billings!" she panted. "I need to speak to you."

He pinched the bridge of his nose. "Miss Everly, in case you aren't aware, we have a bit of a situation here."

"Yes, but—"

"I'm sure Inspector Sinclair will be back within the hour if you would like to return at that time to speak to him."

Though Louisa would have much rather spoken to Malcolm, she didn't enjoy being tossed off either. "There's an ashtray in Paul's room," she said, ducking under the rope barrier.

"Miss Everly." The sergeant tried to cut her off and escort her away.

"It's on the bedside table. The first time I went to his room, it was full—"

"Miss *Everly*!"

"But when I was there the other day—after the shooting—it was empty!"

At last, Sergeant Billings hesitated. "And? What of it?"

"I need to know if one of your officers emptied it."

"They might have done." He screwed up his eyes, thinking. "Yes, I'm sure they must have if it was empty. I can check the file later."

"There's no time to wait for later!" Louisa cried. "If the police didn't empty that ashtray, then someone else did. And if someone risked going back to Paul's room to empty the blasted thing, then you have to ask yourself—why did they do it?"

"It sounds like you already have a theory."

"Inspector Sinclair said he had all the food in the room tested for poisons, and the scotch."

"True enough."

"Did you test the cigarettes in the ashtray?"

Billings looked like he wanted to dismiss this question as nippily as all the rest, but he paused despite himself and pondered it. And then, to Louisa's inexpressible shock, he waved over one of the constables. "Go straight to the station," he muttered, "and check the evidence log in the Rosemont file for cigarette butts. I'll have a man waiting by the phone in St. Stephen's for your answer." He turned back to Louisa. "There." He said the word as though he was merely placating her. "You'll have your answer soon enough."

Louisa had never been good at waiting. Back in school, she was always getting in trouble with the teacher for cutting in line, and she'd never been able to sit still long enough to sew or crochet anything. When Christmas came, she whirred about the house for days, begging to try one of the treats that had been set aside for Christmas Eve, and whenever her mother made biscuits, she always filled herself up on dough before any of them had made it into the oven to bake.

Sergeant Billings had banished Louisa from the tea tent, informing her they'd be in touch once they had news. She'd called him an odious man and trudged off, buzzing all the while with nervous energy. It might be an hour or more before the constable called with an update about the evidence list, and even then, she had a feeling the sergeant wasn't going to be particularly forthcoming about the results. There was little point in waiting around for Malcolm. Depending on how his conversation went with the poor doctor's widow, and how much he enjoyed the company of Dorothy Simms, he could be away for hours.

As she waited to hear from the sergeant, Louisa considered the ashtray again. If the officers had emptied it, then she'd lost a promising lead and was nowhere nearer to uncovering the truth. But if her suspicions were true—if someone *had* sneaked into the flat and emptied the ashtray when no one was looking—then the evidence was gone regardless. It was all starting to look rather bleak.

It didn't help matters that Mrs. Watson kept trying to force-feed Louisa sandwiches. "You must eat something," the older woman said, nudging the plate closer to Louisa's side of the table. "You'll wear yourself out worrying like this."

When a sopping mess of egg salad materialized in front of her, Louisa folded forward, pressing her hands to her eyes. She felt like she was finally stumbling somewhere near the truth, and yet there were too many moths in her brain to think clearly. She remembered how strongly she'd sensed Paul's death on the night of the fire; why didn't she feel something now? The bond between them, which she'd only recognized at the moment of his death, had been severed before she ever realized it was there.

As usual, it was the frustration that fired her guilt. Every night, she'd lain in bed and prayed that her brother had forgiven her for all the horrible things she'd said to him, but at the moment all she could hear was the sound of his sneering laughter, so spiteful, as a puff of cigarette smoke slipped from his lips . . .

Louisa flinched and gasped, her hands falling away from her eyes.

"You've thought of something," Mrs. Watson whispered with anticipation, "haven't you?"

Louisa smiled faintly and, this time, accepted a sandwich when it was offered.

34

Louisa zipped back to Everly Hall in Mrs. Watson's car. By now her headache had shifted and settled behind her eyes, and so she kept the windows rolled down, breathing in the balmy currents of fresh summer air. Mrs. Watson had stayed behind at the fete to wait for Malcolm, and she promised to call as soon as they heard back from the sergeant about the evidence log.

Louisa hadn't been willing to risk waiting a moment longer. Somehow she knew. She knew that the culprit, whoever they were, had broken into her brother's room and emptied the ashtray. The evidence, such as it was, had been carried away—it was gone. *Or so they thought*, Louisa reminded herself, tapping her fingers impatiently on the steering wheel as she flew past the last road sign to Wilbeth Green.

Everly Hall was empty when she arrived, but this was not surprising. Her aunt had given everyone the day off to attend the fete. The Cadillac was gone too, which meant her aunt and uncle had left, probably to fret over the flower arrangements again. *And so much the better*, thought Louisa. For it ensured that she wouldn't be interrupted.

Her legs were shaking as she creaked open the door to her uncle's study. Assuring herself that it was empty, she darted over to the fireplace and dropped to her knees. It was just as well that her aunt couldn't tolerate soot, for if the fireplaces in Everly Hall had been in regular use, Louisa never would have had a prayer. As quietly as she could, she slid the grate aside while her quarrel with Paul looped again and again through her mind:

"*I think you're drunk,*" she'd told him just before the fire.

"*Think whatever you'd like,*" he'd said and then flicked his cigarette stub into the fireplace.

Louisa yanked off her gloves and felt along the cool stone hearth until her fingers closed around it. And as they did, a film of tears blurred her vision as weeks of regret culminated in one swift moment of piercing relief. For if she and Paul hadn't fought, he never would have tossed his cigarette aside. She never would have known it was there, would never have found the evidence of his innocence.

It felt as if his hand were somehow stretching out to meet hers.

It felt like absolution.

The feeling was severed by a thudding crash upstairs, which was accompanied by the unmistakable sound of breaking glass. Hand fisting reflexively around the cigarette, Louisa straightened and lifted her eyes to the ceiling. She expected to hear a scream, but the silence that followed chilled her all the more.

Since she didn't have a pocket, she slid the cigarette butt into the base of a potted philodendron as she tiptoed over to the telephone in the hallway and snatched up the receiver. "Hello, hello," she whispered, cupping her hand around her mouth to muffle the sound. "This is Louisa Everly. I need you to put me through to St. Stephen's Church. There should be a policeman there, waiting by the telephone!"

Perhaps it was fate that Sergeant Billings was the one who picked up.

"Miss Everly." He spoke slowly as though summoning patience. "I told you to stay put and wait for word."

"Yes, but—"

"This meddling has to *stop*, Miss Everly!"

He hung up on her again, and Louisa hissed a word that most certainly would have made Mrs. Watson tattle on her to the vicar. Perhaps she ought to have tried the station next or else run out of the house, but she didn't move, except to lower the receiver gently into its cradle. She thought of the vicar and of Thomas Sykes, both of whom had been clouted on the back of the head by an unseen assailant. She thought of the bullet in her brother's room and the doctor's lifeless body. There wasn't a moment to spare. Not if someone was to be hurt. Not if she could perhaps do something to save them.

Her hand was sweaty on the banister as she climbed the stairs, imagining all the things Malcolm might have shouted at her if he knew what she was about to do. Holding her breath, she listened at each door in turn before stopping outside the door to her own chamber. And there it was—the muted sound of scuffling footsteps coming from the other side of the oak door. She might have felt better about entering if she'd had a weapon on her person. A knife, perhaps, or a gun. She might have even settled for Malcolm's umbrella, but that had been tossed to the bottom of her closet in a moment of shortsighted stubbornness.

As it was, the only available objects in the hall were a small statue of the Greek goddess Flora, likely too little to inflict any real damage; a vase of white lilies; and a hideous painting of a goose. Naturally, Louisa chose the statue. She weighed it in her hand before hefting it over her head. If she chucked the thing with impeccable aim . . .

Her heart was squarely against her in this decision, trying to batter its way out of her chest, but she pressed the door open, certain she was about to discover another dead body—

Instead, she came face-to-face with the barrel of a gun.

35

ouisa had never, not once, seen Fernsby with an actual
expression on his face, and yet his eyes widened a fraction when she stepped into the room. Though she was
petrified by the sight of his weapon, she refused to let on.
"Drop it," she ordered, nodding to the gun in his hand and
taking a stance that said she was prepared to lob the statue
at him.

Fernsby smiled faintly. "You first," he said.

Louisa wasn't about to comply, but she did appreciate the
simple dignity of being treated as though she posed a threat.
She scanned the room behind him. It appeared her bedside
lamp was the only casualty thus far. Fernsby seemed to have
been in the process of gathering the shards of it into a nearby
wastebasket.

"Knocked it over," he explained in his customary drone.
"As you can see, no real harm done."

"What are you doing in here?"

"I was looking for something."

"Oh? What sort of something?"

He lowered his gun, wincing slightly, but he didn't set it

down. "You're just like your brother. He never knew when to
let well enough alone either."

Louisa sucked in a breath. She wondered if, like her brother,
she was about to be silenced for her curiosity. But Fernsby only
stared at her, then finally put down the gun and began depositing lamp fragments into the wastebasket. "I know what you're
thinking, Miss Everly. You think your brother was set up for
the fire, that someone might have hurt him. And you've been
speaking with my sister, so you know I have a colorful history. But I can assure you that it wasn't me. I abhor violence."

"And yet blackmailing my family doesn't seem to tug at
your conscience overly much."

He stopped tidying to peer up at her, and she thought he
almost smiled. "So," he said, "you've seen the photograph."

"Young woman wearing a locket?"

"Yes. I've been trying to get my hands on it ever since you
and your inspector friend started sniffing in my direction.
I've never been able to leave a mess lying about."

"The gun is a recent acquisition, then."

He narrowed his eyes. "What makes you say that?"

"Well, I'm assuming you wouldn't have bashed poor Thomas
Sykes with a shoehorn if you'd had a gun with you. And I
would imagine that getting yourself shot in my brother's room
might have relaxed your position on violence. I know you were
there because you winced just now when you lowered your left
arm, and I've heard bullet wounds hurt like the dickens. But
if you're searching my room in the hope that Paul passed the
photograph off to me, I'm afraid you're only half right. I came
into possession of the photograph, true enough, but the police
have it now. The locket as well."

"Locket?" Fernsby jolted. "What locket?"

Now that he was unarmed, Louisa was beginning to feel a bit silly standing over him with the statue in her hand. She plonked it down on the mantel and folded her arms nervously. "I found it in my uncle's room. It was a perfect match to the locket in the photograph, but that's as much as I've been able to piece together. You were blackmailing him, I suppose?"

"I was."

"And Paul knew about it?"

"He found me out. He uncovered the photograph in your uncle's study, and the note on the back. I'd tried to mask it, of course, but I've always had a distinctive *S*. Paul noticed things. Little things. He'd seen me jot down notes for the staff a time or two and recognized it."

"I would imagine he confronted you about it."

"On the morning of the fire. Yes."

"Did he threaten to expose you?"

"On the contrary. He was searching for proof about something, though he didn't go into detail—said it was too dangerous to involve anyone else—but he promised to keep me out of it."

"And you believed him?"

"Of course. Your brother was honorable enough, in his own way."

Louisa swallowed hard. She agreed with what Fernsby had said, but she also felt a sister should have known as much far sooner, and so she gave no answer. "Who was she?" she asked at length. "The woman in the photograph?"

Fernsby had finished cleaning up the broken lamp and, proving himself a butler through and through, began fluffing the pillows in the window seat. "She was my mother." He spoke the words faintly but with frankness, and Louisa was so surprised to hear them that she had to catch her weight on the back of a chair.

"Your mother!" she cried. "But what does she have to do with my uncle?"

She'd never heard Fernsby laugh, but the sound that scraped his throat might have passed for one. "I can imagine your surprise," he said. "What could a wealthy blighter like your uncle have in common with a poor, unremarkable seamstress? That's how your uncle must have thought, at any rate. My mother begged for us to write to him when she realized she was dying. She wanted to see him just one last time before she went. She held on for as long as she could, but he never sent word. He never came to see her."

Louisa's thoughts were foggy as she rubbed her tired eyes. She thought he was trying to imply that Uncle Archie and his mother had been romantically involved, but something about this wasn't matching up with everything else she knew. After all, Fernsby wasn't much younger than her uncle, five years difference at most, which meant the woman in the photograph would have been old enough to be Uncle Archie's . . .

And there it was. All along, Louisa had assumed the wisp of hair in the locket had belonged to a woman, but it didn't. It belonged to a baby.

"He's your brother," Louisa whispered, "isn't he?"

"Half brother," Fernsby corrected with an upward turn of his nose. "My mother was a laundress here during your grandparents' time. She found herself in some difficulty and pleaded with them to help her, to find a home for her child if they could. Your grandparents had been trying to start a family of their own for years at that point, and so they offered to adopt the child and raise him as their own. Imagine their surprise when, three years later, your father came along—the full and rightful heir to the Everly fortune and estate."

Louisa shook her head. "My grandparents wouldn't have thought about it like that."

"And yet, in the eyes of the world, your uncle was the bastard-born son of a first-class nobody. It's the kind of secret a man in his position would pay handsomely to bury for good, don't you think?"

Or kill for, Louisa thought uneasily.

"My mother never told us or tried to seek him out," Fernsby went on. "She feared the truth would only hurt him, and besides that, she'd married and started a family of her own. And yet on her deathbed, she spoke only of the child she'd lost."

"That must have been tremendously painful for you."

He lifted one shoulder in a stiff shrug. "It was actually my mother's nurse who struggled most of all. She sent letter after letter, begging for your uncle to come and ease our mother's anguish. I didn't realize she'd sent him the locket as well. My mother was never without it. She worked like a dog from the day she was born, but she was a softhearted, sentimental creature."

"Like your sister."

This time there was no mistaking his laugh. "Well spotted, Miss Everly, yes. She never knew who your uncle was—not by name—but she said we ought to try to understand his position and forgive him for not answering the letters. But I couldn't forgive him. When our mother died, I got the nurse to give up his name and then came looking for work at Everly Hall. As soon as I could safely do so, I began sending the blackmail notes. Your uncle never suspected it was me, although he did test me once. For three months, he refused to pay me."

"What did you do?"

He lowered his eyes as if here, at last, he knew he'd crossed a line. "I threatened to send word to your father. I'm sorry to say his heart gave out before my letter ever reached him."

Though Louisa's legs still felt uneasy, she drew herself up, her fingers clawing into the upholstered chairback for support. "You needn't have bothered sending it in the first place," she said. "I am sorry for what you've been through, but I know exactly what my father would have done. He'd have burned your letter."

"You can't possibly know that."

"Of course I can. My uncle was wrong to disown your mother, but nothing you could have exposed about his past would have changed the fact that he *was* my father's brother. My grandparents lived and died claiming Uncle Archie as their oldest son and heir. My father would have had to disown him to claim the inheritance, and he *never* would have done so!"

They both heard the sound of a car approaching on the drive below. Before Louisa realized what was happening, Fernsby's gun was gripped in his hand again. It occurred to her that she ought to raise the hue and cry. The butler wasn't guilty of murder—in this, at least, she believed him—but he was guilty of plenty else. Her window was cracked. How easy it would have been to scream, and Fernsby would have been caught red-handed with a gun in her room.

Louisa pitied him. The man had been driven by vengeance for so long. He'd carried it with the same sense of devotion that his mother had in always wearing her locket. The passing of years had poisoned him against his own brother; it must have been exhausting.

"Go," she said in a quiet voice. "Quickly."

Fernsby's brow dipped as his eyes darted from her to the door. "You really aren't going to turn me in?"

Louisa sank into the chair. "I haven't the heart for it," she answered.

As Fernsby made his silent escape, she pressed a hand to her chest, shaking her head slowly. Twelve years ago, Fernsby had threatened to send word about her uncle's birthright to her father, but her father had suffered a heart attack before the news could reach him. Now, just as soon as the doctor's alibi for the night of the fire had been dismantled, he too had suffered a heart attack. It might have been a coincidence. No doubt that was what Sergeant Billings would have said had he been there, and Malcolm might have agreed if only to vex her.

And the killer? Well, she thought, they probably would have told her to leave well enough alone if she knew what was good for her, but what was the point in starting now?

36

There had been footsteps on the stairs. On the landing. Now they were right outside of Louisa's bedroom. Without the prelude of a knock, the doorknob turned. After her recent standoff with Fernsby and his gun, Louisa thought she was prepared for pretty much anything. So she stood to face the newcomer. Without warning, her headache sharpened like an ice pick between her eyes. She winced and toppled forward, seizing the bedpost for balance.

"Louisa!"

She heard her aunt's worried wail a second before the older woman's hands slipped beneath her elbows, supporting her. "Are you all right? What's the matter?"

Louisa tried to look up at her, but the lamp was casting the same strange halo of light that she'd seen when she stepped outside the tent at the fete. She curled forward and wished she'd taken the time to eat another sandwich. "My head," she muttered, "it hurts terribly."

Her aunt was still wearing her gloves when she set a soothing hand on the back of her neck. "Poor dear," she said, guiding her back to sit on the bed. "Rest here a moment and I'll get you something to drink."

Aunt Agatha snapped out the light. She was gone and back in an instant with a tall glass of cold lemonade. By then Louisa could open her eyes without wincing. As her fingers curved around the glass when it was offered, she lifted her head and tried to smile.

Her aunt was sitting in the chair beside the bed, setting her handbag beside her on the floor. Her eyes, when she looked up at Louisa, were creased with worry.

But her lips were Pippin Red.

Louisa's heartbeat jumped, then jolted. It was the same shade of lipstick she'd seen on the doctor's collar. All at once, a number of disjointed thoughts tumbling in her mind clicked suddenly into place.

She already knew that her aunt had been in love with someone else when she married Uncle Archie. Someone unsuitable, she'd said on the night of the disastrous dinner party. Someone with gray eyes, which really ought to have struck Louisa as odd, for they'd been speaking of Malcolm at the time, and his eyes were brown.

The doctor's eyes, however?

Without a doubt, they were gray.

But even if Louisa's aunt was the doctor's secret lover, she couldn't possibly have been his alibi on the night of the fire. She'd been with Louisa that entire evening, from the time of the party to the moment the abbey was ablaze. Besides that, her aunt didn't smoke, and Mr. Hexam had said the doctor was in the company that night of someone who undoubtedly did.

Unless . . . Louisa's head reeled again as she mulled it over. Unless he hadn't been with a woman at all, for he might have been moving a body that night. A body that smelled like cigarette smoke!

Did that mean her aunt was a convenient excuse the doctor had leaned on to cover his own tracks, or did it mean that she was involved in whatever had happened to Paul?

As Louisa considered this, her aunt cocked her head to the side. Her hair was smoothed back into an elegant French knot. In her dainty white gloves and belted blue sundress, she looked too *chic* to be a killer, and yet . . .

"You aren't drinking the lemonade," observed her aunt.

"I'm not thirsty," said Louisa, and she might have laughed if she wasn't so panicked, for this was nearly the same exchange she'd had with Malcolm at The Three Foxes. This time was different, however. This time she didn't think she was mistaking the dangerous calm in her aunt's eyes as she pushed upward on the glass, angling it toward Louisa's lips.

"Take little sips," Aunt Agatha instructed. "You'll feel much better."

Louisa brought the rim to her mouth, but didn't drink. "Have you come from the fete?" she asked.

"I have. Mrs. Watson told us you weren't feeling well, so I came as soon as I could to check on you."

"Have you heard the dreadful news about the doctor?"

"Yes, it is dreadful."

Louisa thought her aunt looked somber enough about it, but not at all surprised. Discreetly, Louisa glimpsed the felt handbag still resting on the floor beside Aunt Agatha. She said she'd come straight here from the fete, which meant any evidence of what had happened to the doctor might yet be there inside her handbag.

What Louisa needed was a diversion, and since her head

was already causing her a fair amount of trouble that day, she could think of only one. It was a bit old-fashioned, but as Malcolm had told her, there was no arguing with its results.

Louisa swayed forward and collapsed, spilling her second glass of lemonade in as many hours as she slumped onto the carpet. Her aunt wasn't as prepared as Malcolm had been for her fainting ruse, and so Louisa jammed her shoulder painfully on the corner of the table before toppling into the handbag. In the chaos of flailing limbs, she managed to spill a few items on the floor beside her. She spotted a handkerchief, a few makeup compacts—including lipstick—and a medicine bottle in the second before she closed her eyes and lay prone.

Aunt Agatha called out Louisa's name and rattled her sore shoulder, but Louisa forced herself to be deadweight, all the while analyzing what she'd seen spill out of her aunt's purse. Far as she knew, her aunt wasn't taking any medications. But then Louisa remembered what Mr. Hexam had said about his own prescription, which had been given to him by Dr. Clarke that very morning: he took it for his *heart*. Could too much of the medicine, sinisterly administered, have caused a heart attack?

Yes, she decided, that made sense. The doctor had been serving abroad with Louisa's father at the time of his death, and she already knew that Fernsby had threatened to contact her father about his supposed birthright. It would have been all too easy for Aunt Agatha to have written to her lover, pleading with him to administer something to keep the truth from coming out.

Louisa was so alarmed by the thought, so stricken, that her eyes flew open to find that her aunt was pale and peering at her very closely. "I'm sorry," Louisa murmured, pushing herself up onto her knees. "I don't know what's come over me today."

She glanced at the door, wondering how she could possibly extricate herself from the situation long enough to telephone Malcolm, but her aunt sighed and straightened, setting the empty glass of lemonade on the bedside table. "You needn't have worried," she said. "It wasn't in there anyway."

"What do you mean?"

"The poison, dearest. It wasn't in the lemonade. I put it in your tea this morning. You see, it dissolves a good deal more thoroughly in a hot liquid."

At first they only stared at each other. Despite her own misgivings, Louisa was certain she had misheard, for her aunt's smile was entirely calm and ordinary. Then the fragments slid together in her mind.

"You killed them." Though Louisa spoke the words, she still didn't believe them, not quite, and so she licked her lips and tried again: "You killed Paul. And Father."

Her aunt bent down and scooped the fallen articles back into her handbag. "I quite did away with them, yes."

Because Louisa was stuck in disbelief—or was it shock?—the terror didn't strike her all at once. When it did a second later, however, a searing pain ran straight through her like the tip of a spear. This time when she collapsed, it wasn't a ruse. With a keening cry, she folded at the middle, scraping her cheek against the carpet as a torrent of tears wet her face. She'd hoped that discovering the truth about Paul's death would bring some small measure of peace, but it brought only anguish and fury, and the sudden, bone-chilling realization that she and her brother were to be killed in the exact same way—at the hand of someone they ought to have trusted.

"I know you felt him die," said her aunt calmly. "On the night of the fire. As soon as I saw you lying there on the floor with that ghastly look on your face, I knew you'd sensed something." She sighed again. "I really do wish we could have avoided all this unpleasantness."

"But how?" croaked Louisa, lifting her face. "How could you have done it?"

"Don't be dense, dear. For weeks you've been everywhere you ought not to have been. Surely by now you've uncovered the blackmail scheme?"

Louisa's vision clouded, tinged with yellow like she'd stepped sideways into an old painting. She wondered how long she had before she suffered the same fate as her brother. She'd consumed the poison at breakfast, but she had no idea how much she'd been given or how quickly it worked. She was already having a hard time standing and seeing straight, yet it was hard to tell where the effects of the poison ended and her own panic began. Maybe if she kept her aunt talking, she'd be able to figure out what she'd been slipped and find a way to escape.

"I saw a photograph," Louisa admitted. "It was of Uncle Archie's mother."

Aunt Agatha laughed bitterly. "Cruel bit of irony, isn't it? For the sake of pride, I refused the man I loved, only to realize my own husband was no more than a lowly laundress's illegitimate son. Your father might have swept in and taken everything from us. The money. The house. Our reputation."

"Is that why you framed Paul for the fire? Because he'd uncovered the truth?"

Her aunt noticed the out-of-place statue of Flora on the mantel and picked it up with a frown. "Yes," she said, turning it over in her hand. "And no. He always was an unlikable boy, though I never knew the two of you together to be so nosy. He'd gone to paint the surgery, as you've already discovered, and cut his hand on a paint can. He was looking for a bandage, it seems, when he came upon a stack of old love letters. The contents were enough to make him question the circumstances of your father's heart attack. Silly Charles. I thought he'd burned those letters years ago, but he was devilishly sentimental about that sort of thing. You can be sure he burned them after your brother had left the surgery, though he called me in the most ridiculous panic. I assured him I would take care of the matter. I sent a note to Paul early on the morning of the party, telling him we needed to speak about whatever it was he *thought* he'd discovered—"

"And then you poisoned his cigarettes."

Chin lifting with surprise, her aunt glanced over and set the statue back on its perch. "How did you figure it out?"

"The ashtray."

Aunt Agatha shook her head. "An unpardonable oversight, don't you think? Charles almost didn't realize what he'd left behind until it was too late. Thankfully, he got to it before the police could double back, with plenty of time to destroy the remaining evidence."

Louisa lowered her head, trying to look defeated, but her thoughts trailed to the cigarette butt she'd slipped into the philodendron—if only she could reach it in time! "And the fire?" she asked, still stalling. "Whose idea was that?"

Her aunt was beginning to pace. "At first I was content enough to swap cigarette packs with him and wait for the poison to do its work. But then I saw him at the party that evening. I'd never seen him looking so smug. So *superior.* By then he was convinced your uncle and I had something to do with your father's death."

"I wonder why he didn't go to the police?"

Her aunt sniffed. "As if anyone would have believed him over us. He certainly didn't have enough evidence. He was also drunk, as usual, and looking for a fight. He called your uncle a 'sanctimonious nobody' and vowed to expose the truth."

"That must have frightened you."

"Fear had nothing to do with it. The poison had already been administered, though I'll admit it was taking much longer to take effect than I'd expected. I could only coat the mouthpiece with so much, you see, and I was beginning to worry that I hadn't used enough. Or perhaps he wasn't smoking like a chimney as much as usual. It's not an exact science, mind you, which is why I was sure to give you and Charles that much more."

Louisa was trembling violently now. "But why burn the abbey," she whispered, "if Paul was already dying?"

"It was the ingratitude!" spat her aunt. "To hear him speak to your uncle that way after everything we've done for him. I didn't just want to kill him. I wanted to destroy him—to *ruin* him. And when I overheard him telling the vicar that he'd be at the abbey that night, I saw my chance. I rang up Charles and told him exactly where he'd be and what to do. Your brother was already dead when Charles got there, and so the rest of it was easily accomplished and far more easily believed. Reputations are such frightfully fragile things. Everyone thought your brother had thumbed his nose at the town for good and run off. Just like the obnoxious coward I've always known him to be."

"He was leaps and bounds braver than you," declared Louisa defiantly.

Her aunt's lips tightened. "Well, you're entitled to your opinion, dear. Even if you won't live long enough to share it."

At that, Louisa tried to stand, her lips parting around a scream, but her aunt didn't even have to raise a hand to subdue her. She had only to cross the room and flip on the light switch to send Louisa sprawling back onto the floor, curling in on herself to get away from the light.

"You needn't bother screaming," said her aunt. "There isn't a soul in the place to hear you."

Louisa sagged on the carpet, too weak to test her. "And what will people think," she gasped, "when they find me here?"

"That you were despondent over the disappearance of your brother. Your uncle—that stupid man—already thinks you were a bit out of your mind about it anyway. The police will find your note and a decent amount of digitalis in your system."

"Digitalis?"

"From the foxglove flower, dear." Louisa cracked an eye and watched her aunt set a finger on one of the purple flowers in the vase on her dresser. The dainty lilac bells hung their heads as though ashamed of their part in the conspiracy. "We have multitudes of them in the garden. And wouldn't you know, you picked some just yesterday. Elegant, aren't they? Lethal too. Consuming a small quantity can stop the heart."

Louisa thought she felt her soul flicker, but she kept talking: "Is that what you used to kill the doctor?"

"I didn't want to, of course, but his conscience was becoming problematic. When he found your brother in the abbey that night, he said his body was curled up in front of the altar. He looked just like an infant, Charles said, and he feared God's wrath for what he'd done, or something like that."

For the second time that day, Louisa heard the fateful sound of wheels crunching gravel in the drive below. And while she gasped, her aunt merely turned her face toward the window, unruffled, quietly picked up her handbag and stepped across the room. "Don't look so afraid, dear," she said, opening the door with that sharp, sophisticated smile that Louisa knew so terribly well. "From the looks of you, I'm sure it will all be over before I even answer the door."

Louisa's heartbeat sputtered again as she tried to straighten. "Please," she whispered, struggling to crawl across the floor to stop her. "Please don't—"

But the door slid shut, then locked, on her plea.

37

Louisa heard voices in the hall below, but like a living nightmare she couldn't summon enough strength to stand, nor even to scream. Was this, she wondered, how Paul had felt as he crawled helplessly to the foot of the altar? It had been years since they'd worshiped together, and yet she imagined she could hear him now, speaking the liturgy beside her in the pew, and perhaps she could. Perhaps he was reaching for her like he used to when she fell and scraped her knee. Perhaps she was edging her way into eternity to stand beside him . . .

The voices were outside now, just below her window.

"Dear God," she prayed, "spare me." She tried but failed to stand. The door was locked, so she didn't bother wasting any energy there. Instead, she crawled like a crab over to the window, which was still cracked open a few inches.

The table next to the window was piled with records. Whispering another prayer, this time for strength, she used the table for leverage, hoisting herself up, but she couldn't make it all the way to the window. Still, she could hear well enough.

"Well, yes, she was here a little while ago," her aunt was saying from the steps below, "but she told me she wanted to walk for a bit in the garden. You really ought to look for her, Inspector—she seemed distraught."

Inspector!

Louisa's heart might have given out then and there from the sheer shock of a near rescue. She could hear Malcolm thanking Aunt Agatha for her time. His footsteps were fading, getting farther and farther away. He was leaving, Louisa realized, and she was dying, but that couldn't be the end of it, could it? She tried to call out for him, but her voice was tired and thready.

Frantic now, she rummaged through the pile of records, looking for something loud, something distinct. She found what she needed: *Rum and Coca-Cola.*

Her arms were weak as putty as she slid the record from its sleeve. With fumbling hands, she crammed it into her player and lowered the needle, then cranked the volume as high as it would go. Her strength sapped, she fell backward, thumping like a corpse onto the carpet, a sickening sound in the otherwise silent room. She lay there terrified, wondering if there was something wrong with the record player, for the song wasn't playing. But then a second or two later, she heard maracas coming from the speaker, followed by the blare of a trumpet.

Louisa thought it was plenty loud enough to be heard outside, but heavens, it hurt her head. She rolled onto her side, whimpering into the carpet, and prayed that Malcolm wasn't too far away, that he could hear and recognize the strident serenade.

Had she just heard a *bang* in the hall below? Her eyes flew open as she waited. But no, it was only the music. She closed her eyes again and listened as The Andrews Sisters warbled on about American GI's and their romances with Trinidadian women, about hard drinks and hot beaches and the attraction of calypso music. She might have laughed if she'd had the strength for it. Even when loitering on death's doorstep, she couldn't help but think it wasn't the sort of song a person could properly die to. Perhaps it was no wonder that Tilly's mother had disapproved of the girls listening to it when they were younger.

The next sound was far less ambiguous. There was a crash downstairs like something had broken, and shortly after that, Louisa heard an even louder banging right outside her door. "Unlock it!" Malcolm was shouting. "Open it now or I'll kick it down!"

Given the mahogany barrier between them, his voice was somewhat muted in Louisa's ears. The flickers within her were growing fainter now. She felt rather than heard the moment he tore into the room, but then something inside of her shifted, reaching for him instinctively before she fully realized he was there. He said her name as he slid his hands beneath her back, trying to help her stand. She struggled to reach for him, drawn to him as if to the light. Then something darker beckoned, and she slumped back to the floor as though pulled down by a magnet.

"What have you given her?" Malcolm demanded furiously, his fingers fumbling to find a pulse in Louisa's throat. "Tell me, woman!" But if Aunt Agatha was in the room with them, Louisa would never have known, for her aunt made no reply.

"Digitalis . . ." Louisa whispered the word, yet she couldn't tell if she'd said it loud enough for him to hear it. She tried again, growing more alarmed when she realized her lips refused to form the word properly.

When this didn't work, she tried to tell him about the ciga-rette butt in the philodendron, but this was far too difficult for her faltering lips, and she didn't think he would understand anyway.

"It's fine," he said. His voice was strong and steady, but his fingers, as they moved from her pulse to her lips, were trembling. "You're going to be all right."

He wasn't fooling anyone, least of all Louisa, but at least he was there. At least she wouldn't have to die alone. She felt the floor drop away as he swung her up into his arms.

It was only then that Aunt Agatha spoke: "You'll never make it in time."

Malcolm's hands tightened painfully around Louisa's shoulders. "If she dies," he snarled, "I'll ask to knot the hang-man's noose for you myself."

And then they were moving, the music dying off to a whis-per, though Louisa realized she was still humming it deliri-ously as Malcolm tucked her head against his chest to keep it from banging into anything on their way down the stairs. She thought that her cheek fit quite naturally against his sternum. And here was comfort too, for even if her heartbeat was, as she feared, unsteady, she could feel that his was pounding hard and fast enough for the both of them.

Fresh air against her skin told her he'd made it down the stairs and through the front door in record time. He jostled her a bit as he opened the car door. "Keep your eyes open," he ordered briskly, lowering her onto the front seat. A second later and he was sliding in beside her and revving the engine.

The first turn had a bit too much adrenaline behind it, the force of which sent Louisa slumping, but Malcolm caught her by the elbow before she flew off the seat. With one hand he held her tightly against him; with the other he gripped the steering wheel. Louisa could tell, even without opening her eyes, that Mrs. Watson would have shrieked in outrage if she'd been there to see how fast he was driving.

Louisa's head was swimming again, and so she turned her face into Malcolm's shirt as he blasted the horn at someone or something in the road. He nudged her shoulder and asked her a question, but she was too adrift inside herself to hear or to answer. Death, she thought, was a good deal quieter, less fearsome, than she'd thought.

"He's a proud beast," she whispered, the vicar's words materializing from somewhere deep within the fog, "but he hasn't got any teeth."

Perhaps that sounded like gibberish to Malcolm. He said her name. Repeated it twice when she couldn't find her way out of herself to respond. She heard him swear, then pray, then swear again. Somehow, hearing his prayer, short and halting though it was, gave her the strength she needed to open her eyes, lift her hand, and rest it gently on his shirtsleeve.

He flinched, then looked down. She'd never seen Malcolm so afraid, but his face was gravestone gray. "What is it?" he murmured. His throat bobbed as he swallowed deeply.

This was the moment when Louisa ought to have come clean. She should have confessed her love for him, said something that was both sweet and unforgettably sentimental. At least this was what she intended, for it would not do for her last words to him on earth to be something ridiculous.

Instead, she blurted out, "Dorothy Simms can't bake a proper cake, can she?"

Then her heartbeat slipped away as everything around her went black.

38

There were far too many flowers on the table next to Louisa's hospital bed. At least that was what the peevish head nurse, Matron Beaufort, had said. And indeed, there was a rather shocking number of them. Mr. Hexam had sent over tulips and pink hyacinth from his garden. The Kittles brought begonias. The daffodils were from Elsie Ann, with a note at the bottom, unsigned, that could only have been written by Fernsby. Even Sergeant Billings had sent a constable to deliver a small nosegay of roses, which was the least he could do for hanging up the telephone in Louisa's last great moment of peril.

"Miss Everly! Yoo-hoo, Miss Everly! Are you awake?"

That exaggerated whisper could have roused the dead, and no one was more grateful than Louisa to be counted among the living. She looked sideways to find the friendliest of the nurses, young Miss Moriarty, who was peering around the partition.

"Yes," Louisa answered, shuffling up to sit. "I'm awake."

Miss Moriarty stepped neatly around the partition. She was juggling a large wicker basket and a vase that was teeming with posies, primroses, and peonies. "These were on the step outside." She jostled them closer so Louisa could read the note, which had been tucked among the blooms:

Swept the cobwebs out of my conscience to send you these. Get well, sweetheart.

Sykes

Louisa smiled and rested her head back against the pillow as Miss Moriarty held out the basket. "And Mrs. Watson asked me to smuggle this in for you," she whispered.

Inside, Louisa found a tin of biscuits (Mrs. Watson was sure they weren't feeding her properly), a thermos of nettle tea, and a bottle of nail polish, something Louisa had specifically requested.

"I'm going to ask that Catholic grandson of hers to nominate her for sainthood," said Louisa, tearing into the biscuit tin.

Miss Moriarty's eyes twinkled. "Patron Saint of Catholic Grandsons!" she declared, fluffing Louisa's pillow. "I'd hang her icon in the infirmary just to see Matron's face when she sees it."

Louisa laughed in agreement. Like England and France, Mrs. Watson was the natural-born rival of Matron Beaufort, who reminded everyone, daily, that her surname meant "beautiful fortress." And a fortress she was. As soon as the doctor had said that Louisa ought to rest and avoid any unnecessary excitement, Matron Beaufort declared that Mrs. Watson was "unnecessary excitement personified" and barred her, and all other visitors, from Louisa's bedside.

"Was there . . . anything *else*?" Louisa asked.

Her indifferent attitude took some doing, for she secretly hoped that Malcolm had sent along a note or a letter or . . . well, something. It embarrassed her to admit it, but when she'd first awakened, having been brought back from the brink of death by a hasty dose of atropine, she'd called out for him six or seven times and cried piteously when she was told that he'd already gone. Three days had passed since then, and still he hadn't come to visit.

"He hasn't come," said Miss Moriarty, patting her hand. "But he will."

Louisa's face reddened when she realized she'd given away far more than she'd intended. "Who do you mean?"

"The inspector." Miss Moriarty sighed dreamily. "I've never seen anyone burst through a door like that. He dropped you on the table right in front of the doctor and said, 'Fix her!'"

"As if I were a broken carburetor," muttered Louisa.

"*Far* more trouble than a broken carburetor."

Louisa had just crammed a biscuit into her mouth, and so she coughed on the crumbs as Malcolm appeared at the edge of the partition. Miss Moriarty took her cue and was gone in a flash, her apron strings flapping behind her. As Malcolm strode to her bedside, Louisa wished she'd had the foresight to freshen up. A bit of lipstick would have gone a long way toward making her feel presentable, even if she was in her nightgown. If Malcolm found the situation as uncomfortable as Louisa did, he didn't show it. He leaned against the wall near her bed, lifting a brow as he waited for her to finish chewing.

She swallowed much too soon, the biscuit dense as a cricket ball in her throat. He stared at her a moment, then said, "You look like a garden gnome surrounded by all these ridiculous flowers."

"I think you're the only person in Wilbeth Green who hasn't sent any," she countered, choosing to ignore the fact that he'd just compared her to a gnome.

"I've brought something better," he said and tossed a folded newspaper down on her lap. Louisa picked it up and, with a growing ache in her chest, read the headline:

Everly Boy Exonerated in Arson, Murder Investigation Ongoing

"There's a fine bit about you in there," he said, poking absently through the various flower bouquets on the table. "At the bottom of page three."

Louisa blinked away tears and set the paper aside without reading more. "I can only hope they've left out my sillier moments."

Malcolm, who had just noticed the floral arrangement from Thomas Sykes, read the attached note, frowned, and then swapped the vase with one of the bouquets at the back of the table. "Most of them, yes," he said. "Though it has been leaked, for public scrutiny, that you have a habit of wearing impractical shoes."

On any other day, the banter would have done her good, but Louisa wasn't having it. "Where have you been?" she demanded, the urge to cry gathering in her throat. "It's been awful here without you. I didn't know what to think."

"I've been speaking with a hundred different people about a hundred different things," he answered, slouching into the chair beside the bed. As he lowered his head, Louisa could see how tired he was. His eyes were rimmed with gloom, his jaw showing the first dark shadow of unshaven stubble. She remembered the morning she'd so foolishly suspected him of murder. He told her he'd tilled through the abbey ruins, fully expecting to unearth his best friend's body.

"Have you spoken to my aunt?" she whispered, realizing they were both, in a way, still surrounded by the debris.

"I apprehended and interrogated her myself. It was like getting blood from a stone, but we think we know where Paul's body might be buried. My men are searching even now."

Louisa must not have looked terribly reassured by this, for he leaned forward and set his hand over hers on the bed. "I'll do everything I can to find him, Louisa. You have my word on that."

Louisa squeezed his fingers, knowing full well what it cost him to make such promises. "And my uncle?"

"He knew nothing of the murders. As you can imagine, he's more than a bit beside himself."

Louisa could only imagine. Long before she'd fully come to, she knew her uncle had been at her bedside because she could hear him shouting at the nurses. She'd awakened before he realized she was coming to, and she thought he looked ashen and aged sitting at the foot of her bed. As soon as he saw her open eyes, he stood as though rising from the dead himself. *"I never really minded the bicycle,"* he'd muttered nonsensically, then was gone from the room like a puff of pipe smoke.

He had not returned since then.

Malcolm stood. "I know this must be painful for you, but if there's anything you remember from that morning, anything that could be helpful . . ."

His notebook was poised in his hand as he awaited her

statement. The sight of it chilled Louisa, and she tugged the blanket up to her chest and answered: "I found one of Paul's cigarettes from the night of the fire. He'd tossed it into my uncle's fireplace while we were talking."

"You hid the cigarette butt in the philodendron, didn't you?"

Dumbfounded, she gaped up at him. "How did you know?"

His lips curved. "Even when you aren't making a lick of sense, I generally know what you're saying."

"And? Has it been tested?"

"Yes. It was positive for digitalis. I do not doubt that the doctor's body will show signs of it as well."

Louisa sighed. "I don't suppose there's anything else that really matters, is there?"

"No," said Malcolm. "Except, well, I understand if this isn't the right time . . ."

Louisa waited for him to finish his thought, but he shook his head as though he'd somehow misplaced it along the way. Then he dropped his notebook onto the bedside table and said, "It was a very near thing, wasn't it?"

Louisa set her hand over her heart to assure herself it was still beating. She'd vowed to find her brother's killer, to clear his name, but even though she'd heard the confession from her aunt's own lips, she still couldn't believe that any one person could be capable of such raw, unmitigated hatred. Five minutes more and Aunt Agatha might have gotten away with it all.

"Thank heavens for The Andrews Sisters," said Louisa quietly.

"Thank heavens for your quick thinking," Malcolm corrected. "You really are brilliant, you know. In case I haven't said."

He hadn't said it, not once, and so Louisa might have rejoiced or even gloated, but alas, she didn't have the heart to do either. "I don't feel brilliant," she admitted. "I feel like a mess. In fact, I've been thinking lately that I wish I were an old woman already so I could tell all the young women that they're doing just fine when they feel like they're falling to pieces."

"You don't want to be an old woman."

"I certainly do. As a matter of fact, I think it might be my one true calling."

"Well," mused Malcolm, "becoming old is most of our callings at one point or another. But anyway, don't go off becoming an old woman quite yet. I'm growing pretty fond of the younger version."

"So you *are* fond of me!"

"Yes, but I'm not really sure what to do about it. Sergeant Billings is the best man I have, and he's already threatened to put in for a transfer if I marry you."

Louisa laughed flippantly, convinced he was joking again. "I expect you told him he has nothing to worry about."

"On the contrary. I told him I'm going to find him a cozy position. In Swindon probably."

The way Malcolm looked at her then . . .

He was dead serious.

This time Louisa's laugh was not as much flippant as it was frantic. She was about to start talking, which would have been disastrous, but of course Malcolm knew as much. Before she could get a word out, he sat down on the side of the bed and, leaning very close, pressed a warm, lingering kiss against the skittering pulse in her throat.

For a second, Louisa leaned into his embrace and allowed herself to feel quite overcome. But then her senses rallied, and she caught his face between her hands, pushing him back a fraction. "You're being ridiculous. What do you want to marry me for?"

His lips were at her neck again like he couldn't help himself. "Well," he murmured, "it's either that I'm barking mad, as Billings says, or else it's because I've been in love with you for as far back as I can remember." Lacing his fingers into her hair, he traced a soft but insistent line of kisses from the base of her neck up to the curve of her ear. "Which do you think it is?"

"I think you must be mad," she answered shakily, "but I don't seem to mind it."

He laughed and drew her face to his. He kissed her lips lightly and then not so lightly. And it was then, right as Louisa was at long last brushing her fingertips through Malcolm's once unruly hair, that they were interrupted by a shrill cry from the vicinity of the partition:

"Inspector Sinclair!" admonished Matron Beaufort. "I told you that Miss Everly is to have no unnecessary excitement!"

Epilogue

It was a right handsome headstone. That was what Biddy said as she stooped to place a handful of flowers at its base. The funeral service had been small and private in accordance with Louisa's wishes. After everything that had happened, especially with all the reporters riled up and circling again, she didn't want to make a spectacle of it.

Paul had always hated crowds anyway.

Mrs. Watson was there, and Biddy, and even Uncle Archie, who had pulled Malcolm aside at the end of the service and told him that just so long as Louisa always came home with shoes on her feet, he was welcomed to marry her at his earliest convenience. This was surprising, of course, but not as surprising as the morning before when he'd called Louisa into his study and told her that he was amending his will and that she'd have the entire Everly estate and fortune at her disposal by the end of the month.

"It should have been yours anyway," he said, "and now everyone knows it. I never should have paid to hush it up, but there it is."

"I won't have a penny of it," insisted Louisa, pressing a

kiss to his cheek and smiling when he grumbled and lightly swatted her away. "You're my father's brother, and he never would have said otherwise."

The skies were bright on the morning of the funeral, but the gray, crumbling stones of the abbey ruins were slick and streaked after an overnight rain. They seemed to sorrow with Louisa as she placed her brother's St. Jude icon, very gently, on top of the headstone. The inscription below had taken her some time to decide, but she was inclined to agree with Biddy that it was both right and handsome:

Paul Everly
Beloved Son and Brother

"One short sleep past, we wake eternally
And death shall be no more; Death, thou shalt die."

"I thought I'd feel better," Louisa mused, sensing the moment when the vicar had come to stand beside her. "More at peace perhaps. Or else more whole. But I'm the last living soul in my family. All except Uncle Archie, that is. And I keep wondering what Paul and I might have been to each other if only we'd been given the time. I like to think that Malcolm and I would have come round to their house on Christmas Eve. Perhaps brought a bar of chocolate for the little ones Paul and Biddy might have had. Oh, we'd have fought like mad, I'm sure, for that was our way. But we would have loved each other, too."

"Your brother loved you, Louisa. Fiercely so. And it is a fine and faithful thing you've done in bringing his body home to rest. But remember this—God has been even more faithful.

Your pain may never fully fade on this side of heaven, but Christ's promise is fulfilled regardless of how you may be feeling now."

"Do you think Paul was afraid in the end?"

"He might have been. But I also know he heard his Savior's voice: 'Young man, I say to you, arise!'"

Louisa smiled through the tears, touching his elbow to thank him before turning to join Mrs. Watson, who stood waiting with Malcolm beside her new sedan. The two of them had called a truce for the sake of the funeral service, but now they were back to quarreling again. When Louisa drew near enough, she heard the words "spots" and "silver," and Malcolm was saying that he didn't particularly care what Mrs. Watson thought of his ability to polish spoons, that he would marry whomever he pleased—with or without her approval.

They both broke off when they saw Louisa approaching. Malcolm had been reluctant to leave her side when she'd asked them for a moment alone, but he'd honored her wishes. Now he stepped close to her, his brow wrinkled with worry. "Are you all right?" he whispered, opening the door for her.

"I'm not sure," admitted Louisa, glancing up one last time at the charred yet christened remains of Rosemont Abbey. "But I will be."

Malcolm nodded and took up his usual place in the back seat as Mrs. Watson slid in behind the wheel, straightening her hat and gloves like a jockey readying to mount. "I've named him Anthony," she said, glancing at Malcolm over her shoulder. "The car, I mean. Like the prime minister. Do you like the prime minister, Inspector?"

"I like to ride in silence," he answered, which made Mrs.

Watson remark, dismissively, that she didn't expect a boy who skipped choir practice to have many useful political opinions anyway. Louisa rolled down her window as they squabbled, feeling the wind on her face as it blew aside her curls. Her laughter could be heard for miles up the road.

Acknowledgments

This book was a joy to write, even if it wasn't always easy. And much of that joy came from working with, and being supported by, so many wonderful people.

Thank you, first and foremost, to my husband, Curtis, for offering endless love and encouragement, and for your constant willingness to brainstorm. In this book, you found the solution to the biggest, most terrible plot hole I've ever encountered, and I am so thankful that you were there to help vanquish that particular dragon, among so many others. I love you.

Hugs and kisses to my children for cheering me on as I was writing. There were days when I think the two of you were even more excited about this book than I was, and that warmed my heart. I love you both so much!

To my incredible parents, William and Shirley, to whom this book is dedicated: Thank you for offering me so firm a foundation by teaching me the faith as a child and for always encouraging me. I'm so blessed to call you mom and dad. And to my amazing mother-in-law and father-in-law, Scott and Diane: Thank you both for taking such a warm and loving interest in all of my writing endeavors; your support has meant the world to me.

No expression of thanks will ever be enough to convey my gratitude to the team at Bethany House. First, to Jessica Sharpe for bringing me into the fold and for proving the age-old adage that two heads are *definitely* better than one; you have helped turn this into the book of my dreams, and I am still so excited that we get to work together. To Luke Hinrichs for your amazing editing work. To Dan Thornberg for designing the perfect cover. And to Rachael Betz, Jennifer Parker, Joyce Perez, Raela Schoenherr, Lindsay Schubert, and Anne Van Solkema for pouring so much time and creative energy into this project. Cheers to you all as we cross the finish line together!

A huge, joyful thank-you hug to Christina MacKenzie and Jenny Maske, two of my dearest friends, both of whom offered invaluable feedback and support, especially when I was cobbling together the first draft.

And to Adria Goetz, who saw potential in this project and encouraged me to pursue it at a time when I was beginning to feel defeated. Your enthusiasm has always been a tremendous blessing to me, Adria, and I am grateful to you for knocking on so many doors on my behalf.

A special thank-you to Dr. Kathryn Harkup for answering so many rapid-fire questions while I was working on the rough draft; to Ruth Boeder for sharing insights on vintage cocktails; and, again, to my mother-in-law, Diane Stephens, for a hands-on lesson about pin curls.

Lastly, to my readers: God has blessed me time and again through each and every one of you. Thank you for taking the time to read my books and for sharing them with others. I couldn't do this without you.

Soli Deo gloria.

Read on for a *sneak peek* at

The NEXT EXCITING MYSTERY *from* NAOMI STEPHENS

AVAILABLE IN THE SPRING OF 2026

Keep up to date with all of Naomi's releases
at NaomiStephens.com
and on Facebook and Instagram.

CHAPTER ONE

The first body was exactly where it was supposed to be.

The vicar, Ignatius Cole, stood over the casket wherein it rested, his hands gripping a worn copy of *The Book of Common Prayer*. "'In the midst of life,'" he read, "'we are in death . . .'"

The widow jostled her umbrella to dab at her tearless eyes. The son, who had come rocketing up the drive in an Aston Martin five minutes before the service began, stood at the head of the grave with one hand in his pocket, staring at nothing in particular.

Hippolyta Halfpenny had never seen an earl before. Not even a newly minted one. He looked rich enough in his Italian overcoat, she decided, though somehow not much like an earl. The society columns had been even less generous than this in their estimation of him. If the headlines were to be believed, Crispin Cavendish had spent the three weeks leading up to his father's death attending wild parties, gambling in a London slum, and breaking off a long-standing engagement to a Russian ballerina (though perhaps not in that order).

Thankfully, he hadn't seemed to notice Hippolyta's brief

inspection of him. She'd staked out a fairly secluded spot near the back of the crowd, huddled beneath an umbrella of her own and attempting to blend in with the cluster of willow trees behind her. She didn't know much about the family beyond the salacious details she'd read in the newspapers on the train ride over. She'd certainly never met Lord Basil Montfort, the poor bloke in the casket, though if anyone asked, she'd claim to be his third cousin twice removed.

She was always the third cousin twice removed.

This alias afforded her enough closeness to be considered one of the family, but there was also a sense of safety and anonymity in it. No one ever questioned a third cousin twice removed, nor were most people in the habit of remembering Hippolyta to begin with, for she always wore a simple black suit-dress, a no-nonsense pair of pumps, and went by the most unremarkable name she could think of: Ethel Jones. The only embellishment she ever allowed herself for these events was a black, beret-style fascinator with a birdcage veil, which had once belonged to her mother.

Her younger sister, Cordelia, always said Hippolyta lacked "creative vision." And though Hippolyta might have quipped that each one of her siblings had three times as much creative vision as could naturally fit in a single personality, it couldn't really be helped. Their parents had fallen in love on the stage, and so theatrics were in their blood. Her older brother, Horatio, had shown up to the funeral that morning wearing an ascot and claiming to be a member of the baronetcy. And Tybalt, having been forbidden by their father from wearing fake mustaches (for he was only sixteen and couldn't grow one the natural way), arrived at the gravesite with a newly acquired limp and a gaudy, silver-tipped walking stick.

Their father was still glowering at them both.

"'Like as a father pitieth his own children,'" quoth the vicar, "'even so is the Lord merciful unto them that fear him.'"

A middle-aged woman, whisperingly referred to as "the American," leaned forward and murmured something into the son's ear, which relaxed his blank stare into something more like a smile. Cordelia wept like she was auditioning for a Hitchcock film. She wore a wide-brimmed hat with a chin-length veil and copious black feathers, most of which had already withered in the October fog.

"'For as much as it hath pleased Almighty God of his great mercy to take unto himself the soul of our dear brother here departed, we therefore commit his body to the ground—'" the vicar bent down, scooped up a clump of cold, rain-soaked earth into his hand, and tossed it in to christen the casket— "'earth to earth, ashes to ashes, dust to dust; in sure and certain hope of the resurrection to eternal life through our Lord Jesus Christ, who shall change the body of our low estate that it may be like unto his glorious body.'"

Hippolyta had heard this part of the service dozens of times, and yet it still stole her breath. It still made her tremble and think of her mother, as did the voices which answered in chorus: "'Blessed are the dead which die in the Lord.'"

Hippolyta's vision clouded with tears at the haunting refrain, while the rest of the mourners were already beginning to shuffle on their feet. One chap cleared his throat and discreetly checked his pocket watch. Another, who was holding a porkpie hat, smothered a yawn. Even the undertaker, from his place on the perimeter, looked like he might have been planning out in his mind what he hoped to eat for lunch. Hippolyta squinted from one downturned face to the next, but apart from Cordelia and the usual rabble of extras her father hired for higher-paying clients, she couldn't spot a single tear-stained cheek.

This wasn't surprising exactly. Professional mourners were hired for a reason. Sometimes it was because the family was afraid no one would attend otherwise. Sometimes it was because the deceased came from a small family, and some kin or other felt they deserved a larger send-off. Sometimes it was merely to satisfy a dying person's vanity. Even people who didn't care a mite about being disliked while they were living had a strong aversion to this being made apparent in death.

But it was still heartbreaking.

Most of what Hippolyta knew of Lord Basil Montfort, famed recluse that he was, was limited to the contents of a crumpled letter in her father's waistcoat pocket, which contained specific instructions for their arrival and reception at Montfort Manor. No one, not even Lord Montfort's wife, was to know who they were or why they were there.

"I demand dignity and discretion," he'd written just two short weeks before his passing. "A few damp eyes will suffice; after all, this is England. Besides that, I'll have already paid you in advance, and as I don't imagine I'll be able to hear you from the casket, I won't be in a position to pay you extra, even if I might have otherwise appreciated the theatrics."

Given these directions, Hippolyta doubted very much if Lord Montfort would have wanted anyone flinging themself upon his casket, but Cordelia was inching forward and wringing her gloved hands as though strongly considering it.

The vicar displayed ecclesiastical expertise by pivoting slightly, obstructing Cordelia's path to the departed one. "'Grant unto him eternal rest,'" he read from his book without looking up.

"'And let perpetual light shine on him,'" chorused the congregation.

"Perpetual light, eh?"

Hippolyta flinched as two men in stained work clothes shuffled out from the trees, shovels in hand, to stand beside her. The first stood gloomily by, his tweed flat cap pulled low over his brow so only his cheeks and chin were visible. The second man, the one who had spoken, was old and bent, his voice more wheeze than whisper. He crossed himself and spat on the ground, and the two of them vanished into the gray drizzle before the next versicle was spoken.

Long after the men had gone, their spiteful presence chilled Hippolyta. She tried to focus on the prayers but found herself thinking of Lord Montfort instead. The society columns had not been particularly generous to him, and this might have been merited. Perhaps he really was a scoundrel. Perhaps he was the kind of man who'd never spoken a kind word to anyone in all his life.

Did that mean he deserved this pathetic farce for a funeral?

She closed her eyes and pressed the toes of her shoes forward until they began sinking into the wet sod. She'd done the same at her mother's funeral, for it had rained that morning as well. Nine years old and wanting nothing more than to slip through the grassy layer of earth, not to join her mother exactly but so she might avoid all the people who were staring at her.

And yet there hadn't really been many people at her mother's graveside.

There was the stage manager from the last play her parents had been in, two neighbors, and Auntie Joan, the only relative who was willing to look after Hippolyta and her siblings when Father was still in hospital and the funeral arrangements had to be made.

Three weeks after the accident, he'd awakened to learn that his wife had not survived it. He wept into his hands when he heard how small her service had been. "She deserved better!" he cried hoarsely as the nurses struggled to calm him. "If anyone deserved better, it was her!"

Hippolyta opened her eyes. She clutched her umbrella and stared at the gaping grave without blinking, no longer trying to hold back the tears that were coming quite naturally now. They fell for her mother, for her father, for everything her family had lost and become since the accident. But she made sure to spare a few for Lord Montfort as well.

For years, her father had lived by the philosophy that everyone deserved a proper funeral. And though Hippolyta had always struggled with her place in the so-called family business—for she'd always hated making a spectacle—she also knew this: that if the only person who could manage to cry real tears that morning was a phony third cousin twice removed, then so be it. She'd be the finest phony third cousin twice removed Lord Montfort had ever had.

She didn't bawl like Cordelia. She didn't blubber or scrub her sleeve against her eyes every two seconds like the extras were in the habit of doing. She didn't even sniffle. Her sorrow was softer than all of that, the tears silent but insistent, slipping off her nose and chin until she felt a strange, inward pull from somewhere between the shifting sea of black-clad shoulders. When she looked up, she realized Crispin Cavendish, the new Lord Montfort, was no longer staring at nothing in particular.

He was staring at her. Staring as if, somehow, he knew she didn't belong there, as if he could already tell that the girl beneath the umbrella wasn't at all who she seemed to be.

Naomi Stephens (NaomiStephens.com) is a bookworm turned teacher turned writer. Her first novel, *Shadow among Sheaves*, was an INSPY Award short list contender and the winner of the 2020 Carol Award for Debut Fiction. Though Naomi has called many places home over the years, she currently lives in New York with her husband, her two children, and a rascal of a dog named Sherlock.

Sign Up for
Naomi's Newsletter

Keep up to date with Naomi's latest news
on book releases and events by signing
up for her email list at the link below.

NaomiStephens.com

FOLLOW NAOMI ON SOCIAL MEDIA

Naomi Stephens, Author   @AuthorNaomiStephens